HUNTING
PEARL

C.J. PETIT

C.J. PETIT

Printed in the United States of America

First Printing, 2017

ISBN: 9781081862961

HUNTING PEARL

C.J. PETIT

TABLE OF CONTENTS

HUNTING PEARL

PROLOGUE

April 19, 1873
San Miguel, New Mexico

Will had never really paid any attention to such things before because he was an eleven-year-old boy and only concerned himself with things that ran around on four legs, swam in the stream, or anything that went boom.

But that morning before school, he'd overheard Ellie Fitzpatrick tell Mary Hinkley that her mother was going to have a baby and Mary replied that she hoped Ellie didn't have another stupid brother like Freddy but wouldn't find out until almost Christmas. Will thought that it was pretty funny at first, because his good friend, Freddy, was a bit dim. But then after he took his seat in the classroom, he recalled the second part of what Ellie had said; that she wouldn't know until Christmas. It was only April, and Christmas was more than half a year away.

It wasn't the mention of Christmas itself that was important to him, at least not now, but the fact that it was six months away was. He kept popping numbers in his head for most of the morning and it had resulted in a couple of smacks in the head for woolgathering from Miss Bloomfield, who they all called Miss Broomstick behind her back.

He was going to be twelve on October 5th, and his younger sister, Sarah, was going to be eleven next month, on April 7th. If what Mary Hinkley said was true, then there was something wrong. He was only six months older than his sister.

Now, he needed verification, *but who could he ask?*

HUNTING PEARL

He was absolutely sure that he couldn't ask his father about it when he got home. His father always got angry when he asked questions like that, and that was above the almost constant level of dislike that his father seemed to hold for him. Once, he had asked why he was the only one in the family with blue eyes, and it had cost him a severe beating. He never got an answer, either.

He couldn't ask his mother because he knew that if he did, he'd get her in trouble with his father, too. His father seemed to hate everyone in and out of the family. Will had never seen him smile and it was one of the reasons that they could never keep the same ranch hands for more than a season.

If he wanted to guarantee a beating from his father, all he had to do was to ask any question that was even remotely connected to the family. As a result, Will had no idea who his grandparents were or even if they were alive. He could have lots of uncles and aunts and dozens of cousins out there and he wouldn't know.

Probably the most sensitive area was his older sister, Pearl. He discovered just how touchy his father was about it when just last week, he started to tell Sarah that she was a pearl compared to the other girls in class, but never got two words past pearl when his father had not only snarled at him to shut up but had grabbed him by his britches, taken him outside and whipped his butt raw with a leather strap that had come from an old harness.

Pearl was a lot older than he was, but he really wasn't sure how old she was because she was already married and lived with her husband, and he wasn't sure exactly where she was living now, either. He was six when she had been married and moved away, yet that day was burned into his memory.

Sarah was sitting with him on the front porch as Pearl's new husband loaded up the waiting wagon with her things as she quietly sat on the driver's seat with her head down. He had wondered why his parents weren't there to say goodbye to Pearl and kept glancing back at the front door expecting that at least his mother would come out of the house and go to the wagon to kiss his sister goodbye, but she never did.

When he finished the loading, her new husband, Oscar, climbed onto the seat, and as he took the reins, he heard Pearl almost begging him, "Please, Oscar. Please." He never said a word as he released the handbrake, snapped the reins and the wagon began rolling.

But the most memorable thing about that day was after the wagon wheels began rolling, as he and Sarah stood and waved goodbye, Pearl suddenly turned with tears in her eyes, looked straight at him, and shouted, "I love you, Will."

What had startled him was that she hadn't said anything to Sarah. He remembered having to comfort his little sister after the wagon left and wondered why Pearl had neglected to tell Sarah that she loved her too, which disappointed him because he always thought Sarah was a better person than he was.

He didn't remember her face that well anymore but would never forget how much he had liked her. She would sneak him treats whenever she could and tell him stories when he was small, acting more like a mother than a big sister. He recalled how sad he was to see her leave, and that sorrowful day had never left him, despite his young age. He hadn't liked her new husband at all either and not just because he was taking his beloved sister away. Oscar had despised him from the very start, which had surprised him because he had tried to be nice to him for Pearl, but he acted like Will was a skunk or something.

But now, the inability to ask his father or mother about the nine-month question was compounded by his inability to ask anyone else. He couldn't ask his friends, of course, because guys didn't talk about babies or girls. The one person he could always talk to about anything was Sarah, but this subject involved her, and he was worried enough not to ask her about it. Because if it was true, then that meant Sarah might not be his sister at all. Either he or she must have been adopted, and he didn't want to hurt her feelings.

His naivete about how babies were conceived prevented him from even considering the much more obvious answer.

So, for the time being, Will set it aside and just let it simmer in the back of his mind.

———

The question slid into the background until the answer practically knocked him over when he was thirteen and another of his friends, Charlie Blanton, confided to their small circle of friends in between giggles, that his fifteen-year-old sister was going to have a baby because she had been fooling around with one of the ranch hands and his father was going to make the man marry her.

He had laughed along with the other two boys in the little huddle, but he wasn't laughing inside. Suddenly, the explanation for those missing three months was readily apparent, and he was embarrassed at his ignorance.

He left school that day numb with the knowledge, and as he walked home with Sarah, he knew he couldn't tell her what he had discovered. It meant that one of them, probably him, belonged to Pearl. The reason he was sure that he was her son was that miserable day when Pearl had been taken away and she had shouted that she loved him but hadn't said the same to Sarah.

Pearl was telling him that he was her son, and it had taken him more than seven years to realize it. What really bothered him was as much as he remembered about that day, he couldn't remember his real mother's face any longer. He felt ashamed, and he felt cheated somehow.

He didn't say anything to anyone, not even Sarah, for the same reasons he hadn't asked the questions all those years…his father's temper. But he began to study Sarah and his mother more closely, even though he was sure that his mother was really his grandmother now. He also began to understand why his father hated him so much. His father may be his grandfather, but he surely wasn't a friendly grandpa, either.

That year had also been the last one he was allowed to attend school because his father said it was a waste of time and he wanted him working full time at the ranch now; he was a big boy and it was time he pulled his weight. He'd been working as a ranch hand since he was ten but had been allowed to go to school as long as he did his work. It made for long days, but Will was determined to learn as much as he could despite his father/grandfather. Maybe it was to spite the cruel man who hated everything about him, but whatever the reason, Will studied and read harder after he'd been forced to leave school than he ever had while in the classroom.

But he also vowed that as soon as he was able to leave, he'd go and find Pearl. He'd hunt for his mother if it took the rest of his life.

CHAPTER 1

April 17, 1879

Will was out with the small herd mounted on Buster, his six-year-old black gelding when he heard the dinner bell ringing in the distance. It was only mid-afternoon, so it surely wasn't because it was time to eat. He was the only ranch hand now, so he knew his mother wanted him back at the house, and that there was trouble.

It wasn't a big ranch, so as soon as he turned Buster, he spotted his mother and Sarah waiting on the back porch near the dinner bell, and less than a minute later pulled his gelding to a dusty stop near the back hitchrail.

"What's wrong, Mama?" he asked as he dismounted.

"Come inside, Will. Quickly," his mother said before she and Sarah turned and entered the house.

Will had seen the distress on both of their faces and was sure that it had something to do with that thug who pretended to be his father.

He didn't bother taking off his beat-up old hat as he walked through the door and spotted Joe Houston's body lying on the floor and his mother and sister standing alongside staring at him.

He didn't ask any questions, but said, "I'll get him out of the house, Mama," then walked close to the body, dropped to his heels, picked it up, bad smells and all, stood and carried it out of the kitchen and through the door.

He carried it all the way to the barn, just dropped it like a sack of flour onto the wagon's bed, then turned and headed back to the house. He soon realized how foul he must smell, so he stopped, took off his foul-smelling shirt, walked to the trough, and began dunking it in the water.

After wringing it out, he continued his walk to the house and soon entered the kitchen again and found Sarah and his mother on their knees scrubbing the floor. When they heard him enter, they both stopped, dropped their bristle brushes into the bucket, and stood, drying their hands on their dresses.

"What happened, Mama?" Will asked.

"I really don't have any idea. I was doing laundry with Sarah when he came in and he just began screaming at Sarah because she was just standing at the time waiting to take over the scrubbing. Then, he just collapsed to the floor as if he'd been struck by lightning. I checked and found that he was dead, then we went outside and rang the dinner bell."

"Maybe God finally recognized that he belonged in hell rather than on earth, Mama. I'll go and harness the wagon and bring his body into town. I'll be back in a couple of hours."

"I think Sarah and I should come along, Will. We were both here."

"Okay, Mama. I'll go and hitch up the team and be back in ten minutes."

It took him almost twenty minutes to get the team in harness and throw an old canvas tarp over the body. But ten minutes after that, he was driving the wagon out of the ranch and onto the road to San Miguel, six miles away.

HUNTING PEARL

Now that the biggest obstacle was finally gone, Will felt he could talk to his mother about Pearl without fear of anyone paying the price. He was pretty sure that Sarah knew that he was her nephew and not her brother, too, but with the ogre gone now, they could broach the subject.

"Mama," he said as he straightened the wagon onto the road, "is Pearl my mother?"

He expected her to be shocked, but he probably shouldn't have as she quickly replied, "I'm surprised it took this long for you to ask, Will, but I suppose I shouldn't have been. Not asking was probably the only reason you're still here."

Sarah leaned forward past her mother and said, "I've known for a long time, too, Will. I just didn't want to say anything that might get you hurt."

Will smiled at Sarah. She was always so considerate. Then he waited for his mother to continue what he knew would be a long response to his short question.

"Pearl was my first child. She was born on the eleventh of June in 1845 when we lived in Kansas. I was just seventeen when she was born, and yes, before you ask, that monster in the back of the wagon was her father. He was a farm worker on the neighboring farm owned by the Andersons. My father made him marry me for what he'd done when he found that I was carrying Pearl, and he was never happy about it.

"Then, after living on the farm for eight more years, he finally took me and Pearl to New Mexico Territory to get away from my father who detested him. I think he stole our family's money, too, because he forbade me from ever contacting them, or else he would make me and Pearl sorry.

"We stopped in Santa Fe and he took a job in a livery for a while, then bought this ranch. It was never that much, but it let him be the boss for a change, and that was what mattered most to him. I gave birth three times after Pearl was born, but none survived more than three days. What made him most angry was that two of them were boys. He began to blame me for it, and his temper only got worse, if you can imagine it.

"Then, when shortly after Pearl turned fifteen, she confided in me that she was pregnant and was terrified, but she wouldn't tell me who the father was or even the circumstances of the conception. I had just lost my third baby three months earlier and told her not to worry about it yet. I knew I had to tell my husband about Pearl's condition before she began to show, but I knew that there would be hell to pay when I did. But I was fortunate when just two weeks later, I caught him in a decent mood because he had sold six head of cattle at a very good price and told him. He was very angry, but because he had made some money, he only slapped me around a little and said it was my problem now."

Will shook his head, knowing full well that being 'slapped around a little' was much worse than it sounded. He'd used the phrase himself and hadn't been able to sit for days afterward.

His mother continued after taking a sip of water from one of the two canteens.

"The only thing that kept him from throwing Pearl out of the house back then was when I told him that she might be carrying a boy. So, when she went into labor, I was praying heavily that she had a boy and not a girl for Pearl's sake. When you were born, I literally dropped to my knees and thanked God for giving you to Pearl. You didn't know that you had probably saved her life.

14

"It was after you were born that I finally told him that I was pregnant again, too. I had known that I was for a month, but I was holding back from letting him know in case I had to somehow use the news as a tool to keep Pearl if she had a daughter.

"He was actually in a good mood for a while when he found that there was a baby boy in the house and there might be another one soon. You were a robust little boy and grew quickly, which almost made him human, but when Sarah was born, he reverted back to his nasty former self. That was when he began threatening to keep Pearl and send me and Sarah away, but Pearl said she'd take you away, too."

Will then asked, "But, why did he hate me so much? If he wanted a son, why did he treat me like dirt?"

"He didn't for the first year or so, but when he realized that your blue eyes were always going to stay blue, he knew that everyone would at least suspect that you weren't his son. Then, with each passing year, everything about you proved that he wasn't your father and he grew to despise you and blame Pearl for having you in the first place.

"He began to shop for a husband for her and found Oscar Charlton in San Miguel. Your father had just won a big hand of poker and Charlton was close to being, how do you say it? Tapped out. That's when your father said that he'd let Charlton take the pot if he'd marry Pearl and take her away. He'd even provide the wagon to leave town. Charlton took him up on his offer and Pearl had to go through with it because if she didn't, my husband said he'd take it out on you."

Will exhaled and said, "I remember the day he took her away. It was that memory that convinced me that she was my mother when I finally figured out that both Sarah and I couldn't be your children because of the age difference."

"I'm so ashamed for not being able to tell you both, even in private. I knew that if I did, sooner or later, you might say something, and I have no idea just how angry he would be. I just hoped that when you each figured it out, you'd both be smart enough to keep it to yourselves."

Sarah then said, "I figured it out when I was twelve and you had to tell me how a girl becomes a woman and has babies. I remember that I didn't get much sleep that night when I realized that Will was probably either an orphan or Pearl's son. I wanted to tell him, but I was worried he'd get angry and say something to father and be beaten to death."

Will smiled at Sarah and said, "That's where you had the advantage over me, Sarah. No one ever told me about such things. I had to learn about how a man became a father from the stories that my friends told and even that ended when I stopped going to school."

His mother then asked, "Will, how much do you know now, if you don't mind my asking?"

Will blushed and replied, "Probably not as much as I should, but now that he's gone, I can go and talk to Mister Chavez or somebody else."

"Did you want me to tell you?" she asked.

Will squirmed a bit and answered, "If you don't mind, Mama, I'd rather a man tell me."

"I understand, Will," she replied with a slight smile.

Then Will asked, "Mama, do you mind if I still call you mama, even though you're my grandmother?"

Emma looked at him and said, "If you ever call me grandma, I'll wash your mouth out with soap."

Will grinned and said, "Okay, Mama."

Then he asked seriously, "What are you going to do now, Mama?"

Sarah leaned forward to hear her reply because she had the same question.

"I can't stay in that house any longer than I have to. I want to sell the ranch and buy a big house in San Miguel and make it into a boarding house."

Sarah was relieved, because she didn't want to stay, either.

But Will was now in a quandary, and as he sat between the two women, he didn't know how or what he should do.

Emma may not have been his real mother, but she was the woman who had raised him and knew him better than anyone except for Sarah, so she understood what was bothering him.

She asked, "Will, can you wait until we get the boarding house up and running before you leave?"

Will turned to her and asked, "How did you know, Mama?"

"I'll bet Sarah knew, too. You want to go and find your mother."

"Yes. I have to, Mama. I need to know how she is and more than anything else, I need to talk to her and tell her…well, just tell her."

Sarah took her brother/nephew's hand and said, "Yes, Will, you do need to tell her."

He then turned and smiled at Sarah and said, "You sure that you're my Aunt Sarah?"

Sarah started laughing at the sound, but then said, "I'll always be your sister, Will."

Will then said, "I'll do all I can to help with everything, Mama. When you think it's okay, I'll go and find Pearl. Do you have any idea where she might be?"

Emma sighed and said, "Not much. I only received one letter from her, and when that bastard lying dead behind us found me reading it, he ripped it out of my hands and threw it into the cookstove's firebox. All I know was that she had arrived in Santa Fe but was leaving soon and heading southwest."

"And that was almost twelve years ago," Will said as he looked straight ahead.

Emma nodded and said, "Will, it's a hard country out there, and I know that you want to find your mother, but you're not even eighteen yet. It won't make much difference if you wait a year or two to prepare yourself better for the journey."

"No, Mama. I can't wait any longer than I have to. It's been burning inside me since I first realized why Pearl shouted from that wagon that she loved me. I owe it to her to find her."

Emma acknowledged defeat but wasn't convinced that Will had any idea just how difficult his search would be. She had some vague inkling but was sure that it would be much worse than that and it might even cost Will his life.

———

They arrived in San Miguel an hour later and dropped the body off at the mortuary. Doctor Hector Ramirez did the examination and said that it was probably a burst aneurysm but didn't explain what it was as he wrote the death certificate.

They stopped at the bank on the way back and Emma signed a contract with Henry Simmons for the sale of the ranch and mentioned that she wanted to buy a large house with the proceeds of the sale before they went to the cantina for dinner.

As they drove back to the ranch, Sarah and Emma were both in a decidedly good mood as the worries that had hung over them daily for so many years were buried along with Joe Houston.

Will remained relatively quiet on the drive, thinking about how long it might take to find Pearl. Despite what Emma believed, he had long suspected that it would take him some time to even find where she was. After his grandmother had told him the circumstances of Pearl's marriage, he wasn't even sure that if he even found Oscar Charlton, he'd find his mother. He sounded like a worthless, selfish man and Will doubted if he would take care of her.

He also began making a list of what he would need for the journey, realizing that he didn't have much now, other than Buster, two pairs of britches, three shirts, four pairs of underpants, three pairs of darned socks, one pair of boots and his sad hat. His father hadn't even let him have a pistol, probably because he was worried that Will would use it to shoot him, which was a valid concern. But now, he'd at least have his father's Spencer and Colt New Army pistol and enough time to practice with both weapons.

Maybe, if there was enough money left over after the sale of the ranch and cattle, he'd be able to buy a Winchester, but until he left, his focus had to be on helping with the transition to the boarding house. It might take months before that happened, too.

———

As it turned out, the sale of the ranch and the purchase of the house only took three weeks. The ranch sale netted over three thousand dollars, and the house only cost eleven hundred, so there was plenty of cash left to reconfigure the house as a boarding house. There were six bedrooms, two bathrooms, and a large kitchen, but it still took an investment in time and money to convert it into a boarding house.

When it was done four months later, and Emma finally began accepting tenants, Will knew that any money left over should stay with his mother, so she could afford to buy the food and other necessities to keep the place profitable.

During those four months, he'd been practicing with the Spencer and the Colt and had achieved an acceptable level of proficiency with both guns. Joe Houston may have been a horrible man, but he took good care of his weapons and even had a good store of Spencer cartridges and powder and ball paper ammunition for the Colt and a large box of percussion caps.

On Monday, the fifteenth of September, Will left his room after the guests had finished their supper and walked to the kitchen where Sarah and Emma were cleaning the dishes. He normally helped, but this time, he'd spent the time packing.

When he entered, Sarah turned and asked, "Are you leaving tomorrow, Will?"

"Yes. I think the boarding house is doing well now. If I don't start now, then I don't know if I'll ever go."

Emma took her hands out of the soapy water, dried them on her apron, and stepped across the room to face her grandson.

"Will, I can't tell you not to leave, even though my heart is begging you to stay. I understand why you have to go, and I respect your decision. You've worked so hard for as long as I can remember without any compensation at all, and I want to give you some money to help you find Pearl."

"Mama, I have some money that I made when I helped Mr. Donahue over at the livery whenever I could. I'll work as I search. Folks out in the country always need help."

"How much do you have, Will?"

"Um…almost a hundred dollars," he replied as he looked down.

"How much?" she asked again.

Will sighed and answered sheepishly, "Thirty-two dollars and eleven cents."

"I thought so," she said, then pulled out an envelope and offered it to him, adding, "Here's two hundred dollars. We still have almost a thousand dollars in the bank, so don't you dare tell me you won't take it."

Will looked at his grandmother, smiled as he accepted the envelope, and said, "Thank you, Mama."

She smiled back, kissed him on the cheek, and asked, "Are you all packed?"

"Yes, ma'am."

"Did you ever have a talk with anyone about men and women?" she asked.

Will blushed, which answered her question before he replied, "No, ma'am. I've been pretty busy, and it just didn't come up."

Sarah laughed, then walked across the kitchen, hooked her arm through his, and said, "Mama, I'll take Will to his room and educate him."

Emma grinned and said, "As long as there are no demonstrations, Sarah. You're still his aunt."

Sarah was still laughing as she led a beet-red Will out of the kitchen and to his room.

For more than an hour, Sarah expanded his pitiful knowledge of the world of sex, and he began to wonder how she knew so much. But the advantage of having Sarah explain it to him rather than an older man, or even a parent, was that she gave him the woman's perspective about the male-female relationship and that of a young woman who was able to pass along her own expectations of what she hoped was waiting for her.

At one point, Will asked Sarah why she knew so much, and all Sarah did was smile and tell him that it was none of his business.

But what he did learn, aside from the very critical basics was how women thought and what they wanted. What he had learned from his friends back when he was in school was almost in direct conflict with what Sarah was telling him, and he believed her rather than his friends because Sarah never would lie or mislead him in the slightest. It also gave him insight into why he even existed when he began to understand how his mother might have given in to promises and the emotional lure of love.

When they finally finished, Sarah who had been sitting next to him on his bed, surprised him when she put her hands on both sides of his face and kissed him on the lips as he'd seen boys and girls kiss.

Then she leaned back, smiled, and asked, "How did that feel?"

"Odd. How was I supposed to feel?"

"I wanted to be sure that you and I were still brother and sister. I love you, Will. I'll always love you as my brother, but I had to be sure."

Will smiled at her and said, "That's how I felt, too. Have you ever felt any different, you know with other boys?"

"Of course, I have. I'm not a prude, Will."

"You're the prettiest girl I've ever seen, Sarah. I would have been surprised if you hadn't been kissed before."

"And you, Will James Houston, are the handsomest, most manly young man I've ever seen, and I'm shocked that you haven't been at least kissed before."

Will blushed again, as he had many times in the past hour as he said, "You know why, Sarah."

Then he effectively ended the lesson when he said, "Thank you, Sarah. This meant a lot more to me than you'll ever know. I'll miss you terribly while I'm gone."

"Then you'd better write to me and mama, Mister Houston."

He smiled, gave his sister a brotherly peck on the cheek, and said, "Yes, ma'am."

Sarah rose and smiled at him before she left the room, leaving Will sitting on his bed amazed at just how ignorant he had been. He was almost eighteen and readily admitted to himself that he was probably inadequately prepared to make the lonely and difficult trek he would be undertaking tomorrow, but it didn't matter. He would have to learn as he went, even at the cost of his life. He had to find Pearl.

———

Then next morning, Will was up early, dressed, belted on his Colt New Army, donned his jacket and sad hat, took his saddlebags, walked quietly out of his room, and left the house through the front door.

He walked around the house in the early sunshine, entered the barn, and began to saddle Buster.

"Are you ready for a long ride, Buster?" he asked, not really expecting an answer.

After the gelding was saddled, Will did a final check of his horse, running his trained hands over his joints and muscles, then checking each of his shoes. Working part-time in the livery had helped him understand horses much better than he would have if he had only listened to his father.

Satisfied that Buster was in as good a shape as he ever had been, Will led him from his stall to the back of the house and tied him off on the hitchrail. The Spencer was in the scabbard and he had four boxes of boxes of the heavy .56-56 cartridges but knew that they were common enough that he could get more if necessary. He estimated he had about fifty rounds worth of ammunition for the Colt, so he should be okay for a while. He still thought about using some of the cash he'd been given to buy a Winchester when he got to Santa Fe, where he'd start his search, but he put off that decision until he got there.

He then took a deep breath and stepped up the back steps of the porch and entered the kitchen where Sarah and his mother were cooking breakfast.

"Sit down and eat before you leave, Will," Emma commanded.

He smiled and said, "Yes, ma'am."

Sarah and his mother then began setting food before him in massive quantities.

"You expect me to eat all this," he asked as his eyes bulged at the piles of eggs, bacon, biscuits, and flapjacks.

"Every bite, mister," Sarah replied as she poured a cup of coffee.

He began eating as Sarah and Emma then put their normal breakfasts on the table and joined him.

"Where are you going first, Will?" Sarah asked.

"I'll start in Santa Fe, where they went, but I don't think I'll find them there, or even if anyone remembers them. It was so long ago."

"It's going to be that way everywhere, Will," Emma said quietly.

"I know. The only fortunate thing about this is that Oscar Charlton is an unusual name. If he'd been Joe Smith or John Brown, it would be a lot harder," he said before shoveling in a large forkful of eggs.

Sarah asked, "What if he changed his name?"

Will just shrugged as he chewed. He knew it would be difficult, but he knew he wouldn't change his mind.

Throughout the breakfast, they talked about his journey and as they progressed, it seemed more and more like the ultimate act of futility.

When he finished, and Sarah stood to take the two large bags of prepared food that she and Emma had made for him, she asked, "Will, how long will you keep going? What if you haven't found her in a year?"

Will took a sip of his lukewarm coffee and replied, "I don't know, Sarah. If I haven't had a clue in a year, maybe I'll come back. I just don't know yet."

Sarah put the two bags on the table and sat down again.

"Don't take any chances, Will. I want you to come back, and hopefully, it will be with my sister."

"I'll be okay, Sarah," he said as he stood.

Emma and Sarah both stood as well, and he hugged and kissed each woman before he took his two bags and headed for the door as they followed.

He crossed the porch, trotted down the steps, and after putting the two bags into his saddlebags, untied Buster and mounted.

"I'll be back, but I'll write, too," Will said from the saddle as he looked down at his sister/aunt and mother/grandmother.

Emma and Sarah were already crying, and Will knew he'd start soon, so he waved, wheeled Buster away from the house, and set him off at a walk. But as he turned the gelding onto the street, he looked back, saw them walking along the wraparound porch, waved once more, and then set Buster to a slow trot leaving San Miguel and heading for Santa Fe.

His search for his mother had officially begun.

CHAPTER 2

May 17, 1880

Will spent his nineteenth birthday as he had spent his eighteenth, on the back of Buster as he trudged wearily across the scalding sands of the southwestern desert. There was no birthday cake, but he sure could feel the heat from countless candles.

He recalled one of the last questions that Sarah had asked him, 'What if you don't find her in a year?', and even though he knew it would be a difficult quest, he didn't believe it would take this long. Now, it was more than a year and he wasn't much closer to finding his mother than he had been after that first day.

After he'd left San Miguel, he'd ridden to Santa Fe as planned, hadn't found any clues whatsoever, as he had expected, then ridden southwest. He'd decided not to buy a Winchester in Santa Fe but conserve his cash. He'd regretted that decision within a month when he discovered that the Spencer cartridges weren't nearly as popular as he expected, but the .44 ammunition for the Winchesters was everywhere and a lot cheaper.

So, when he reached Val Verde, he bought a Winchester '73 carbine and six boxes of the cartridges but kept the Spencer. The Winchester, while a very good weapon didn't have the Spencer's range or stopping power.

But in every town where he stopped over the next few months, he got the same answers, if he got any at all. Usually, the person he asked would stare at him and laugh at the absurdity of asking about anyone who'd passed through town twelve years ago.

He finally shifted his direction of inquiry to just ask if anyone had heard the name Oscar Charlton, which at least resulted in just head shakes.

He'd work at a ranch or a farm, usually only get fed and a place to sleep for his labors, but sometimes he'd earn fifty cents or even a dollar. But at each farm or ranch, he found that most of the folks were decent, hard-working people who were doing everything they could to get by, and he made sure he gave them their money's worth of labor, even if there was no money.

He kept the envelope of money in a money belt he'd made out of leather scraps, and still had most of the two hundred and thirty dollars he'd had when he left Santa Fe because he wasn't sure when he'd need to spend a large portion of the money for a new horse. Buster was holding up well, but one could never predict accidents or the appearance of Apaches.

He'd get to a town and ask the local law first, if there was any, which there usually wasn't. Then he'd find the postmaster, where he'd leave a letter if he had written one, and then to his best sources of information, the livery and the dry goods store.

When he had first started out, the saloons presented a problem. More often than not, he'd been either politely told to leave or impolitely ejected through the batwing doors. But, after a year, with some growth in stature and bulk, and the sun's relentless aging, he could pass for a man much older than his tender nineteen years.

He finally left New Mexico and wandered into Arizona Territory where he was now. It was here that he had his first real clue, and it wasn't even really in a town. The settlement had four structures clustered around a water hole and none were significant enough to be called buildings or have anything more than a few letters scrawled across one of the adobe walls. But when he was in the trading post adding to his dwindling supplies and had asked the proprietor, the man remembered Oscar Charlton quite clearly when he stopped at the trading post, and it wasn't for a good reason.

He remembered him because he and two other gents were playing poker with Oscar and had taken him for thirty-seven dollars. There was a large pot on the table and Charlton had offered his wife as collateral in the final hand.

Jake Henry, the man who was telling him the story, had said he threw away a full house rather than have the good-looking lady suffer the humiliation of being little more than a poker chip, and he was sure that the other two men did the same. After Oscar had gone away with his money and supplies, Jake said they all checked the hands and found that Oscar had been holding a pair of eights. Any of the other hands would have beaten him yet he'd offered his wife to back his play. Then Jake said that Oscar had said he'd have better luck down south and headed that way with his wife.

That was eight months ago that he'd had that valuable clue and had headed directly south but his brief glimmer of hope had soon been replaced with the much more prevalent feeling of frustration when nothing developed from Jake's story.

He did get a possible clue when the liveryman in Bear Springs said he had to shoe some horses for a man and a woman driving a wagon, and that hint had taken him in a southeasterly direction. He had misgivings about it because there were only two tiny towns in that direction, but lots of Apaches, and lots of hot desert.

HUNTING PEARL

Now, several months later he was still going, only due west now. It turned out that there had been only one town when he had gone southeast, the second having been absorbed by the relentless sand. After finding nothing but remnants of man's feeble attempts to hold back the desert at the second town, he turned west toward the larger settlements along the Gila River.

He should stop and rest for a while and then start again when the sun was down, but he didn't want to be caught alone in the desert at night so close to yesterday's incident.

A small group of Mescalero Apaches had moved in to relieve him of his supplies, especially his weapons and ammunition. He hadn't seen them, but Buster had alerted him when he nickered. He barely fought them off, but it had cost him more than half of his Spencer's ammunition. They had given up after losing two warriors and he hadn't had to fire the Winchester, but he was down to just eleven rounds for the Spencer now, and he'd have to find a town, or at least a trading post to replenish his supply.

He came close to thinking about just returning to San Miguel after the close brush with the Apaches but finally created an ultimatum for his search as he rode through the desert. He would follow the Gila River and its bend to the southwest corner of Arizona Territory. If he hadn't even found a substantial clue as to her whereabouts, then he'd just go home before leaving the territory.

Although he still had no idea where his mother lived, it was now a secondary search for him as his immediate goal was to find water. He finally climbed down from Buster and began walking himself, leading the tired gelding. He knew the Gila River was due west, but he wasn't sure of the distance.

Without looking up at the horse, he asked, "Buster, you don't know where there is any water nearby, do you?"

Buster didn't reply.

"Didn't think so."

He snickered at himself. Talking to a horse in the desert. He'll know he's in trouble if Buster starts giving him an answer.

Buster had proven to be a reliable mount for two years, and he really only had one serious flaw...Buster was a coward. Will wouldn't dare fire a gun from his back, because as soon as he fired, the gelding would bolt in a different direction. Loud noises from the east would send him racing to the west.

Will had discovered that fault in his character early in their relationship when he had been caught in a thunderstorm. When the storm had finally blown out, Will felt as abused as a rag doll and had no idea where he was. But once he knew about the problem, he had to live with it. He thought of trading Buster many times, but never quite managed to get it done.

Now he was just putting one foot in front of the other and was mentally drifting in the afternoon heat, which was a good way to get yourself killed in this territory. Suddenly, the rhythmic sounds of his and Buster's plodding steps were interrupted by the nearby buzz of a rattlesnake issuing its warning.

He snapped out of his woolgathering and saw the big diamondback curled up not six feet straight ahead of him. Buster reared slightly and stepped back, Will joined him, letting the snake keep his territory for himself.

They swung to the north to go around him. When he did, he noticed smoke on the horizon. *How could he have missed it?*

It wasn't signal smoke because it was constant. Something was burning. *But what could be burning out here?* The nearest water was to the west, but that was another ten miles or so. He changed direction and headed for the smoke. It was only a couple of miles away, and his curiosity outweighed his common sense.

He didn't increase his speed because he still needed water, so it took almost an hour to get close enough to make out the source of the smoke. It was a wagon, or what was left of it. He pulled his Winchester out of its scabbard as they neared the still smoking wagon. It hadn't been a covered wagon as what was left of the wheels was much more robust, making it look more like a freight wagon. It would have been stripped, of course. The Apaches didn't let anything go to waste.

Will was within fifty yards and quickly scanned the area. He couldn't see any movement, but that didn't mean a lot. He knew he could almost step on an Apache without realizing he was there. He kept moving at an ever slower, more careful pace, listening as well as scanning the landscape for anything that looked out of place. There were no signs of survivors, which again, was no surprise. He saw one body near the front right corner, and it looked like they had used oxen to pull the wagon, but there was no sign of them, either.

When he was finally close enough to investigate in detail, he hitched Buster to the remnants of the right rear wheel. The charred wood of the wagon's bed was bare of cargo, but the good news was that it had a water keg strapped to the side of the wagon that looked untouched. He wasn't going to rush in and start drinking it, though. Apaches had been known to foul the water and leave it for others to use at their peril. He opened the barrel, gave it a sniff, and didn't smell anything bad. He dipped his hand into the warm water and smelled it closer before he tasted it. It wasn't great, but it didn't taste like it had been tainted. He left it for the time being and walked to the opposite side of the wagon and found the second teamster. Both men had been scalped. He went through their pockets and to his pleasant surprise, found almost fifty dollars in cash. Apaches didn't care about money at all, so it seems.

He was debating about burying the two when he heard Buster whinny. He snapped his head up and saw movement to his right, quickly cocked the hammer of the Winchester and swiveled it into position, then discovered that he was aiming at a dog. At first, he thought it might be a wolf, it was so large, but it was just a dog. He lowered his carbine and stepped toward the animal. It had been injured, and there was blood on its right hind quarter.

"Come here, boy," he called as he crouched to his heels.

The dog limped toward him. He didn't know much about dogs and hoped this one didn't suddenly see him as his dinner. This one had intelligent eyes, but he could tell it was in pain.

He rose, walked to Buster, pulled a piece of jerky out of his saddlebag, then returned to the dog who was now sitting down and just staring at him.

He took two slow steps toward the dog, then dropped to his heels again, holding out the dried meat. The dog rose, then trotted towards him when he got the scent, and Will stayed in a crouch as the dog finally took the jerky and wagged his tail.

Will took a big risk when he reached out with his bare hand and held it in front of the dog. The dog sniffed his hand, smelled the jerky scent still on his fingers, and licked them. Will smiled and scratched the dog behind his ear as the dog wagged his tail again, and Will knew that he had a new friend. For more than a year, his only companion was Buster, and as well as he and the gelding got along, he already felt a stronger connection with the big dog. Maybe it was because of his eyes that seemed to be talking to him.

The trouble with his new companion was that he was an injured friend. Will sat on the remains of the wagon's bed and wondered what he could do to help the hurt canine. He hopped back from the bed, took off the Stetson he'd bought in some forgettable town along the way, walked to the water barrel, and stuck his hat inside, filling it with water. He walked to Buster first and let him drink, then filled it again and let the dog drink. Will still didn't want to take a risk, so he let Buster finish it, and then he took a swig from one of his two canteens, the one that wasn't empty. He filled the empty one with the almost depleted water barrel.

With both animals in better shape, he wondered if the dog, as injured as he was, could walk to the next water hole or the Gila River. Regardless of whether he could or not, he knew that he'd better get moving again before the Apaches came back, sure that they knew he was there. He took out two more pieces of jerky and gave one to the dog, popped the other in his mouth, and started walking. After he'd walked a hundred yards, he glanced back and saw the dog following, which made him smile.

The small parade of man, horse, and dog pressed westward toward the Gila River.

Will looked back at the dog and said, "I'm going to have to give you a name. You look like a German shepherd or maybe a wolf, so how about Otto? It's a good German name. What do you think?"

The dog wagged his tail, more than likely because Will was talking to him, but it didn't matter, from that moment on, he would be Otto.

They continued walking even after the sun had gone down. Max had shared his jerky with Otto and had given both animals more water. It was almost dark when Will saw lights almost directly ahead. It wouldn't be Apaches, so it was either white men making camp or a trading post and he hoped for a trading post. You never know what you'll find when you discover men this far away from civilization.

After another ten minutes of walking, the lights grew more defined and Will identified it as a trading post. Will breathed a lot easier when he saw the windows, and it took them another half an hour to reach the building. There was a corral in back with a couple of horses, and two more were hitched in front.

Will was about to tie off Buster at the hitching rail when he heard loud voices from inside the post.

He stepped quietly toward the door and listened.

"You better give us the money, old man!"

"I told ya. You have all that was here. There just ain't no more!"

"We know better. You gonna come clean or do we have to shoot you first and then hunt for ourselves?"

Will pulled his Colt and cocked the hammer, stepped quietly to the door, and tried to open it, hoping it was well-greased. It wasn't, so it squealed loudly when he began to pull it open.

As soon as it began its screech, he yanked it open and aimed his pistol at the two men standing in front of the proprietor. Only one had a pistol out, but he quickly turned toward Will at the sound, then snap-fired when he spotted Will's drawn pistol.

Will had no idea where the man's shot went, but wasn't about to give him a second shot, as he had the man in his sights and pulled his trigger. His heavy Colt bucked, and the .44 blasted across the sixteen-foot gap into the man's chest, smashed through two ribs, then punched through his right lung before destroying his seventh thoracic vertebra and exiting his body, burying itself into the far adobe wall. He cocked the hammer again and rushed inside to see the second man grabbing the dead man's fallen pistol.

"Don't do it, mister!" Will shouted.

Either the man was stupid, deaf, or just trusted that the kid couldn't be that lucky again, because he continued to reach for the pistol and after he had grabbed it, quickly turned it in Will's direction.

Will didn't wait for him to pull the hammer back and fired again. The second would-be robber grunted, then grabbed his stomach before he fell forward and hit the floor. Will rushed in, sending the clouds of gunsmoke into miniature tornadoes as he approached both men. He quickly found that the first one was dead, but the second was moaning and holding onto his stomach as his blood pooled on the floor beneath him.

"You murdered me, you little bastard!" he snarled.

"No, sir. I didn't murder you. I may have killed you, but it sure wasn't murder," he answered as he pulled the pistol out of the man's hand.

He looked at the revolver. It was a Colt 1873 model and used cartridges instead of the ball and powder his New Army used.

Will finally turned to face the man behind the counter. They had called him "old man", but he didn't seem that old.

"Are you all right, mister?" Will asked.

"Fine, son. Just fine. I'm right glad you showed up when you did. I was thinkin' that I was a dead man."

"I'll get them out of here."

"I'd appreciate that."

Will slid the new pistol under his gunbelt at his waist, grabbed the collar of the robber who had shot at him, and pulled him across the floor. As he waddled backward dragging the heavy load, Will looked at his chest, unsure if he shouldn't be sickened by the carnage the bullet had done. When he'd shot the Apaches, they were so far away and had been taken away by the others, so he never saw the damage. This was a lot of damage.

But he didn't feel upset by what he had done as he pulled him outside and then dragged him west, away from the trading post. He peeled off the man's gunbelt, noting the absence of cartridges in the loops, then on the way back to the trading post, dropped the gunbelt to the ground near Buster.

When he returned, he found that the second man had stopped moaning, and it wasn't because he was silently enduring the pain. He gripped his collar and dragged him outside to join his companion. He wasn't as heavy as the first man, so it was a bit easier.

As he passed their horses, he noticed that one had a Spencer like his in his scabbard and the other had a Winchester, but it was a '66, not like the '73 he already had.

He went inside the store, spotted the proprietor, and said, "I just left them a bit west of the building. I can bury them in a little while if you don't want them stinking the place up."

"You'd do that?"

"I don't mind work, mister."

"The name's Harvey. Harvey Freeman."

"Will Houston," he replied, offering his hand.

Harvey shook his hand and was trying to get an estimate on Will's age. He looked so damned young, but then, at the same time, he didn't.

"Mr. Freeman, do you have a shovel I can borrow. I'd like to get those two under the ground to keep the coyotes away."

"Oh, sure. But do you want something to eat first? I just made some beef stew."

"That sounds really good. I've been living on jerky for a few days now."

"Come on back."

Will followed Harvey to a back room which obviously functioned as both a storeroom and his living quarters. He could smell the stew and his mouth erupted in saliva.

Harvey put out two bowls and poured two cups of coffee, then handed Will a spoon before they both sat down.

"So, Will, what are you doing way out here? I usually only get customers on the north-south road about a quarter mile west, and they always show up during daylight. Well, except for those two and the Apaches."

"I'm looking for my mother, but I don't know where she lives. I was following clues and the last one must have been total nonsense. It sent me southeast and there wasn't anything there, so I turned west. I need to find her."

"How'd you lose your mother?" he asked before he took a big bite of stew.

"I didn't lose her so much as some man took her away. I didn't even know she was my mother until I figured it out a few years ago. I grew up believing that she was my sister. It turns out my mother was my grandmother, and my sister was my real mother."

"You know, that's a lot more common than you think. Girl gets herself in trouble and they let her have the baby and her mama pretends it's hers."

"It does?"

"Yes, sir. All the time. What's your mama's name?"

"Pearl Charlton. She's married to a man named Oscar."

"Don't recall the name, but most folks that pass through don't leave 'em."

"I don't have any idea where they might be, but I've searched most of New Mexico and a good part of Arizona over the past year, and I figure if I haven't found any real clues about where she could be by the time I left Arizona, I'd just go home."

"Well, your best bet from here is to head to Gila City and then to Arizona City. Gila City is maybe a good day's ride from here and Arizona City is another a day or two beyond that. Maybe you should try those places."

"I'll do that."

While they talked, they ate. Will felt his stomach churning as it finally had something to digest. It may not have been the best stew in the world, but it was filling and more than tasty enough for his needs.

When he was done, he took the shovel that Harvey let him use and went outside while the owner cleaned up the blood from the floor. After leaving his gunbelt and the new Colt with the gunbelt near Buster, he hunted for a place for the grave. He didn't want to bury them so close to the trading post, so he dragged them another fifty feet before starting to dig. He'd only dig one hole, and it wasn't going to be six feet deep either. Four feet ought to be enough to keep the night critters away.

It took him almost an hour of what many would consider back-breaking work, but not for Will. He'd done a lot worse over the past year and before that, too, when he had to do what his father told him to do. It wasn't too hot, considering he was in southern Arizona, but the sweat still poured off him. He was getting ready to dump both men into the hole when he noticed that the big man had almost new boots, then checked the size and pulled them off his feet. They were really nice boots and appeared to fit his large feet. He rolled both bodies into the hole and spent another twenty minutes covering them up. He may not have broken his back, but he was exhausted when he was finished and in dire need of water.

He carried the boots and the shovel back to the trading post, leaving the boots near Buster with the two gunbelts, and went inside again.

"All done, Mr. Freeman," he announced as he walked inside.

"Here, you need some water, Will," he said as he handed him a large glass of water.

Will swallowed it down without stopping, then handed the glass back to Harvey and said, "Thanks, Mr. Freeman."

"Will, call me Harvey, will ya?"

"Thanks, Harvey."

"What can I do for you to thank you for saving my hide?" he asked.

"Oh, I'm fine. I'll probably take that Winchester out there in that man's scabbard, though. Maybe they have some ammunition for that Spencer, too."

"You need Spencer ammunition? I got eight boxes of that stuff. You can have two."

"Thanks, Harvey. I'm going to go out and check to see what they have in their saddlebags. Maybe I won't need them."

Will left the trading post, approached the two horses at the hitchrail, and slid the Winchester '66 from the scabbard to take a quick look at the Yellowboy. In the low light, it was hard to examine well, but when he cycled the lever action, no cartridge was ejected. It was empty. The action felt good, though.

He took the Winchester and the scabbard over to Buster and slipped it into his bedroll, then returned, pulled the Spencer out of the second horse's scabbard, and found four rounds in its stock's loading tube. He removed the cartridges before going through the saddlebags and found another eight rounds of Spencer ammunition, some jerky, which he tossed to Otto, and then just some clothes that were a bit ripe. There were two canteens, though, which he appreciated. He took both of them and hooked them over his saddle horn, then strapped on the gunbelt with the Colt Model '73 and carried the now-empty Spencer back inside with him.

"What did you find, Will?"

"A total of a dozen rounds for the Spencer and another carbine. Did you want it? I don't have any use for two of them."

"Sure. Folks are always looking for good guns."

Will pulled the Colt from the holster and said, "I like this '73. It's chambered for the same .44 cartridge as my Winchester, too."

"I'll give you four boxes of those cartridges. I have plenty of 'em in stock. They're mighty popular."

"What about their horses and saddles, Harvey. You want those?"

"I'd recommend that you take one with you. I'll take the other for resale, though."

"Alright. I'll look at them in the morning. I need to get them stripped and fed, though. My horse needs more attention than they do, I think."

"Go ahead and put 'em in the corral. There's plenty of water and hay for 'em back there."

"I'll be back shortly," Will replied as he leaned the Spencer against the wall.

Will went back outside, stripped the saddles off each horse, and walked them back to the corral. He checked out the two horses and liked the mare a lot. She was tan with a dark mane and tail. He didn't know if it was black or brown in the low light, but she seemed like a pleasant animal. After twenty minutes, all three horses were in the corral and munching on the hay.

"Did you find one you liked, Will?" Harvey asked as he walked back inside.

"The tan mare seemed like a gentle soul. I'll take her along with the saddle and saddlebags. It'll be like having a light pack horse."

"You gonna need anything else?"

"I'll need some food before I leave and that should do it."

"That's all I can do for you, Will?"

"That's more than enough, Harvey. I need to get some shuteye, though. I'm a bit tuckered from digging that hole."

"Why don't you bed down here? You can put your bedroll on the floor."

"I appreciate it, but I'd rather be outside. I have a dog that needs company."

"You have a dog? Why didn't you say so? I got a big chunk of beef that I smoked earlier. I could carve out a piece and you could give some to your furry friend."

"I'm sure he'd be grateful."

"What's his name?"

"Otto. I just found him about ten miles east of here. Apaches took out a freight wagon, stripped it, and scalped the two freighters. The dog must have run after it took a hit. Doesn't look bad though."

"How long ago was this attack, you reckon?"

"I'd think earlier this morning. There was still smoke from the wagon being burned, and those two men hadn't been attacked by critters yet. I didn't even see any vultures, for that matter. I guess the smoke kept them away for the time being."

44

"Why would freighters be over there? There's nothing out that way at all. My supplies come from Gila City, and all my customers come from the north-south road."

"I have no idea. The wagon was empty, so I don't know what they were carrying."

"I'd be bettin' that they had rifles and ammunition. Some of these low-life bastards think that they can make money runnin' guns to the Apaches. They get there, and they think they can pull one over on the Injuns by selling them old Springfields or Burnsides. But them Apaches ain't stupid. They want repeaters like that Winchester. They'll even settle for Spencers, but not the single shot guns."

"That makes sense."

"Hang on. I'll give you a piece of beef for the dog."

He disappeared inside and returned a minute later with a piece of beef that must have weighed a pound and handed it to Will.

"He's going to be a happy puppy. Thanks, Harvey."

Will left the trading post and found Otto sitting next to the door, then dropped to his heels.

"You sure are well-behaved, Otto."

He took out his knife and carved a piece of beef out and handed it to Otto. The big dog dropped down and kept the beef between his paws as began ripping it apart.

Will cut off a second piece and began chewing it himself as he watched the big dog wolf down the meat. It was a pleasant change from the jerky. When Otto finished, he gave him the last piece, which he gratefully accepted, in that he didn't take Will's fingers off when he took the meat.

Will walked to his saddles and rifles and dragged them to the western side of the trading post closer to the corral. He spread out his bedroll and pulled off his boots. The new boots he placed near his saddle with the carbine and the Winchesters. His new Colt and his old Colt he kept within reach, each in its own holster. The difference between the gunbelts was the absence of cartridge loops on his, but they both had knife sheaths with nice blades. He hadn't been exaggerating when he said that he was exhausted and fell asleep in five minutes.

––––––

Will's eyes cracked open as the just risen sun sent a harsh ray of light into his face. It was chilly, relatively speaking, of course. He slid out of his bedroll and turned the new boots upside down and shook them. No critters toppled out, so he slipped them on and was pleased with the fit. They were in much better shape than his. He stood, took care of his immediate morning needs and walked to the back of the post, and looked at the mare in the corral. She was as nice as he expected, so he walked over to the corral fence and Buster trotted over to him. He thought of making the mare his primary mount and Buster a pack horse, but she wasn't that much of an improvement to warrant the change.

"Buster, it looks like we're going to have female companionship for a while. What do you think of your new girlfriend?"

Will laughed at the thought. If he had lost his manhood like Buster had, then he wouldn't have thought it was so funny. He took a look at the two extra saddles and picked out the nicer of the two and set it aside. He then examined the Winchester in the morning light. The '66 Yellowboy seemed to be in decent condition but decided he wouldn't need two, so he thought he'd leave it with Harvey. He hadn't found any money on the two miscreants, so he guessed that they were out of food and ammo and thought they could just help themselves. He pulled the new Colt from the holster and checked its load. Sure enough, there was only one more round left in the cylinders. He'd need to clean both weapons, so he needed a new cleaning kit.

He walked to the trough and washed, or at least as well as one could clean himself in water shared by horses and probably all manners of nighttime critters.

He walked to the front of the post and opened the door, finding that Harvey was already awake, then carried the Winchester '66 inside and set it near the Spencer.

"I found that on one of the horses, Harvey, and I don't need a second Winchester."

Harvey was surprised, and said, "Are you sure, Will? I mean, it's a repeater."

"I know, but I already have my Spencer and a '73 that I bought a few months ago."

"Well, I appreciate it. Now, do you fancy a real breakfast?" he asked as he smiled.

"You don't mean with eggs, do you?"

"Eggs and bacon. Come on in."

Will almost sprinted into the back room. He hadn't had eggs in almost a month.

The smell of bacon took control of his senses as Harvey cracked the eggs into the pan. There were eight strips of bacon on the plate, so Will had to sneak one. Harvey noticed and laughed.

After Harvey placed the plate in front of him, Will inhaled the four eggs and remaining three strips of bacon as Harvey asked, "So, you'll be moving on now, Will?"

"Yes, sir."

"Well, good luck in finding your mother. I've packed one bag with food and the other with your ammunition."

"Harvey, do you have any cleaning kits for that Colt and Winchester?"

"Sure do. I'll get you one of each."

He went to the counter and reached underneath, picking out two boxes, then walked over to the smaller bag and slipped them inside.

"Thanks, Harvey. How much do I owe you?"

"You must be joking, Will. You saved my life, my money, and gave me an extra horse and two guns to sell. I owe you much more."

Will wasn't about to argue, but said, "Well, thank you anyway, Harvey," then stood and offered his hand.

They shook hands before Will turned, then walked back outside with the two heavy bags and carried them around to the back of the post where the horses waited. He set the bags down, led Buster out of the corral and saddled him first, tied his reins to the corral rail, then put the Spencer and the Winchester back into their scabbards. He led the tan mare out of the corral, saddled her, then hung the two bags over her saddle, tied them

48

down, and then filled all four canteens. He may only have forty miles to ride to Gila City, but it never paid to take chances, even with the Gila River a mile or less to the west of the road. His last step in his preparation was to make a trail rope for the mare and hook it to Buster.

He handed Otto a few pieces of jerky, then mounted Buster and trailing the mare, trotted past the front of the trading post and waved at Harvey before he headed west to pick up the road to Gila City. Just a few minutes later, he was riding south, hoping to find some clues to his mother's whereabouts in the biggest town he'd been to in a few months.

He kept Buster at a walk so Otto could keep up. The dog seemed to be doing much better as he trotted alongside with no sign of a limp.

They had been on the road for about three hours when Will spotted the vultures that should have been at the wagon and wondered if more Apaches were nearby. They were circling about a half mile off the road to the west and he was keeping an eye on them when Otto suddenly veered from the road in the direction of the big birds.

"Otto!" he shouted, but the dog kept trotting in that direction. Now, Will was curious to find what interested Otto, hoping that the dog would spot any hidden Apaches.

Otto must have spooked the vultures because he could see two of the large birds taking to the air ahead.

He angled Buster in the same direction, pulled his Winchester, but kept him at a walk. After a few minutes, he could see a body on the ground. It looked like a boy, maybe an Apache or Navajo boy, judging by the long, black hair. Otto had already reached the body and was just sitting about three feet away, apparently guarding it from the circling vultures.

Will grew closer and was stunned to find that it wasn't a boy at all. She was a girl, had been stripped almost naked, and was lying half on her stomach with dried blood caked on her back and legs. He stepped down and let Buster stand untethered.

He warily approached the body. The two dead men from last night didn't bother him, but this one did. He wondered why she was here, so far from the road. He could see hoofprints and signs of struggle around her, which suggested the reason for her presence out here in the middle of nowhere. She was so thin it was difficult to guess her age. It could be anywhere from twelve to twenty.

He stepped quietly to the body and was already wondering where he should bury her when he saw her left foot move just a twitch, but it was enough to tell him that there was still some life in her. He ran back to Buster, pulled open his saddlebag and yanked out one of his three spare shirts, grabbed a canteen, and rushed back.

He covered her with his shirt and knelt near her head before he pulled the stopper out of the canteen and poured some water slowly over her forehead.

"Ma'am? Ma'am?" he said in a normal voice but received no response.

He rolled her gently onto her back, keeping the shirt over her. In addition to protecting her modesty, it would keep the sun from frying her skin to a crisp, even though she had darker skin that probably wouldn't burn as quickly as his had when he first started his journey. Will was well-tanned after two years crossing the southwest, but hers was natural. He looked at her face and tried to get a sense of who she could be. She looked like an Indian, but not completely because her cheekbones weren't as pronounced. He guessed she was a half-breed. Probably the product of a white father and Indian mother. It was

50

very common in the Southwest, but right now, none of that mattered. She just wasn't responding to anything he did to bring her out of her unconscious state.

He stoppered the canteen and set it down, then pulled out his Colt New Army and cocked the hammer. He pointed it to the west and squeezed the trigger. The loud report did what the water had failed to do when her eyes flew open as Will was holstering the pistol.

"Ma'am? Can you hear me?" he asked.

She just looked at him with wide eyes filled with fear.

He picked up the canteen again, pulled out the stopper, and offered it to her. She closed her eyes and said nothing.

"Ma'am? How can I help? What do you need me to do?"

She finally spoke when she just croaked, "Let me die."

Will was stunned by her response and said, "I can't do that, ma'am. You need help. Can you get up?"

"Just leave me," she whispered hoarsely.

"Sorry, ma'am. I'm not going to do that either. You need a doctor."

"No. Let me die."

Will began slowly pouring water over her face. Involuntarily, she began moving her tongue across her cracked lips. The water must have modified her wish to die, if only slightly.

"Just let me stay here. I want to die," she said in a slightly stronger voice.

"Dying is kind of permanent, ma'am, and you can't change your mind later."

"It won't matter. Leave me alone," she said as she closed her eyes and turned away from him.

Will knew he couldn't just leave her here to die, so he stood, then walked to Buster and removed his bedroll. The girl acted as if he wasn't there as she stayed lying on the sands with her eyes closed. He carried his bedroll to the girl, stretched it out on the ground four feet from her, then laid down on his back and pulled his Stetson over his eyes.

She opened her eyes, turned her head to the side facing him, and said, "What are you doing? I told you to leave."

"I'm going to keep you alive until you stop this nonsense of wanting to die. You're too young to die."

"What do you know about anything? Just go away."

"No."

She turned away from Will again, and he wondered how long she had been there.

"How long have you been laying here?"

"It doesn't matter. I will die here. Leave me!"

"I'll give you one thing. You sure are stubborn."

She didn't reply.

"It looks like you've been assaulted, ma'am. I don't suppose that it was by two men who kind of smelled bad, was it?"

She turned her face back toward him, glaring at him despite his face being hidden under his hat, but said nothing.

Will then said, "Last night, I found two men trying to rob Harvey Freeman's trading post about three hours' ride north of here and killed them both. One of them was riding a pretty tan mare. The horse is right there," he said as he pointed toward the horses with his Stetson still covering his face.

The girl looked at the horse and recognized it as one of their horses but wondered if he had really killed the two men. He didn't look much older than she was, so she remained silent.

"You're hurt, ma'am. I'm sure your folks will want you back home."

That statement inspired a surprising and angry response when she almost swore, "No! My father won't want me back. He'll send me away. I can't face them. Let me die!"

"So, the two men that did this to you. Did one ride the mare or not?" he asked.

Finally, she admitted, "Yes. That's one of the horses."

"Now, I killed those two men last night. They're not coming back to hurt you again."

"They are really dead?"

"Dead and buried, ma'am."

She closed her eyes and whispered a quiet prayer that Will couldn't recognize.

He didn't know if it was one of thankfulness or forgiveness, but she seemed more at peace when she finished even as she kept her eyes closed.

"So, are you still wanting to die, or will you rejoin the land of the living?"

Again, she provided no answer, but after having seen her pray, he changed his approach.

"Ma'am, you're going to go to hell if you just die."

Her eyes flew open as she glared at him and croaked, "Who are you to judge? I didn't ask for what they did to me! They violated me!"

"I wasn't saying that you'd go to hell for being attacked, ma'am. I was saying you'd go to hell for letting yourself die. That's suicide and it's a mortal sin."

"It's not suicide. It's just letting God take me."

"It's not any different than just walking off a cliff and saying God is letting you fall to the earth. It's a lousy excuse and you know it."

She squirmed when he said that because deep down, she knew he was right, but still didn't know if she could trust him. *Did she have a choice?*

Will's face was still under his Stetson as he said, "You'd better drink some water, ma'am. I don't want to have to bury you like I did those two that I tossed into their grave last night."

"Why did you bury them after killing them? They didn't deserve to be buried. They should have been eaten by coyotes and vultures."

"I didn't care either, ma'am. I just didn't fancy waking up to the smell. They smelled bad enough while they were alive."

She almost snickered but didn't, as she reached over and picked up the canteen, pulled the stopper, and poured the water down her throat.

Will could hear her drinking but wasn't sure he should look. She might be exposed because she'd have to be sitting to drink and the last thing that she'd want is a man looking at her.

"Would you like something to eat now, ma'am?" he asked, reasonably sure that she'd changed her mind about dying once he heard her drinking.

Finally, she answered his question when she replied, "Yes."

"I'll get you something, but before I do, I need you to put on the shirt, so you don't get embarrassed."

She wondered why she should be embarrassed. He had seen her naked, and she had little to show anyway, but she pulled her arms through the shirtsleeves and buttoned the front.

"I have your shirt on."

Will sat up and shoved his Stetson back onto his head, then stood and walked toward the bags.

Before he reached them, she said, "I am naked below the waist. Do you have anything else to cover me, so I can stand?"

"I have an extra pair of britches you can wear. I have some extra boots, but they're probably too big. You have small feet."

"I'll wear the britches and go barefoot."

"Stay there then. I'll go and get the britches."

He stood and walked back to Buster, pulled back the flap to the saddlebag, and pulled out his only pair of spare britches. He'd buy some more in Gila City after he dropped her off.

He walked back to her, handed her the pants, and said, "These are going to be pretty baggy on you, but I'll get you something to hold them up when I get you some food. I won't turn around until you tell me you're dressed."

"Alright."

Will headed back to the tan mare and lifted the two bags from the horse. He opened the smaller, heavier bag and took out a box of .44 caliber ammunition. Then he opened the large bag with the food and stared inside. It was quite a haul. There was also a piece of paper, which he pulled from the bag and unfolded. It was a note from Harvey.

Will:

I know you wouldn't accept this while you were here. Thanks for what you did. I'll make the money back from selling the horse, saddle, and Spencer.

Harvey

He was confused until he looked deeper into the bag and found some folded bills and pulled them out. It was a hundred dollars. Between that and the fifty he got from the teamsters, he now had over three hundred and fifty dollars in cash. It was a lot of money. He stuffed the bills into different pockets until he could put them into his homemade money belt and took out a small ham. He cut off a piece and tossed it to Otto, who had remained on guard the entire time, then he cut off some more pieces and added some biscuits that were wrapped in a cloth.

He waited until she said, "I'm dressed, so you can turn around."

Will closed the bag and took four biscuits and four slices of ham over to the girl. She looked a lot different wearing the shirt and britches, especially as both were much too large for her. She looked almost like a boy, except for her big brown eyes, long black hair, and smooth face. He stepped over and handed her two of the biscuits and ham, then watched as she devoured them as quickly as Otto would have.

He was going to eat two himself but held off until she finished, then handed her the other two. She didn't question why he wasn't eating as she accepted them both and ate them, but more slowly. He pulled another canteen off Buster and gave it to her to wash down the biscuits. She uncorked it and drank deeply.

"I'll hang the bags on the mare and then I'll take you back to Gila City."

She quickly lowered the canteen and surprised him when she said, "I can't go back home. Not like this. If you won't leave me here, then you must take me with you."

Will didn't like that idea at all and said, "Ma'am, you've got to understand. I'm heading all over the place looking for my mother and I don't know how long I'll have to keep hunting for her. It could be months. I can't take care of anyone, and you're just a young girl, so it wouldn't be right."

She snapped, "Then let me stay here. Maybe more men will come and abuse me again. You wouldn't care."

Will felt backed into a corner as he replied, "Ma'am, that's just not fair. I can't let that happen, and I can't take you with me. You can understand that, can't you?"

"No, I can't. I'm coming with you or I'm staying right here."

Now, Will was seriously conflicted. *What were his options?* Maybe he could let her come along for a while and then talk her into staying in Gila City. It was still a day's ride away and it would buy him some time and he might find some way out of this dilemma.

"Alright, you can come along."

She almost smiled at her victory but instead upended the canteen again.

As she drank, Will looked a little further away to where she had obviously been assaulted and saw the remains of her clothing and some blood on the ground. She didn't seem injured at all, so he wondered if she was hurt inside.

When she finished drinking, he asked, "Ma'am, are you okay? Are you cut anywhere? Or are you hurt inside?"

"No, I'm not cut. I'll be better soon."

Will didn't want to press the issue, but asked, "Can you ride, or do you want to rest for a while?"

"I don't know. Let me get into the saddle and I'll see."

She walked over to the mare and put her bare foot into the stirrup and pulled herself up. She was grimacing as she swung her leg over the saddle, then when she started to sit, she quickly pulled her leg back and stepped down.

"I think I need some more time. Can we stay here for a while?"

"Alright. I'll put out the blanket, so you can just lie down. I'll unsaddle the horses again. Water might be a problem, though."

"There is a seep about a mile down the road on the right or the Gila River about a mile west."

"Okay. I'll leave you here with the mare and some food. I'll leave you with a pistol, too. Do you know how to shoot a gun?"

"Yes, but not a pistol."

"I'll give you a quick lesson before I go to fill up the canteens and let Buster get something to drink. I'll take the mare as well, so she can drink, too."

"*You're going to leave me, aren't you?*" she asked with panicked eyes.

"No, ma'am, I won't. I promise you that I'll come right back."

"Promises mean nothing."

"They mean everything to me. I've never broken one before and I won't this time."

She just looked at him, not knowing what to make of him.

He pulled out his blanket and spread it on the ground, then he unsaddled the mare and put the saddle near the blanket, pulled out his Colt New Army from the saddlebag, and walked over to her.

"I can't keep calling you ma'am. What's your name?"

"Mary Fleming."

"I'm Will Houston. Let me show you how to use the pistol. It's really simple."

He showed her how to cock the hammer, point it, and pull the trigger, which is all she needed to know for the time being.

"There are only three rounds left in this gun. I'll reload it when I come back. If you like, you can wear it. I'll leave all the food and ammunition with you, so that should make you feel better."

"It does."

"Go ahead and drink some more water and I'll be back with the full canteens in about half an hour."

"The seep is easy to find, there are tracks going to the west."

"Thank you, Mary. I'll be back shortly."

He climbed on board Buster and swung him diagonally southeast to intercept the road closer to the seep. He reached the road after just ten minutes and, as Mary had suggested, found the seep easily. He filled all four canteens before letting both horses drink their fill, then he headed back, following his own tracks back to Mary.

He was thinking as he rode. *How would he be able to convince her to stay in Gila City?* Maybe her father wouldn't be such a jerk. He also wondered about the blood. If she wasn't cut, then it meant that she had been deflowered by those bastards. Rape was bad enough, but to have it happen to a young girl was a crime beyond punishment.

He found Mary stretched out on the blanket with her eyes closed, and he thought that she needed a hat or something to keep the sun out of her eyes. She didn't even look up as he approached.

Otto had come along with Will, so he was well watered, and trotted ahead, then sat down almost protectively next to Mary, just as he had before, even though the vultures had already flown off in search of better pickings.

Will stopped about fifty feet away and stepped down, ground hitched Buster, and began to unsaddle him. He would glance over at Mary from time to time and began to worry that something had happened to her in the brief time he was away.

He had Buster unsaddled and carried the four canteens to the blanket and the hopefully sleeping Mary, then walked quietly to the blanket and knelt beside her.

"Mary? Are you all right?"

Her eyes popped open and she turned her head.

"Of course, I'm all right. I was just resting. It felt good to just lay here and feel the sun on my face."

"I was worried that something had happened to you. The blood scared me, and I didn't know if you were still bleeding inside or something. I had to make sure."

Her eyes grew even wider as she looked at him and asked, "You don't understand, do you?"

"Understand what?"

"What those men did to me."

"Yes, I do. They raped you, and you were still a virgin. I'm sorry. I knew that, but I just didn't want to bring it up. I was worried you might be still bleeding from other injuries."

Mary said angrily, "They hurt me! I wanted to kill them but could do nothing! *Do you know what that's like? To be violated and have no way to stop it*? Of course, you don't. You're a man.

Men don't have it happen to them. My mother did and now I did. Maybe I'll have a baby just like she had me. You'll never understand!"

Then she did something that surprised Will when she began to cry. Will had wondered why she had suffered through such torment and been able to act so normal, except for wanting to die. Now, she sat on the blanket and just shook as her tears washed over her.

Will was at a loss. She was right in her accusations. He didn't understand at all, but he did know better than to go over and hold her while she cried. She was probably a lot more upset than she let on.

Will may have been very ignorant in that area before his talk with Sarah, but after the past year, he was no longer new to the pleasures of the flesh. On his trip, he had enjoyed the pleasures of four daughters of farmers and ranchers. One, Carla Gomez, he had enjoyed almost a dozen times before he left, but he knew that Mary was strictly hands-off for more than just her situation. Aside from her boyishly thin appearance, he still had no idea of her age.

As she continued to weep, he said, "I'm sorry, Mary. You're right, I don't understand. I'm ignorant of many of those kinds of things. But there's nothing I can do to change what happened to you. If you'd rather that I just give you the horse, some water, and food and then just leave, I'll do that."

Mary suddenly wished she hadn't vented at Will. It wasn't his fault. He just seemed so innocent and really had no idea what she had gone through, and even worse, he had no conception of what she would go through if she went home.

As she wiped the tears from her face, in a much gentler voice, she said, "I'm sorry, Will. It's not your fault. I'm just so angry for what they did to me. I'd rather you stay. Besides, I need to be your guide. Why are you looking for your mother?"

Will was glad for the change in the topic as he replied, "When I was just a kid, I realized that I was only six months older than my sister, Sarah. I couldn't ask my father, because he'd probably beat me like he did when I asked why I had blue eyes and everyone else in the family had brown eyes. It wasn't until after he died that I finally was able to get the whole story from my mother, who was really my grandmother.

"She told me that I wasn't her son, but her grandson and I was the son of the woman I thought was my older sister. Her name is Pearl. I left home just before I turned eighteen and I've been searching for her over a year now. I've had to work along my way to keep my belly full, so it's taken me a lot longer to get here. I've made up my mind that if I don't at least find a solid lead to where she is before I leave Arizona, I'll go back home."

Mary knew it was a common tale, but Will had made it uncommon by traveling hundreds of miles in a search for his mother. Most just acknowledged the change in parentage and continued on with their lives.

Mary looked at him and said, "So, neither of us knew our real fathers. Unless your mother married the man who made her pregnant."

"She didn't. My mother, or rather, my grandmother, said that Pearl never said who he was. I'm not sure it really matters. I just remember when she went away with her new husband. She was crying and begging that I come along, but he didn't want me. I was six years old when they left."

"You are nineteen now?"

"Yes. How old are you, Mary?"

"I'll be eighteen in two months."

Will must have looked surprised because Mary continued, "You thought I was much younger, didn't you?"

"Yes. I thought you were fourteen or fifteen."

"It's because I'm so thin. We never had much to eat in the house, and my mother's husband ate most of what we did have. He is fat and I am thin."

"That's terrible, Mary. A man should take care of his family first."

She laughed before she said, "You don't know him. It's why I know he will use this as an excuse not to take me back. Besides, he was going to try to sell me in two months anyway."

Will was shocked by her comment and the casual nature of its delivery before he asked, "*What do you mean sell you? Like a slave?*"

"No. As a wife to anyone who would pay for me. Now, I am damaged, and he'll be very angry if he knows that I am no longer a virgin and would have to lower his asking price."

Will sat back on his haunches and asked, "Are you afraid of returning to Gila City?"

"I do not have to be afraid, because I will not go back there."

"I need more food and some clothes, Mary. I don't have enough to last all the way to Arizona City."

"You could leave me outside the city and get your things and come back for me."

"Do you trust me already?"

"No, but I have little choice. If you leave me with the mare and some food, it is better than I was before."

"Alright. We'll do that. But when we set up camp, I'd rather do it further from the road. I don't want any nighttime visitors."

Mary just nodded.

Then, there was a dead period of about two minutes where neither spoke a word.

Mary broke the awkward silence, when she asked, "Where are you from, Will?"

"Northeastern New Mexico. A town called San Miguel."

"Did you live there all your life?"

"Until I left to begin my search."

"Why has it taken you so long to get here?"

"I had some money, but still needed to work my way. Some places I stayed longer than others. Some were just a day or two and others were two or three months. It kept my belly full and at the very worst, didn't drain my cash."

"Do you have much money?"

Will was tempted to say 'no', but if he did, it would mean she'd know sooner or later that he didn't trust her.

"I have enough."

"I won't cost you anything, Will. I can work."

"No, Mary. You won't need to work. I'm close enough now that I'm not going to work either."

"What happens when you find your mother?"

Now that was an interesting question that he surprisingly hadn't thought of before. He'd been so intent on finding her that he really hadn't applied much attention to what would happen if he did finally locate her.

"I hadn't really thought about it much. I wanted so badly to find her, that I didn't think about what to do after."

Her question then plunged him into deep thought. *What would he do? Say, 'Hello, Mama. Remember me?' and then shake hands? What if she was dead?* It had been thirteen years since he'd seen her. A lot can happen in that time, especially to women. So many died during childbirth. He'd known several women in San Miguel who had gone to meet their maker that way. *What if she didn't want to see him anymore?*

He came out of his reverie and saw Mary staring at him as her almost cow-like brown eyes studied him.

"Mary, what about your mother? When I go into Gila City, did you want me to tell her that you're safe?"

Now it was Mary's turn to drift off and think about the question, which she finally answered, saying, "I'm not sure. My mother is afraid of her husband. He hits her often."

"Do you have any brothers or sisters?"

"No, do you?"

"That's a good question, because I always had Sarah, who I thought was my sister, but she's now my aunt, and my other sister, Pearl, turned out to be my mother. So, unless my mother, Pearl, has had children, then I guess I don't have any brothers or sisters either."

Mary grinned and said, "That's confusing, isn't it?"

Will smiled back at her and answered, "I still think of Sarah as my sister and my grandmother as my mother, though."

"Do they know where you are?"

"Sort of. I write letters to them, about once every two or three weeks, but because I'm rarely in the same place very long, I've never received any because I don't know where I'll be. I'll write to them again in Gila City, though."

Mary sighed, looked down, and said, "I never could write or read because I am so stupid."

"Mary, that's not true. You may be ignorant, but you're not stupid."

"It's the same thing."

"No, it's not. Being ignorant just means that you don't know something. You don't know how to read or write, so you are ignorant about it. But stupid means you can't learn. You seem smart enough to learn. You speak English very well. I know of many people who have finished schooling and don't speak it nearly as well as you do."

"That is from my mother. She is Navajo and when she learned to speak English from the priests, they taught her to use it properly."

"I'll bet her husband doesn't speak well."

She smiled and asked, "How did you know?"

"Because any man that hurts his wife really is stupid."

Mary laughed, a sound that Will found hard to believe possible she could make after what she had been through.

"Mary, can I ask you something that I'm very curious about?"

She studied his face for a moment before replying, "Alright."

"You went through a terrible ordeal less than a day ago, and you seem to have put it behind you very quickly. I knew one other woman who was raped when I was fifteen, and she was upset for a long time."

Mary looked down at the blanket and replied, "Most of my anguish was burned from me by the time you arrived. All that was left was emptiness. It happens to many young women in our part of town. I had expected it to happen to me long before today, but maybe because I was so thin, I wasn't considered worth violating. I vowed then, that if it did happen, I would seek vengeance, not sorrow. But you already avenged what they did to me."

"If I had known what they had done, Mary, I would have made them suffer more."

"Thank you, but it doesn't matter. I must go on now."

"Then why did you tell me to let you die?"

She looked at him as she answered, "As I said, I was empty inside. I'm not sure I really wanted to die, but I wanted you to go away. I didn't know what you were going to do. I was helpless again. If you were another man like those two, I don't know if I could have survived."

"Mary, if I was another man like those two, telling me to let you die wouldn't have made any difference. They weren't men at all. They were animals."

"It was the best I could come up with at the time. You were suddenly there, so I pretended to be dead, but you surprised me. Once you knew I was alive, all I could do was hope you would leave me alone. I'm glad you didn't, Will."

"What's your mother's name?"

"Her Christian name was Maria. Her Navajo name meant White Cloud. She is a very pretty woman."

"Then why did she marry your father?"

"She was already pregnant, and he offered my grandfather money to marry her. He only found out about her pregnancy after they were married, but she was so beautiful that he kept her. Now, I think he is tired of her and treats her badly."

"Does he hit you?"

"Sometimes. But not as often or as hard as he hits my mother."

"Want me to shoot him?"

The question took Mary by surprise. She had wished her father dead many times as he hit her mother, *but to actually have it done?*

"No. You would go to prison or hang for it. God will punish him."

"I'd like to pound him a while, though."

"He is a big man, Will. I think it better if you let it go."

"Can your mother read?"

"Yes. The priests taught her."

"How about your father?"

"A little bit. But he cannot read handwriting."

"If I left your mother a note saying that you are safe and protected, would that be alright?"

Mary thought about it. She loved her mother and it would help her to know that she was alive and safe.

"I think so. If you ask anyone where Joseph Fleming lives, they should tell you."

"Okay. I'll try and do that. What happened to your boots or moccasins?"

"I was barefoot when they caught me. It was dusk, and I was outside the city picking some flowers, so I could sell them in the square the next day. They were leaving town and saw me. I tried to escape, but they were on horses and there were two of them. They smelled bad."

"I know. I have a spare pair of boots that are too large, but if I put some cloth inside each one, you could wear those."

"I'll go barefoot. It's all right."

"Are you still hungry?"

"Yes. I'm always hungry."

"I'll start a fire and we'll have some lunch. I could use some food myself."

Will dug a small pit and began picking up pieces of old wood that seemed to be scattered in a decent quantity in the area. Some were natural, but most were pieces of wagons or discarded furniture. He started the fire and set his cooking grate over the top, poured some water from one canteen into his coffeepot, and set it and his skillet on the grate. He walked quickly to the food bag, pulled a can of beans and some onions, and cut some pieces off the ham. He tossed the ham and onions into the frypan and then opened the can of beans and dumped that in. As the mix began bubbling, Will started stirring their dinner and sprinkled in some salt. He only had one plate and one spoon, so he'd need to share with Mary.

The water was boiling, so he pulled it off the grate and added some coffee which he'd have to share with Mary using his lone tin cup.

"Mary, we're going to have to share until I can get another plate, spoon, and cup in Gila City."

"That's fine."

He spooned the mix onto the plate and filled the cup with coffee, then handed the plate to Mary along with the spoon. She took a spoonful and blew on it before putting it in her mouth. It may not have been a culinary masterpiece, but Mary seemed more than pleased as she put it into her small mouth. After she swallowed, she handed the plate back to Will.

"No, go ahead and finish that. There's more in the frypan. Do you drink black coffee?"

"When I get a chance."

She devoured the entire plate in less than a minute before Will handed her the coffee and refilled the plate, emptying the fry pan. He took three bites and then handed the plate to her.

"That's yours, Will," she said, still sipping the coffee.

"I'm full. You go ahead and finish it."

She knew he was far from full but gratefully accepted the food. She ate the last of the bean and ham mix more slowly, but soon the plate was clean. She handed the plate and empty cup back to Will and promptly belched.

Will started laughing as Mary just smiled sheepishly.

He poured himself some coffee, then remembered he had forgotten to take care of Otto.

"I forgot Otto. Just a minute."

He went to his saddlebag and took out four pieces of jerky. Otto watched closely as Will tossed one in his direction. The big dog caught it on the fly and inhaled it, but just handed to rest of the dried meat to him.

"He's a handsome dog. How long have you had him?"

"Just a day. I found a wagon that had been raided by the Apaches about twenty miles northeast of here. The dog came out of his hiding place when he saw me. He'd been injured but seems okay now. He's a smart dog too, so I named him Otto."

"Why Otto?"

"He looks like the German shepherd that one of my friends had back in San Miguel, and the only German name I know is Otto."

"Can I pet him?"

"I'm sure he wouldn't mind. He seems to be a friendly dog, but I imagine if he doesn't like someone, he'd be anything but friendly."

Mary reached out to Otto and he sniffed her hand, then took two steps closer to her before she rubbed him behind his ears and Otto had a new friend.

Will cleaned the plate and frypan in the sand rather than waste any water, then put them back in his saddlebags and returned to the blanket. Mary had stretched out and had her eyes closed, so Will just sat nearby and looked at her.

He was still astounded that she seemed to be so normal after what she had just endured, and even more astonishing was her apparent acceptance that such behavior was viewed as almost normal and expected.

But one thing he knew for certain was that if she continued to eat as she just had, he'd need a lot more food. He'd see what he could get in Gila City tomorrow or maybe the day after. Tonight, they'd camp about another half mile away from the road and then start south in the morning. They should reach Gila City by mid-afternoon.

Those two bastards that he buried must have carried her off quite a way from the city to make sure she couldn't run back, or anyone could hear her screams. At least no one would hurt her now. His plans to leave her in Gila City just evaporated after learning about her home life. *Her father was going to sell her off to the highest bidder? What was wrong with the world? And she didn't even seem to understand how wrong that was!*

He watched Mary as she slept. She looked like a fifteen-year-old boy from the neck down and still didn't look like she was eighteen in her face. She looked as if she was no older than sixteen and he wondered if she wasn't exaggerating her age, so he wouldn't be so worried about having her along.

Mary wasn't sleeping, she was thinking. She suspected that Will wanted to leave her somewhere. Gila City was off the list, but he would probably leave her in Arizona City, especially if he found his mother. She thought Arizona City would be worse because she knew no one there, but he seemed to be kind and that meant he wouldn't leave her, or at least she hoped that he wouldn't. That was three or four days from now and a lot could change.

Eventually, her pretend sleep transitioned into a genuine siesta before Will also succumbed to the afternoon doldrums and drifted off.

———

His eyes snapped awake less than an hour later, feeling foolish for having fallen asleep. He stood, stretched, and scanned the road for potential visitors. There was a small dust cloud from the north, probably about two or three miles off.

He quickly saddled both horses and put the two bags on the mare as he kept glancing at the approaching dust cloud. It was getting noticeably closer and was probably just some freight wagon, but he didn't want to take a chance out here in the middle of the empty desert.

"Mary! We've got to move," he said loudly.

Mary's eyelids fluttered as she returned to the live world. She sat up and then saw the cloud of dust on the road and needed no more incentive. She quickly hopped to her feet and began moving away from the road.

Will snatched up the blanket and led Buster and the mare right behind her. She was moving at a good clip and was pulling away from Will as he, Otto, and the horses hurried after her.

Five minutes later, they were another quarter mile from the road and found a shallow gully. They entered the gully and turned to watch the road. It was a good distance away now but they both had young eyes.

When the cloud-makers finally were close enough to pick out, Will saw that they were three riders. He couldn't make out their faces, but two were dressed as American cow hands and the third like a Mexican vaquero. They were all armed.

"What do you think, Mary? Do you know those guys?"

"No. But I don't like them."

"Neither do I. We'll let them go. This is a good place to set up camp, anyway. It's hidden from the road."

"You said you'd let me wear the gun. Could I do that?"

"Sure, but first I need to clean it and reload it. I'll do that in a few minutes."

"I'd feel better if I had a gun."

"So, would I. Unless you plan on shooting me."

She laughed and said, "Why would I do that? You're the only one who's been good to me."

Will smiled but felt uncomfortable. He couldn't get attached to Mary for a number of reasons. She was probably only sixteen and couldn't stay with him for very long. It wouldn't be right. And the biggest reason was that she was probably still afraid of him, despite her saying differently. *But those eyes!*

He mentally shrugged then pulled the blanket from Buster and laid it on the ground again, slid the bags off the mare, and then unsaddled the horses.

Mary was already sitting on the blanket when he pulled out the Winchester, and the Spencer and set the two Colts on the blanket.

"I've got to clean the pistols. The two Colts have been fired recently, but the Winchester is clean and so is the Spencer."

She didn't answer as he took out the cleaning kits. He laid them on the sand, so the solvent and oil didn't get on the blanket, then started with the New Army. After it was cleaned and oiled, he put powder and balls into the cylinders and then put new percussion caps on the nipples of the cylinder's filled chambers. He slid it into his old holster and took out the new Colt. He emptied the cylinders and cleaned and oiled it before sliding five new cartridges into the pistol.

"Why do the pistols use different bullets?"

"They're different models. I've had this one, called the Colt New Army for almost two years. I picked up this Colt 1873 from one of those two I buried. Did you know that they had no money at all and only two bullets for the pistol?"

"No, but I know they didn't spend any money on soap, either."

He smiled at her and then had her stand up. He gave her the New Army in its holster and told her to strap it on. She tried, but it just slid past her hips. She started laughing after the second attempt.

"I told you I was skinny."

"I'll punch a new hole in the belt."

She stepped out of the fallen gunbelt before Will picked it up, then used the tip of his knife blade to make a new hole and had her try again. It stayed put the second time, but it did have almost a clownish appearance around Mary's thin waist.

"Mary, those are sixteen-year-old hips. Not eighteen," he said as he stepped back and looked at her.

Her head jerked up when he said it. *He knew!* She had just turned sixteen five weeks ago and had been a bit surprised that he hadn't questioned her age earlier.

She quickly asked, "You're going to get rid of me now. Aren't you?"

"No, Mary. Nothing has changed. I'm just in more of a bind. I can't be seen riding around with a sixteen-year-old girl. Everyone would think I was taking advantage of you."

"But you aren't! Can't we come to some arrangement?"

"Sit down, Mary. Let me think of something."

She sat down sullenly, almost certain that he'd leave her in Gila City now. She was in serious trouble.

Will knew what difficulties she'd face if he left her in Gila City. She couldn't go home, and he surely couldn't just abandon her. If only she had been a boy. The moment he thought of it, the idea stuck in his mind.

He looked at her closely. Her face was too female, but if no one looked too closely, maybe it would work.

"Mary, I'm going to try something. Come here."

She stood and walked to Will, then stopped when she was three feet away before she stood in front of him and he said, "Put your hair up for a second."

She did, and he then removed his Stetson and put it on her head. It was too large and slipped down past her forehead, but he stepped back and looked at her. This might work.

"Go ahead and walk away from me."

She did, getting the gist of his plan. She tried to walk like a man, but Will noticed that she wasn't close to walking like a man or even a boy. It must be something in the hip joints or somewhere else in the construction of females that made the difference.

"Alright, Mary. Here's what we'll do. When I get to Gila City, I'll buy some more shirts and three more pairs of pants, including two that are smaller. I'll buy you a sombrero and something you can use to tie your hair up. As long as you don't walk, you'll be okay. Just stay on the mare when we're around anyone and don't talk."

She was ecstatic inside. *He wasn't going to get rid of her!*

"I can cut my hair short."

"No, Mary. Don't do that."

"Why not?"

"Just don't do it. I don't want you to be a man, just look like one from a distance."

She smiled at the hidden compliment and answered simply, "Okay."

He set up the camp and spent almost an hour hunting for enough wood for a fire then brought back a full armload and dropped it down next to his fire pit.

"Will, what did you do in San Miguel?" Mary asked as she sat near the future fire.

"I worked at my father's ranch and went to school until I was twelve, then I worked on our ranch before my father died, and then helped to set up my grandmother's boarding house with my sister, or my aunt, Sarah, before I left."

"What did you do while you were coming here?"

"Anything that was available. I did repair work, tilled fields, branded and rounded up cattle, and even some storekeeping. There were a couple of places where I had the joy of slopping hogs. Now, that wasn't a job I'd recommend."

She laughed, and Will grinned at her before he asked, "What did you do, Mary? I mean, for men, we can do anything we want, but women can't. I know that because Sarah was always complaining that she could either be a schoolmarm or a housewife, but little else."

"I cleaned around the house. I cooked, too. I don't know if you'd like the food, though."

"Why not?"

"It was mostly Mexican style. My mother's husband didn't really like it though. He called it greaser food. But there wasn't much selection in the market with our budget, so he would go to the café a couple of times a week and buy himself a steak."

Will shook his head slowly and said, "While you were staying skinny, he was buying himself a steak. He's slipping lower in my estimation every time you say something about him."

She didn't tell him about the other things he did that would probably drop him down a few more rungs because she might need them later. He would bring strange women into the house and have his way with them while she and her mother were in the next room with no door for privacy. She was disgusted by everything he did, but that was the worst.

After another bean and ham dinner, with tomatoes instead of onions this time, Will cleaned up and pulled out his bedroll.

"You get the bedroll, Mary. I'll just sleep on the blanket."

"Will, it'll get chilly at night."

"I know, but I'm used to it. I'll feel better if you're inside the bedroll anyway. They had two, but I sure wasn't about to take either one. You can imagine why."

Mary laughed and said, "Yes, I can. Thank you, Will."

The sun had barely set when Mary slipped into the bedroll, and Will stretched out on the blanket, leaving the pistols and Winchester between them. The Spencer was on Will's right side. Neither was asleep as they lay in the darkness, thinking about Gila City.

It wasn't until an hour later that they finally drifted off to sleep as coyotes howled in the night.

CHAPTER 3

They were back on the road to Gila City just an hour after sunrise. Will had made breakfast with two cans of beans because he knew Mary would be hungry, and she didn't disappoint him. They were low on supplies now, even with Harvey's infusion of food. The new question was if Will bought enough food for both of them, *how would he arrange the transport?* With Mary on the mare, there wasn't much room to spare. Two sets of saddlebags didn't leave much room either, especially with the added clothing. He'd just have to see what he could do.

He was riding next to Mary and she seemed to be in a good mood, so he asked, "Does it still hurt, Mary?"

"Not too much. It'll be better by tomorrow. Will, why are the rifles so different?"

"The Winchester is a new repeater that has fifteen cartridges. It uses the same cartridge as the Colt 1873. The Spencer is an older model, but it's a repeater that carries seven shots. The bullets are much bigger and can go a lot further."

"Then why make a newer gun that doesn't shoot as far?"

"Most people shooting a rifle can't hit anything beyond a hundred yards anyway, so the folks who designed the rifle figured that if they designed it to use a smaller cartridge, it could hold more shots. The Spencer can shoot almost five times as far, but, honestly, I couldn't hit anything that far away. I could hit something consistently at three hundred yards but almost guaranteed at two hundred yards. With the Winchester, I can hit targets at a hundred yards or a little more without any problem. The Winchester is also very simpler to load, too. The Spencer has a problem with ejecting the hot brass sometimes, too."

"How are you with the pistols?"

"I'm above average with the New Army, so it'll probably be the same with the newer one."

"Can I practice with the pistol sometime?"

"After we get out of Gila City you can."

"Good. I'll look forward to that."

———

They rode until noon and took a break at a watering hole for the animals to drink and fill the canteens. They let the horses graze on some sparse grass for about twenty minutes before they set out again. Will gave the last two biscuits and some ham to Mary, then let Otto finish the ham off and also got the bone, which Will was sure he appreciated.

As much as Mary was consuming, he wondered if she'd be a chubby sixteen-year-old girl before much longer and smiled at the idea.

Around mid-afternoon, Gila City came into view on the horizon.

Will looked to the right toward the river, pointed, and said, "Mary, see that arroyo over there? Why don't you ride down there and wait for me? It curves to the south, so you'll be safe."

Mary looked in that direction, saw the arroyo, and said, "Alright. Be back soon, Will."

"I'll be back as soon as I can."

She smiled at him and turned the mare due west to the gully, and he kept an eye on her until she was hidden from sight, then he rode to Gila City.

He wanted to make this quick, so his first stop was at the first livery he found. It was situated right on the edge of town on the eastern side of the road and he spotted some animals in the corral in back, so maybe he'd get lucky. He reined in Buster, dismounted, and tied him to the hitching post.

As he entered, he said, "Howdy!", to the liveryman, a heavy-set Mexican.

"Hola! What can I do for you?"

"I need to go and buy some supplies, but don't have a lot of room, so I need a pack horse."

"I think you'll be better with a pack mule or even a burro."

"Do you have any for sale?"

"I have a burro, but no mules."

"How much is the burro?"

"Twenty dollars, but I'll throw in a pack saddle that is made for a burro."

"Let's go see him."

They walked out to the corral and hidden among the horses was the grayish burro. He stood about forty-four inches at the shoulder and looked healthy.

Will walked him around the corral and his gait seemed normal, then, when he returned, Will checked his joints and teeth and was satisfied.

"Okay, I'll take him."

Will counted out the money and handed them to the liveryman. After fitting him with the pack saddle, they led the donkey to Buster and hooked up a trail rope. Will waved and set off for the dry goods store. He figured it was on the main street and wasn't surprised when he found it six buildings down on the left. He dismounted, tied off Buster with his new companion, then went inside and began loading up supplies.

He bought all the standard items: beans, coffee, a slab of bacon, and salt. Then he found a lot of Mexican food items that he bought for Mary. He picked up two more tin plates, cups, spoons, and forks before he walked to the clothing area and picked up four shirts, another pair of pants in his size, and two more of a smaller size along with a leather belt.

He found a pair of boots for Mary that looked about right and a pair of moccasins as well, in case he was wrong. After leaving his first armloads at the counter, he returned to the aisles and bought three pairs of socks, some underwear, a sombrero, a new bedroll, and four towels. He then bought some soap, two more toothbrushes and tooth powder, a hairbrush for Mary, and some hair ribbons. He picked up two pencils and a notepad, too, then set it all down on the counter and added some penny candy on a whim. He finished the order with two panniers and some cord to get it secured to the burro.

His bill came to just over forty dollars, which was his biggest single expense since he'd left San Miguel. The proprietor helped him load the full panniers onto the pack saddle as the patient burro stood there nonplussed. He left the sombrero on top of the panniers, then mounted and turned Buster, heading for the central square. After he arrived, he sat in the saddle and wrote on the notepad, then pulled the page off and looked around.

There was a group of children playing on the opposite side of the square, so he walked Buster over to them, stepped down, and called over a boy that looked about eight years old.

"Do you know where Senora Fleming lives?" he asked.

He nodded.

"Bring this note to her and I will give you a nickel, but I need you to come back and tell me what she says. When you return, I'll give you another nickel."

His eyes lit up as he snatched the note from his fingers and Will handed him his nickel, smiled, then watched him go flying off.

When he returned a few minutes later, Will already had the second nickel in his hand.

"Yes?"

"She read it and cried for a little while and then said to tell you 'Go with God and thank you'."

He handed the boy his second nickel and watched him run off to join his friends and show them his newfound wealth.

He climbed on board Buster, then trailed the loaded burro out of Gila City heading north back to Mary.

He walked Buster until he spotted the arroyo and turned west, then, when he reached the gulch, he walked the animals down the slope to the bottom of the gully.

"Mary! I'm back!" he shouted.

They heard the sound of hooves and Mary came trotting around the corner with a big smile on her face, probably relieved that he returned, thought Will.

"I see you have a burro," she said as she grinned.

"He was cheap. Are you ready to go, Mary? I'd rather we move to the south of Gila City some distance away before we camp."

"Okay. I'm ready."

He handed her the sombrero and she flipped her hair under the hat and put it on.

"Do I look like a boy now?" she asked, still smiling.

"Not to me, Mary," he replied as he smiled back at her.

They left the arroyo and headed south, then skirted east around Gila City and regained the road a mile outside of town.

They walked the horses another ten miles before the light began to fade, and luckily, there was no shortage of gullies. They found one about a quarter mile off the road and walked their animals down to the bed. It wasn't deep, about eight feet from the flat ground, but it was broad at the bottom.

Will stepped down, tied off Buster to a boulder along the wall, and began preparing camp.

Mary got off the mare, tied her off at a different rock, and helped gather wood. Once they were more or less settled, Will unsaddled the two horses and unloaded the donkey.

They were fortunate in that the gully had some depressions where there was still water, probably from a very recent flash flood as they would have evaporated quickly after a few days. The horses and the burro drank one large puddle empty in less than a minute and Will directed them to a second.

Once they seemed quenched, he hitched them to a larger boulder and walked to where Mary sat on one of the saddles near the panniers.

Will opened the first pannier and began emptying items as he said, "Mary, I bought these boots for you. If they don't fit, I have a pair of moccasins that will. Here are some socks, some pants that will fit you and some underwear. I picked up another bedroll and some more plates, cups, and spoons, along with a few other things."

He handed the bag of candy to Mary, who smiled, accepted the bag, opened it and selected a cherry drop, and popped it into her mouth as Will kept unstacking the clothes and other supplies. She didn't tell Will that she'd never had a piece of candy before but had only wistfully looked at the treats behind the glass counter. As she sucked on the sweet, she closed her eyes and enjoyed every second.

The Gila River ran just west of town and paralleled the road about a mile so away from their camp. If either of them wanted to bathe, that's where they could do it.

Mary opened her eyes as the last of the cherry drop dissolved and they grew large at the sight of some of the items. She saw soap, clean towels, toothbrushes and powder, and finally, the hairbrush.

Mary slowly picked up the hairbrush and began sliding it through her long black hair, almost numb with disbelief as she did. *Why had Will bought it for her?* And the candy was probably for her, too. *Did he think of her as a child?* She ran it through her hair, watching him for three minutes while Will continued to unpack.

After everything was unpacked and piled on one of the blankets, Will dug his fire pit and took out his cooking gear before finally starting the fire. Its flames were going strong, and he was preparing to start cooking when Mary stepped close to him.

She asked, "If you don't mind, I'll do the cooking. Is that alright?"

"I'd be very grateful, Mary," he replied as he stepped away from the fire.

He returned to the horses and the burro to brush them down as Mary began cooking.

She was pleased with all the different foods that Will had purchased and had never had this much to choose from before, but the real reason for her to make the offer was to show him that she wasn't a child, despite her obvious affection for the penny candy.

Will hadn't even considered Mary as a child after his initial discovery, but even as a sixteen-year-old girl, he knew that he had to be careful with her, not realizing that he was just three years older than she was.

Twenty minutes later, as they were eating their supper, Will quickly agreed that having Mary cook was a significant improvement over his filling, but less tasty creations.

After dinner, Will and Mary cleaned up and put everything away before taking seats before the glowing embers of the dying fire.

Will said, "Mary, when I was in Gila City, I wrote a note to your mother telling her that you were safe and that you would be taken care of. I had a boy deliver it and return to tell me her reply. He told me that she said to go with God and thank you."

Mary didn't cry, but her eyes glistened with moisture as she said quietly, "Thank you, Will. That will ease her heart."

"You're welcome, Mary."

"Will, you told her that I would be provided for. How can you make that promise?"

Will hadn't realized that he'd unintentionally made a commitment, so he blew out his breath and replied, "Because I will, Mary. I'll make sure that nothing bad happens to you if I can help it."

Mary wasn't sure what kind of commitment it was, but she felt better for it, nonetheless.

Will began setting up the bedrolls, then after they were set out, laid the blanket between them and set the guns on top.

"Mary, I left your new pants and shirts on the blanket. There are socks and underclothing, too."

She smiled and replied, "Thank you, Will. These were a bit baggy."

"Hopefully, these will all fit better, and that belt will keep them in place. I was worried when you put on the gunbelt that they'd yank those baggy pants down to your ankles."

Mary laughed and said, "That would have been funny."

Will smiled but thought it could have been embarrassing for
Mary rather than funny.

He left both the boots and moccasins near the socks as well
before they turned in.

———

In Gila City, Frank Gilford, Paul Winston, and Raoul Gutierrez
were enjoying themselves at a cantina. Each had a young
Mexican girl glued to his side as they partied the night away.
They had made a good haul in Mohawk, almost six hundred
dollars. They had already gone through almost a hundred of that
in two days and were probably going to spend another fifty
today. Money was easy to get if you knew where to find it and
didn't mind hurting people to take it away.

Most of these towns didn't have any decent law enforcement,
so they could just ride in, hold up the bank, or any other place
that might have money worth stealing, and ride out. As long as
they didn't shoot anybody, they wouldn't even be trailed.
Somehow going after three heavily armed men for a few dollars
just didn't seem worth the risk.

As long as they stayed with the small-town banks, they were
okay.

Forty minutes later, they escorted their female companions
upstairs to their rooms, and ten minutes after that, each of the
rooms was filled with assorted sounds of laughter, moaning, and
more passionate noises as beds rocked against the walls.
Tomorrow morning, they'd continue heading south to look for
smaller towns that didn't need their money. Gila City was too big
to do anything other than party.

———

Early the next morning, they had breakfast in the cantina, then picked up their horses from the livery, mounted, and left Gila City in a good mood as they headed south.

———

Will and Mary slept in a bit and Will finally made the fire for breakfast about an hour after sunrise and Mary insisted on taking care of the cooking duties.

When they had finished eating, Will took the plates and frypan to the nearest puddle and washed them then returned to the camp.

"Will, can you show me how to shoot the pistol before we go?"

"Sure, Mary. Go ahead and get the gunbelt."

Mary eagerly trotted over to the blanket where the guns were laid out, picked up the New Army gunbelt, and strapped it on while Will waited nearby, smiling as she hung the heavy pistol around her waist. It probably increased her weight by five percent.

Once she was armed, they walked a few feet from the base of the camp and Will pointed out a hole in the side of the wide arroyo on the west wall.

"See that hole? That's about thirty feet away and about the size of a man's head. Go ahead and unhook the hammer loop, that's that string of leather that keeps the pistol from being bounced out of the holster. Now when you pull the pistol, use your left hand to pull the hammer all the way back. Your hand isn't big enough to just let your thumb do it as I can. Once it's cocked, it can be fired, so be careful. After you cock the hammer, slide your left hand to the base of the pistol and let it support your right hand. Then just point the gun at the hole. Aiming a pistol can be annoying, so just point it like you're pointing your finger. Got all that?"

She nodded as Will stepped back and slightly behind Mary. He should have had her dryfire the Colt a few times, or at the least shown her how to hold it, but he had already loaded the New Army and didn't think getting close enough to her was a good idea.

She drew the pistol slowly, cocked the hammer with her left palm, and then slid it to the base of the pistol handle and pulled the trigger. The Colt kicked in her hands, surprising her as it blew gunsmoke, flame, and the lead projectile out of its muzzle. The dirt on the side of the gully exploded about a foot and a half to the right of the hole.

Will was surprised that she'd done so well and hadn't put that first shot into the sky.

"Very good, Mary, but don't pull the trigger back so quickly. It causes the gun to jump, so just squeeze it. You should be surprised when the thing goes off. Try again."

"Okay. But I was surprised the first time because it was so loud."

"Fine, just squeeze the trigger this time."

She repeated the sequence, only a little more slowly on the trigger action. The Colt bucked, and the shot hit just below the hole.

Will turned, grinned at her, and exclaimed, "Outstanding, Mary! That was very good for your first shots."

Mary smiled as she slid the smoking pistol back into its holster.

―――

Out on the road, Frank, Paul, and Raoul were startled by the gunfire, turned their eyes west, and quickly spotted the smoke rising from the gully.

"What the hell is that?" asked Frank.

"I'm thinkin' someone is target shootin'," replied Paul.

"Let's ride on. It's no concern of ours," Frank said.

Then Paul changed his mind and said, "Wait a minute. I don't like having someone behind us. Let's at least go and check them out. They won't see us comin'."

"Paul, it's just not worth it," Frank replied.

Raoul backed Paul's idea when he said, "Come on, Frank. Let's go look just to be sure."

Frank gave in, so they turned off the road and headed toward the smoke.

―――

Will accepted the gunbelt from Mary and said "I'll clean and reload the gun tonight. We're running a bit late."

Just five hundred yards east, the three outlaws were walking their horses toward them. Frank may not have agreed with the idea, but now his curiosity was piqued, and he wondered who was down there. He doubted that whoever it was could pose a threat, but he wasn't as high-strung as the other two.

Will and Mary were starting to saddle the horses when Otto started growling.

Will felt the hairs on the back of his neck stand up at the instinctively fearful sound. He looked at Otto and saw that the dog was staring to the east with his hackles raised and his fearsome teeth showing.

"Mary," he said quickly, "get over to the east wall and press yourself against it."

Mary glanced at Otto, then Will nodded and plastered her back against the eastern wall of the arroyo.

Will grabbed the Winchester, handed it to Mary, and said, "Hold onto this until I ask for it."

After she took the repeater, he turned back to the blanket, snatched the Spencer, stepped back to the east wall of the arroyo, then stepped onto a small boulder. Before looking over the top, he removed his Stetson, tossed it back to the blanket, then slowly stuck his head over the top and saw the three men coming toward them. He instantly recognized them as the same three men that they had seen the day before yesterday, was sure that they weren't good men, and each had his pistol drawn.

Even though they were all ready with their revolvers, they had no idea that they were being watched by a man with a rifle. They were already under a hundred yards now, and Will decided he wanted the faster firing Winchester, so he lowered the Spencer toward Mary.

"Winchester!" he loudly whispered.

She took the Spencer and handed him the Winchester. He cocked the hammer as Mary set the Spencer against the side of the gully and unhooked the hammer loop from her pistol.

The men continued to approach, listening for any signs of the shooter in the gully. When they were within thirty yards, Will slid the Winchester above the arroyo, sure that they'd see the sudden movement and hoped that they'd be smart enough to wheel their horse around and run away.

The men all spotted his sudden appearance and while they were smart, they were also ruthless and didn't hesitate in their universal decision to fire first.

Even though they were about a hundred feet from a shooter armed with a Winchester, they opened fire with their pistols, hoping the single shooter would duck down and then they could rush to the edge of the gully and fire down on him. There was also a good chance that they'd kill the man with their fusillade of gunfire.

The ground around Will exploded as their 44s slammed into the dirt, but he already had his target and at less than twenty yards, it wasn't going to miss, despite the volcanoes erupting all around him.

He fired the Winchester, and the center man, Frank Gilford, barely had a chance for his brain to register the .44's arrival as it passed through the left side of his chest before he fell to the ground in a cloud of dust.

Will had already swung his sights to the man to his right before Frank fell from his saddle, levering in a second round as he did, and hastily pulled the trigger. He should have missed in his haste, but his shot and Paul Winston's were both on line and probably passed each other by just inches.

As Paul felt the hammer blow of Will's .44, the dirt just a foot in front of Will created a dirt and dust geyser that blew into his face.

Paul dropped his Winchester and clutched at his wound just above his belly button before falling backward over the rump of his horse, his abdominal aorta pouring blood into his gut.

"Damn! I can't see a thing!" Will shouted even as he rapidly worked his Winchester's action and fired at the moving blur.

Raoul heard him shout, and fired, cocked his hammer but held his fire as he pulled his horse to a halt and looked almost straight down at Will as he rapidly blinked his eyes.

Will knew the last shooter was close, and he was going to die soon, even as he searched for the last outlaw.

Raoul was certain that the blinded man with the Winchester was about to die as well as he brought his pistol to bear, but he was shocked when a shot came from his left and felt the bullet slam into the left side of his chest. He barely had enough time to turn and see the shooter, then began to laugh even as he died and collapsed from his horse to the ground.

Will heard the last shot that had just been fired, but it hadn't been from his front where he had expected it to be. It had come from his left, and then he heard the unmistakable sound of a man thumping to the earth.

He quickly turned in that direction and asked loudly, "Mary?"

Mary was walking towards him, her Colt New Army still smoking as she replied, "I got him, Will. Can you see anything?"

"Not much. Can you get me a canteen?" he asked as he stepped down from the boulder, almost falling on his face when his feet hit the ground awkwardly.

"I'll be right back."

Will's vision was coming back as his eyes watered, but he waited for Mary. He felt her more than heard her as she appeared on his left. He put out his hand and she slapped the canteen into his palm. He tipped his head back and poured some water onto his eyes, blinking as the water flowed across his face. When it was empty, he dropped his head, looked forward, wiped his eyes with his fingers, and his vision slowly began clearing as the water drained away.

He finally saw Mary's smiling face, smiled himself, and said, "Thank you, Mary. You saved my life."

"You shot two of them, Will."

He set the Winchester down, dropped the canteen, and quickly hugged Mary, but then suddenly remembered what she had so recently gone through, and started to release her, but she would have none of it. She had her thin arms wrapped around him tightly, so they stayed that way for more than a minute.

While she had him held tightly, Mary asked, "Why did they do that, Will? They couldn't even see us."

"I know. It doesn't make any sense at all. They knew someone was shooting down here. As far as they knew, there could be a passel of lawmen taking target practice. This was just stupid. And then when they saw me, I didn't even get a chance to tell them to drop their guns. They could see the rifle and they should have just turned and ran. Maybe they thought it was only a single-shot rifle, I don't know.

'But they started shooting those pistols from horseback at fifty yards, and I knew that if they hit me, they'd be lucky. We'll never know why they did what they did, but personally, I'm just glad they lost. I'm going to go and get their horses and then see if I can find out who they were."

"I'll start cleaning up down here," she said as she finally released him, and he let her go as well.

Will then climbed out of the gully and started collecting horses. None of them had wandered very far, which was quite a cry from Buster who would have been long gone if he hadn't been hitched to a disinterested burro.

The horses didn't seem to mind the change in ownership and came along willingly. When they were all hitched in a small semi-circle, just outside the camp, he returned to check out the three bodies.

He went through their pockets and came out with a staggering $397.60. He shoved it into his pocket, then he pulled their gunbelts before he had to wander around the killing ground to pick up their fallen pistols. All of them were Colt '73s, so he put each pistol into one of the gunbelts, walked to the horses, set the gunbelts on the ground, pulled the rifles out of the scabbards, examined each one, and slid it back home. Each was a very well-maintained Winchester '73. *Why hadn't they approached with their rifles drawn?* Stupid.

He pulled off the first set of saddlebags, and when he checked inside, he found clothes, two boxes of spare .44 caliber cartridges, but no identifying paperwork at all. There was some food, too, but not as much as they should have unless they were planning on riding through to Arizona City. He pulled the second set and found pretty much the same: ammunition, some food, and clothes. The third set also had similar contents. The only difference was the style and size of the clothing and the quantity of ammunition.

He then put the saddlebags back onto the horses, dropped one gunbelt into each set, and then returned to the edge of the arroyo, spotted Mary, and slid down the side.

98

"Did you find anything?" asked Mary when Will popped to his feet.

"They had almost four hundred dollars in cash on them, but no identifying papers at all. They all had newer Colt pistols and Winchester rifles, too, along with six boxes of ammunition and some food. Other than that, they had nothing at all worth keeping."

Mary's big brown eyes grew noticeably larger as she exclaimed, "Four hundred dollars! That's a lot of money, Will."

"I know, and we don't know where they got it from, either. My guess is that they stole it, but we don't know how they got it, so it's ours now. So are their horses and guns. I'll go ahead and bury them as best I can. I don't have a shovel, but the arroyo has some holes already courtesy of the last flash flood, so I'll drop them in one and cover them up. They'll probably float out with the next flash flood, but there's nothing we can do about it."

He headed toward the biggest hole in the arroyo, made sure it would work, then clambered back out onto the flat ground again and began dragging the bodies to the arroyo. Once they were near the edge, he rolled them down the side close to the natural gravesite. One by one, the bodies toppled down the wall and into the hole, or close to it. Then he slid down and after moving the two that didn't make it all the way into their makeshift grave, began throwing rocks onto them first to keep them there. When he'd used all the nearby rocks, he began shoveling sand with his hands like a dog. It took a while, but they were all buried after about half an hour of manual shoveling. The rocks might keep them down there for a while, but as he had said to Mary, he didn't really care. They came to kill him and Mary for no reason at all.

Once the messy job was done, he stepped over to one of the deeper puddles and washed his hands and face, but knew he was in dire need of a bath.

He walked back to where Mary waited, looked at Otto, who was sitting next to her, and asked, "Except for your very handy warning, Otto, what good did you do?"

Mary glanced down at the big dog and said, "I think Otto said that he's not very good with guns."

Will laughed, picked up the Winchester and the Spencer, then walked down the gully to their horses and burro. Mary caught up with him and Otto trotted alongside.

As Will walked toward Buster, he realized that he had almost seven hundred dollars in cash in his pockets and his money belt, and decided he'd better give some to Mary before they arrived in Arizona City.

He saddled both of the horses and packed the burro. Mary mounted the mare as he climbed up on Buster, then they walked them north until the arroyo shallowed enough to walk the horses out of the gully, then climbed out and headed for the three outlaw horses that were all looking at them.

Will finally took time to examine the three horses in detail when he stepped down and approached the tall red gelding that had been ridden by the Mexican. He was a handsome horse with no markings at all, just a dark red with deep brown mane and tail.

"Sorry, Buster," Will thought, "you have just moved into second place."

Not only was the big gelding taller and younger, he had shown his mettle when he hadn't been bothered by the gunfire.

"Mary, I'm going to see how the gelding rides and if he's good, I'll ride him instead of Buster. Buster is a good horse, but he's just not in the same class as this gelding or either of the mares, for that matter, and he's a real coward when there are loud noises, too."

"What will we do with all the saddles?" asked Mary

"As much as I hate to, I'm going to have to chuck the extra saddles into the arroyo. They'll rot eventually, but leading extra horses without saddles isn't that unusual. Leading horses with saddles will raise eyebrows. I'm thinking of cutting the burro loose and transferring the pack saddle to Buster."

"I think the burro will just walk back to Gila City and its barn," said Mary.

Will stepped over to the red gelding and inspected the saddle. It was in excellent shape, as well, so he walked to the other horses and removed their saddles. The second horse was another nice gelding, just not as nearly as good as the red. The third was another light brown mare. She wasn't as nice as Mary's horse, though. The gelding and mare should fetch a decent price in Arizona City.

He examined his saddle on Buster. It was okay, but not as well made as the one on the gelding, so he pulled his saddle off Buster and dragged all three of them to the arroyo and dropped them over the edge. Then he returned, unloaded the panniers from the burro, and removed the pack saddle. It was smaller than one for a horse, but it should fit. He removed all the tack from the burro and let him go, put the pack saddle on Buster, and then loaded the panniers.

It was a break for Buster because he'd carry less weight than his hundred and eighty pounds, then after he added the food from the outlaws' saddlebags and tossed all their clothing into the arroyo, he slid a Winchester into Mary's scabbard and the other two on Buster's and finished his realignment of their resources when he put all three gunbelts in one of the panniers that had enough room.

Satisfied everything was in a proper place, he mounted the big red gelding, looked down at Mary, and said, "Okay, Mary, let's leave this place."

After they reached the road and turned south, Will turned, saw Buster with the pack saddle, and wondered if he was disgruntled about the demotion, snickered, then noticed the burro heading north, returning to his livery in Gila City.

He had thought about trading in Buster rather than the gelding or mare but thought he owed him at least that for staying with him.

———

Back in Gila City, Joe Fleming was standing over his wife as she lay on the floor of their small adobe house, wiping blood from her mouth.

He had his index finger pointed at her as he glared and snarled, "You'd better not be lying, bitch! That daughter of yours is worth seventy-five dollars to me. Juan Nieves only offered me that much because she's unsullied. If she's already spoiled, he's only gonna give me fifty. Where did she get off to?"

Maria looked up at him with a combination of fear and loathing as she replied, "I don't know. The note only said she was safe."

"And you don't know what this guy looks like?"

"No, a boy brought me the note."

102

HUNTING PEARL

"Which boy?"

"Felipe Gonzalez."

"I'll go find the brat, but if you're lyin' to me, you'll regret it."

Joe stomped off to find little Felipe, knowing where he'd be at this time of day as Maria slowly stood, then straightened her dress and walked to the kitchen area.

She slid her fingers across the heavy butcher knife's blade and quietly muttered, "Gringo bastard!"

———

Now that they had switched from the slower-moving burro to Buster as their pack animal, Will and Mary were able to maintain a faster pace as they rode south.

With no other road traffic nearby, Will reached into his pocket, pulled out some bills, and said, "Mary, I have too much money on me, so I'm going to give you a hundred dollars. That way if we get separated for any reason, you won't be broke."

She was going to protest but realized that it was a wise decision, and after the prolonged hug in the gully, she thought that he'd no longer think of her as a boy or a child and wouldn't leave her now.

He peeled off some cash, leaned across the gap between their horses, and handed one set of bills to Mary. She took them from his hands and stared at the wad of currency for a few seconds before she shoved it into her pocket. She looked at Will and was going to say something but instead just smiled at him.

She had never held a single bank note in her hand before until she met Will. All she had ever held was a large half-cent that her mother gave to her on her thirteenth birthday. Now she had a hundred dollars in her pocket and Will didn't seem to believe it was that unusual.

Will then returned most of the cash into his money belt, making sure that Mary had seen him do it, so she'd know where it was if something else bad happened and things didn't work out well.

Mary finally looked up at Will and simply replied, "Thank you, Will."

––––––

Joe Fleming was in a foul mood. He needed to find that girl and find her before she was deflowered. As Mary had told Will, it wasn't uncommon for girls to be taken from the streets and abused, so he had to find her soon. Juan's offer wasn't going to last forever, and the longer she was away from Gila City, the more likely she'd be spoiled.

Felipe had told him that the man who had given him the note had ridden south out of town, rather than north. He'd lied because he had always liked Mary and believed he was protecting her from that mean old bastard who called himself her father. As he watched Joe Fleming mount his mule and head south out of Gila City, he giggled, then rejoined his friends to tell them what he did.

––––––

Will and Mary had stopped for lunch just after noon, letting the horses have their fill of water from a small creek that emptied into the Gila River which still flowed parallel to the road. Four hours later, they had gone more than thirty miles and were only about twenty miles out of Arizona City, so Will suggested that they head due west and camp near the Gila River again, only closer to the riverbank this time.

It was only about a half mile from the road when they reached the river and found a pleasant spot for camp, halfway down the riverbank and out of sight of the road.

Will unsaddled his new gelding and then unpacked Buster, removed the pack saddle, and then unsaddled Mary's mare while Otto rested from the long walk. He led the horses to the river to drink and then returned them to the campsite and let them graze on a good-sized patch of grass.

He set up the campfire and let Mary cook dinner while he walked to the panniers and picked out a new pair of pants, a shirt, underpants, and a towel. He took a bar of regular white soap and without saying anything, walked south along the bank looking for a hidden location that would provide some much-needed privacy.

The river made a slow bend toward the east, so he continued to walk and then found a great spot where the river had created an eddy that had made a deeper pool near the riverbank. He put his things on a nearby rock, then quickly stripped and walked into the water. It was cooler than he expected, which was good, and began to scrub off a week of dirt. He then washed his hair and kept his eyes closed as he did, plunged under the water, and quickly surfaced. He looked north and didn't see any prying eyes, so he stepped out onto the shore and dried quickly. He dressed in his new clothes and took a few minutes to wash his old ones. Once they were clean enough, he wrung them dry and headed back. Feeling cleaner and cooler, he reached the camp and hung his clothes on a tired mesquite bush.

"Take a bath?" asked a smiling Mary.

Will smiled back and replied, "No, ma'am. I'm just all wet 'cause I ran into a thunderstorm around the bend back there. The strange thing is that none of my clean clothes got wet. How do you figure that happened?"

Mary laughed and replied, "Maybe it was a miracle, or you were too stinky, and the raindrops didn't want to go near you."

Will laughed and said, "I was getting pretty bad there, but I feel a lot better now."

"Could I use your soap?"

"You could, but when I bought the supplies, I picked up a bar of scented soap just for you, Mary. I don't think I'll be using it, though. It's in the same pannier as the toothbrushes."

Mary smiled, then said, "I think I'll go down there after dinner."

"I found a perfect spot just past the bend."

"It sounds wonderful."

As Mary spooned their dinner onto their tin plates, she thought about his simple gesture of buying her the soap, knowing it was meant only for her. It was one more sign that Will no longer saw her as a child. She attacked her food with vigor, suddenly seeing it as more than just nourishment. It would help her put some flesh onto her thin frame and make her more of a young woman than a skinny girl.

Will noticed that Mary was still eating heavily and wondered if she was trying to make up for lost meals or trying to fill out. As much as he'd been trying to avoid seeing Mary as anything more than a lost girl, those big brown eyes have been making it very difficult. She was also very pleasant to talk with and just an interesting person overall, not to mention that she'd saved his life with that single pistol shot. He just didn't know how to deal with his growing affection for her. He wished he had Sarah nearby to explain things again.

After he had eaten, Will had a second cup of coffee and looked over at Otto's mournful eyes, smiled, then walked to the pannier. He pulled out Harvey's smoked beef, carved out a large chunk, noting there were maybe two more Otto-sized servings left, and tossed it to their canine friend. When he walked back to the fire he left behind a happy Otto as he ripped at his supper.

"I'll clean up, Mary. You go and enjoy your bath."

She smiled and said, "Thank you, Will."

Mary picked out clean clothes, two towels, and the scented soap and walked off down the bank. With water plentiful, Will washed the dishes in the river rather than sand, returned them to the pannier, and pulled out the bedrolls.

He felt his recently washed clothes and found that they were dry already, which was no surprise, so he folded them and put them back into the pannier. He had nothing else to do, so he sat down near Otto and figured he'd get to know him a little better. He'd already demonstrated his intelligence, so Will wondered how much he already knew from his previous owners.

He tried a few simple commands first: shake, sit, heel. Otto surprised him by responding to each of them without hesitation, then stared at him as if to ask Will if that was all. He rewarded Otto with three pieces of jerky, then just seconds later, after he'd wolfed down the last piece, he got to his feet and stared down at the big dog.

"Try and catch me, Otto!" he exclaimed before he took off at a sprint.

Otto chased him and was on his heels when he cut hard to his right but didn't shake Otto, who stayed just two feet behind him. For more than a minute, he and Otto raced around the campsite, the big dog not missing a beat. When Will zigged or zagged, Otto seemed to be able to anticipate the move and hung right beside him.

Finally, Will came to a stop, breathing heavily, and was suddenly bowled over by Otto, who reared, dropped his front paws on Will's chest, and once he had the human on his back, was threatening to lick the skin from his face.

Will was suddenly well aware just how big Otto was when he tried to sit up but couldn't. He finally wrestled with Otto and rolled him off to the side. To Otto, it was great fun. To Will, it meant he could breathe again.

When he was standing, he decided it would be wise to check on the road from time to time, so he pulled out one of the Winchesters and climbed the riverbank with Otto trailing behind. Will stayed a quarter mile back from the road and looked both ways, didn't see any traffic in either direction, so he returned to their campsite, pulled out his cleaning kit, and started cleaning his rifle and the newly acquired Colts. He'd ask Mary if she would prefer one of the new Colt '73s, as they not only had three of the newer pistols, they had plenty of .44 caliber cartridges.

By the time he had finished the second Colt, he began to wonder what was taking Mary so long. If it wasn't for the fact that she may be naked, he would have gone down to check on her. He'd give her another ten minutes, then naked or not, he'd go and see where she was.

He went back to cleaning the pistols, taking the last Colt into his hands and when he finished loading the last revolver, he knew that the ten minutes were nearly gone. He had just set the pistol down and gotten to his feet when he heard her returning, then breathed a sigh of relief as he sat back down. He had been gone less than fifteen minutes for his bath, including washing his clothes while Mary had been gone for over an hour.

She came into sight, smiling, her long black hair still wet and shining, and her smile grew even larger when she caught his eyes looking at her.

Will said, "You had me worried. I thought you'd be back sooner."

"You must never have been around when a woman takes a bath, Will."

"That's not so. I lived with my mother and sister, or grandmother and niece for a long time, and they didn't take that long."

"You were worried?" she asked,

"Of course, I was," Will replied quickly.

Mary was still smiling as she said, "That's nice to know."

"Mary, from now on, when you go someplace like that, take Otto with you. He'll protect you."

She looked down at the German shepherd, knelt, and said, "Otto, come."

Otto obediently trotted to her and sat down. Mary hugged him, and his wagging tail indicated his pleasure. She looked up at Will, grinned, then stood and rubbed Otto's head.

Will couldn't help but smile as he said, "He seems to like you, Mary. That's good because now I know he'll never let anyone hurt you."

"I'm not worried anymore, Will," she said.

Will looked into those big brown eyes, then blinked and said, "We should make Arizona City tomorrow. I'll sell the spare horses and then I'll start asking around."

Mary could tell he was uncomfortable, so she just asked, "What will I do?"

"That's a good question. Once we get into town, I don't see any reason for you to be a boy when we get there, do you?"

"I can wear a dress again?" she asked with a smile.

"You can. After we get rid of the extra horses, we'll stop at the mercantile and you can pick out two or three nice dresses and whatever else you need, like riding clothes. I'll drop off our horses, and maybe sell two of the Winchesters and my Colt New Army. I'm assuming you'd rather have one of those new Colts that uses cartridges. Is that a good guess?"

"I hadn't thought of that. Does it shoot the same?"

"Yes, ma'am. It loads a lot easier, and I'll show you how to do that when I give it to you. We have plenty of ammunition as well. I'll show you how to shoot the Winchester, too. You'll have one on your horse."

"You're going to turn me into a soldier."

"I hope not," he replied.

She laughed as they prepared for the night. The sun was already below the horizon, but Will didn't want to keep the fire burning after it was dark because even though their campsite was below the line of sight, the light from a fire could be seen from the road and he wasn't about to run afoul of any more gunmen.

They both turned in but continued to talk while in their bedrolls. Will talked about his childhood and his poor relationship with his father and it was only then that he realized that his father and Mary's father shared the same first name – Joseph. Yet neither of them knew their real fathers.

Then it became a contest to see whose father was worse, and as bad as his father/grandfather had been, Will conceded early to Mary because at least his father hadn't tried to sell him for such a degenerated purpose as Mary's pseudo-father Joseph.

One of the other questions Will finally got around to asking that he had thought of asking when she first told him her name but thought it might have been insulting was why she was Mary and not Maria. It turned out that her mother had named her Maria, but never called her that after she married Joe Fleming because it infuriated him. Once she adapted to it, she said she liked it better, even though her mother had really grown to despise white men.

That had bothered Will for a reason he couldn't understand. He really liked Mary, probably more than he had liked any other girl, except Sarah, of course, but that was different. But Mary was sixteen and seemed younger sometimes. Her heritage didn't bother him at all. She had no control over her parentage any more than he had. He knew that many did have a lot of problems with it, and it made no sense to him at all. But the fact that Mary's mother didn't like white men, made him wonder what she would think of Mary traveling with him.

He spent a little time thinking about having killed two more men today and wasn't surprised that it didn't bother him and didn't seem to affect Mary either.

He finally began thinking about tomorrow's arrival in Arizona City, the last stop in Arizona Territory and the place he'd already decided would be the final location where he'd search for Pearl. If he didn't find her there or at least find a solid lead, then he'd just head back to San Miguel.

But then, what would he do with Mary?

It was that last question that was on his mind as he drifted off to sleep.

Twelve miles north of their campsite, Joe Fleming's mood had not improved. Either that kid was lying, and they'd ridden north, or they were going all the way to Arizona City. He was more than halfway, so he may as well go there. If he found out that she wasn't there, he'd find that little liar and make him sorry. And that would be before he made that bitch that he had married sorrier than she had ever been. He didn't know why he even kept her around. Damned squaw. She was darned pretty ten years ago, but she was beginning to sag. Juan had also promised him free rides in his house for a year if he sold him Mary, but only if she was intact, so that damned half-breed had better not be spoiled when he tracked her down. He hated to admit that it wasn't likely that she was still a virgin, if for no other reason than she was riding with some unknown white man. If he had ruined her, he'd kill the bastard, too.

He finally just pulled off the road and laid out his blanket. Luckily, he had some smoked pork in his bag, so he ate the meat and drank his water before laying down, just staring at the Milky Way but didn't see the stars as he fumed.

———

Back in Gila City, Maria was afraid for her life. Joe had hit her before, but usually, after he struck that first blow, his anger abated, and he just left. Sometimes he'd bring his whore back to the house and spend all night with her in their bed while she slept on the floor, listening to the noise of their rutting.

But this time, he left angrier than she had ever seen him. She hoped he didn't find Mary, or that whoever wrote the note could protect her, but knew that there would be hell to pay when he returned either with or without Mary.

She, like her husband, strongly suspected that Mary had been deflowered, and she knew that Joe might kill her for the lost money. He might just take the lesser amount because she was only sixteen and so skinny that he could tell the customer she was thirteen. Some men paid a lot more for girls, even if they weren't virginal. Either way, she knew there was nothing good in her future when Joe returned, and the thought of her precious daughter being turned into a whore made her sick.

She fell to her knees, closed her eyes, and prayed for Mary's deliverance. She prayed to the mother of Jesus to protect her daughter, who bore her name. She also prayed that she wasn't with another white man because they were all devils.

———

Will and Mary woke almost simultaneously. They were facing each other, so the first thing each saw was the other's eyes. Her large brown eyes and his brilliant blue.

"Good morning, Mary," he said softly.

"Good morning, Will," she replied with a smile.

"Shall we go and find my mother?" he asked.

"I hope you find her today, Will."

"So, do I, Mary."

He slipped out first and trotted down to the riverbank and answered nature's call, then returned and let Mary have the river to herself.

As he began adding driftwood to the firepit, he thought about how casually he'd asked Mary about finding his mother. Those last thoughts before he fell asleep were now prominent in his mind. He had set Arizona City as his last hope, and now, because of Mary, he began to think that maybe he should continue his quest into California. He simply hated the idea that today would be the end of the trail without anything to show for it. It would also let him postpone any decision about what to do with Mary.

He had the fire started and the cooking grate in place when Mary returned, and she took over cooking breakfast as Will handled the horses. They were all watered and saddled when they sat down and ate.

Mary could tell that Will was concerned about something, so she didn't say anything, which led to a silent breakfast and cleanup of their campsite.

Forty minutes later, they were on the road to Arizona City.

———

Joe Fleming didn't have anything for breakfast, having eaten all of his smoked pork for his dinner. If his mood could get any blacker, he'd have a small thundercloud over his head as he saddled the mule and was soon on the road to Arizona City. He was still almost twelve miles behind Will and Mary and moving at the same pace.

————

Will and Mary reached the outskirts of Arizona City just before noon.

"Mary, how about if I treat you to a steak lunch?" Will asked.

Mary's face lit up as she looked at him. She wasn't as perpetually hungry as she had been before, but she was still hungry at mealtimes, and was almost trying to will those excess forkfuls of food onto her bones.

Will looked at her face, laughed, and replied, "I'll take that as a yes."

Mary laughed and then said, "I haven't turned down any food yet."

They found a café just inside the city, dismounted, and tied the five horses to the hitching post. Mary slid the sombrero from her head as they crossed the boardwalk, went inside, and took a table.

The waitress arrived, and Will ordered two steaks and baked potatoes.

Mary was antsy, waiting for her meal and Will thought it was cute.

"Hungry, Mary?"

"I don't know why you'd think that," she answered with a grin.

The waitress brought them their steaks, baked potatoes, some butter, and biscuits. They had been drinking coffee waiting for the order, and Mary had put a teaspoon of sugar in hers, so Will reminded himself to add some sugar to their food order, assuming they'd still have to travel even if he found Pearl. Which direction that would take was a whole new question.

Mary attacked her steak like a mortal enemy. She sprinkled on salt and pepper after the first bite and then did the same for her buttered baked potato.

After they had finished, Will paid the bill, then they left the café and stopped on the boardwalk in the heat of southern Arizona Territory.

"Let's head over to the livery first. I want to see if I can sell the extra horses."

Mary nodded, so they untied the horses and led the five horses down the street to a large livery, which was even further on the outskirts, which is where liveries usually were. He had Mary hold the reins as he went inside.

"Hello!" he shouted as he entered the barn doors.

The liveryman looked down from his perch in the loft and shouted, "Howdy. What can I do for ya?"

"I've come to do some horse trading."

The liveryman smiled, dropped down, and asked, "What you got?"

"I have a couple of horses that I'd like to sell."

"Let's look at 'em."

They walked outside, and Will pointed to the two extra horses, the gelding and the mare. The liveryman checked the teeth and legs of the two spare horses, examined their shoes, and then stood back to look at their overall lines. Will knew they were good horses, and he should get about fifty dollars for each one.

"I'll give you seventy dollars for the pair."

"I'll tell you what. If you'll shoe the other three and board them for a day, you've got a deal."

The liveryman's eyes lit up, then quickly said, "Deal," and offered Will his hand to seal the verbal contract.

Will shook his hand and asked, "Do you mind if I leave my dog with you until the morning? Otto is a great watchdog. He saved my hide yesterday when we were jumped by three outlaws. That's where we got the horses, by the way."

"Does he bite?"

"Not if you're a friend. Watch. Otto, come."

Otto trotted into the shop, then stood watching Will.

"What's your name?" Will asked the liveryman.

"Lou."

Will made a show of shaking Lou's hand as Otto watched.

"Otto, this is Lou," he said as he smiled at Lou, then said, "Go ahead and rub his head."

Lou tentatively put his hand near the big dog and Otto just watched. Lou finally rubbed Otto's head and Lou was rewarded with a tail wag.

"Otto will now protect you and yours just like he did for us earlier."

"I'll give him some meat, too. That's a right smart dog."

"He is that."

The transaction complete, he entered his office and returned with seventy dollars, and handed the cash to Will.

"We'll be back in the morning," Will said as he stuffed the bill into his pocket.

"I'll have them shod and looking pretty. I'll store your stuff in my storeroom in back."

"Great. I'll need to grab some of my guns first."

He walked to Buster and removed the New Army, its gunbelt, and two of the Winchesters.

He waved at the liveryman as they walked from the barn.

"Well, Mary, time to do some shopping. First, I'm going to unload these Winchesters and the Colt."

"I'll come along," she said.

They walked on the boardwalk and after two blocks, found the gun shop. Will walked inside trailed by Mary and approached the counter under the watchful eye of the gunsmith.

Mary had a feeling that Will was going to be here for a while, so she asked, "Will, can I go to the general store? It's right across the street."

"Sure. I'll only be here a few minutes."

Mary smiled and left, thinking that it was highly unlikely that Will would be leaving the gun store in less than thirty minutes.

The gunsmith looked at Will and asked, "What can I do for you, young feller?"

"What will you give me for these?" he asked as he set the guns on the counter.

The gunsmith examined the New Army first.

"Good condition, but not much call for these anymore. I'll give you two dollars for it. Now, these Winchesters are different. Lots of folks want them. They look in good condition, too. I'll give you ten dollars each for them. That comes to twenty-two dollars, but I'll give you twenty-five in trade if you'd rather."

"How much for a twelve-gauge?"

"That'll run you twelve dollars."

"Tell you what. If I get a shotgun, I'll need the barrels shortened. Give me four boxes of #4 buckshot, six boxes of .44 cartridges, and a back scabbard for the shotgun and we'll call it even."

"You've got yourself a deal, son. It'll take me a few hours to trim the barrels, and I'll have to modify that back scabbard for the shortened barrels. Can you come back tomorrow morning?"

"I can."

They shook on the deal, and Will noticed something that he would like to have as he examined the newer model 1876 Winchester. He had thought about them before but had hesitated because he'd have to carry two different ammunitions, or three if he included the Spencer's cartridges. But the larger, more powerful .45 caliber cartridges added more stopping power and some added range, so he was still thinking about it and finally asked to look at the Winchester. The gunsmith smiled, handed him the rifle, and began a sales pitch.

"This one is the rifle version with a longer twenty-eight-inch barrel and is chambered for the .45-75 centerfire Winchester cartridge."

"Have you fired one?"

"Now, that's a silly question. Of course, I have. It has a bit more of a kick than the '73 and that heavier caliber round has a serious punch. I don't know why Winchester only claims the same hundred-yard effective range on this model, because I know I can put killing shots at two hundred yards with this weapon."

Will cycled the lever and liked the feel of the new repeater with its longer forearm and even the brass plate on the stock.

The gunsmith then showed him the .45-75 cartridges and that led to more discussion.

————

Mary was crossing the street diagonally toward the store, her sombrero hanging on her back, smiling in anticipation of having the first shopping spree in her life. Her smile didn't last long when she heard a very familiar and terrifying voice behind her.

"There you are! You're comin' home, Mary," Joe Fleming growled.

She knew she should have screamed for Will, but she was terrified and simply froze in place as her eyes stared at her father just ten feet away.

Joe never even left his saddle as he trotted the mule next to her, scooped Mary from the street, and turned the animal back north at a fast trot. Mary was still so horrified that she sat on the saddle petrified, knowing that her worst nightmare was right against her, holding her tightly.

In three minutes, just one hundred and eighty seconds, they were out of Arizona City and on their way back to Gila City, and Mary knew that now, any screaming would be meaningless.

Will gave up on the new Winchester and its twenty-eight-dollar price tag, at least for the moment. There wasn't that much difference, he argued, and that new ammunition requirement was a minus, too. He waved at the gunsmith before he left the shop, then headed across the street and walked into the mercantile.

Once inside, he looked for Mary, but couldn't find her, so he headed down to the women's clothing section, and after still not finding her, he began to worry. He stepped quickly to the counter where the proprietor was already watching him as he walked quickly about his store.

"Excuse me, did you see a young lady wearing pants and a sombrero hanging across her back come in a few minutes ago?"

"No. Can't say I did. But there was a girl that looked like that out in the street a few minutes ago. Some feller rode up on a mule, picked her up, and headed out of town. She didn't scream or anything, so I didn't think much of it."

"Thanks," Will said as he jogged out of the store.

After leaving, he trotted down the boardwalk toward the livery, feeling panic beginning to bubble up inside. He knew it was most likely that it had been her father that had taken her away. She would have screamed bloody murder if it had been anyone else. He could understand why her father would have scared the daylights out of her.

He reached the livery and found that Lou had already stripped his horses, and quickly said, "Lou, I need the red gelding…fast. I've gotta catch some feller that grabbed my girl."

"Let's get him saddled," Lou said, turned quickly, and grabbed Will's saddle.

———

Joe was already three miles out of town and Mary was still so terrified that she was almost comatose.

"You intact, girl?" he shouted almost directly into her ear.

She snapped out of her trance and asked, "What?"

"You heard me. You been ruined or are you still a virgin?"

Mary quickly assumed that it was vitally important that she not admit to having been raped and stammered, "I'm…I'm okay."

"You'd better be. You're worth seventy-five dollars to me from Juan Nieves."

Mary felt a chill permeate her body. *She was going to be turned into a whore!* Then, she glanced past her father's shoulder toward Arizona City. *Where was Will? Where are you, Will? You have to stop him!*

Then she had a horrible revelation when she suddenly realized that she wasn't Will's top priority; finding his mother was. She felt tears welling up in her eyes as she understood the truth. Unexpectedly, being a whore was only her second biggest fear; knowing that she had probably lost Will was worse. He was probably going to get rid of her anyway, so having her father come and take her back to Gila City would probably be the solution that would work best for him, but not for her.

And as the tears flowed, she saw her father looking at her, examining her and she wondered if he would try to inspect her or would even know how to tell if she was ruined.

Through her watery eyes, she kept looking back toward Arizona City fading in the distance. Will wasn't coming. She was alone again.

———

But Will was coming, and he was coming fast. He had the big red gelding moving at a fast trot to conserve his energy. He knew he'd be gaining on her father if he was riding a mule with Mary. They couldn't be moving at a very fast pace and he knew he'd be able to spot them when they were about four miles ahead. He had his Winchester, his Spencer, and he had what he considered his best weapon; he had Otto jogging alongside. The big shepherd seemed to exult in the pace, but he knew that Otto couldn't keep it up very long in this heat. They'd all have to stop in another two miles or so.

———

Joe and Mary had to stop already, too. The mule wasn't accustomed to having over three hundred pounds of weight in this heat. Joe's two hundred and twenty was bad enough, and Joe hadn't watered the mule since he'd left camp that morning.

They pulled off the road and after dismounting, Joe yanked Mary down from the mule, almost throwing her to the ground. She had been terrified by the thought that he was going to examine her to see if she was intact and backed away, but Joe didn't know how to check anyway. He was still seething about having to come all this way to get her but was hesitant to beat her. He knew how thin she was and if he beat her as she deserved, he might even kill her. So, all he could do was glare at her.

"Sit your skinny ass on the ground before I whip you within an inch of your bones, you half-breed bitch! Makin' me drag me all the way down to Arizona City to get you back. That's gonna cost your fat whore mama, too."

Then, he asked, "Who was this bastard that sent that note to your mother?"

Mary glanced back toward Arizona City once more, hoping against hope that Will would come for her, even though she had concluded that he wouldn't.

Then, before she could reply, her hopes skyrocketed when she saw a dust plume in the distance about a mile away, then saw the tall rider and felt her heart explode. *It was Will! He was coming! She was more important than finding his mother!* She totally forgot about her father sitting two feet away. Will was coming for her.

Then he asked more harshly, "Who was he, Mary? You tell me now or I'll whip you even if it's gonna cost me."

————

Will spotted the mule at a half mile off to the side of the road and slowed down to a regular trot. Otto matched the horse's new speed.

He kept his eyes focused ahead and said, "Otto, I think that's Mary and her bastard father."

———

Joe was about to slap Mary's face for her refusal to answer his question when he noticed she was staring south, then whipped his head around and spotted Will just three hundred yards away.

"Damn!" he swore then looked down at Mary and asked, "Is that the bastard that you run off with?"

The sight of Will astride his tall gelding restored Mary's confidence in a flash as she defiantly replied, "No. That's the good man that killed the two bastards that raped me and will save me from the biggest bastard I've ever known."

Joe shouted, "*You been spoiled?* You, lyin' bitch! He ain't gonna save you."

He suddenly grabbed Mary by the hair, stood her up, pulled his big knife, and held it against Mary's thin neck as he glared at the approaching rider.

———

Will saw him yank Mary to her feet, then watched his knife go to her throat and was grateful he had brought Otto along. He walked the gelding until he was about a hundred feet away, stepped down, and began slowly walking towards him, his palms out before him to keep him from hurting Mary.

Will kept his eyes focused on her father and said calmly, "Let her go, Mr. Fleming. She's not even your daughter."

"She sure ain't nothin' to you and if you come any closer. I cut her."

"You know you're in a bad situation, don't you? If you look behind me, you'll see that you're making Otto mad, and you never want to make Otto mad."

Until he'd mentioned it, Joe had surprisingly not noticed the wolf-sized dog behind the tall red horse. But the gray and black canine was now standing just a few feet away and was staring at him, making his neck hairs twitch.

Will could see the growing fear in her father's eyes and said, "You have his good friend with a knife to her throat and he knows that you are threatening her. You are threatening family and dogs like Otto can tell when someone is going to do something bad, and if he sees one muscle on your right arm so much as twitch, Otto will have those big jaws of his clamped on you, his teeth will sink into your flesh, and he will rip your muscles from your bones. His jaws are so powerful, they'll snap the bones in your arms before he starts shaking his head to rip your arm in half. By the time he's finished with you, you'll be begging me to put a .44 between your eyes."

Almost as if he understood Will's threat, a chilling, low growl began rumbling from deep within Otto's chest. Even Will felt the creeping cold from instinctive fear and noted the greater fear in Joe's eyes with satisfaction.

He then said, "One word from me and you're a dead man, Fleming. Now, let Mary go, you can go on your way with both hands still attached, and we'll head back to Arizona City and I'll take Otto with me."

Joe may have been horribly afraid of the huge dog with the big teeth, but he still didn't want to give up on the money he would get for Mary.

He glared at Will and said, "You ain't gonna risk it, mister. If that damned dog attacks me, then Mary's gonna get cut anyway. Now you get on your horse and you and that cur get outta here!"

Will made eye contact with Mary, glanced down for just a moment, and then resumed looking at Joe Fleming.

"Fleming, you just made another mistake when you called him a cur. You insulted him, and Otto doesn't like that."

Otto took two short steps forward, still growling, as the fur on his back bristled. Will's own neck hairs stood higher at the sound, and he trusted the big German shepherd not to make his attack yet.

Will was talking to keep Joe's attention until Mary had understood his visual message to drop to the ground. Mary had seen him glance down, understood, but was still afraid of the knife. *It was so close!*

Will needed to get him to move the knife. He suddenly looked to Joe's right about two feet and shouted, "No! Stay back!"

Then everything happened in a blur.

Joe took a quick glance, the knife moving maybe two inches away from Mary's neck and she dropped like her legs were no longer there.

Otto was already tensed, and when Mary cleared the sharp blade, he charged, taking three running strides then leapt at Joe.

Joe's glance told him almost immediately that Will had tricked him, and he quickly moved his blade back to threaten Mary, but her neck was already gone and before his knife even moved an inch, Otto struck. His ninety pounds of muscle and bone smashed into Joe, sending him flying backward from Mary.

Joe tried to control his knife and stab the big dog, but Otto had his right forearm in his jaws and was twisting his head, neck, and chest in violent swings. Joe screamed as he dropped the knife and began to squirm to try and kick Otto away.

As soon as Otto had Joe Fleming under control, Will quickly ran forward and grabbed Mary, pulling her away from her father, but didn't stop Otto from ripping at Joe Fleming's bloody arm. He had been warned.

Once Mary was safely in his arms, and after Joe's right arm had been mauled into a useless, shredded mass of meat and blood, Will called to Otto. The big dog immediately released Joe and hopped back away from the man. Will then walked over, picked up the knife, then hurled it deep into the desert. As he passed by, he didn't say a word to the blubbering, cursing Joe Fleming as blood poured from his mangled arm.

He walked up to Mary, took her hand, looked into those incredibly grateful brown eyes, and said, "Let's leave, Mary."

She hugged him quickly before they returned to the gelding as Otto trotted behind. Will stepped into the saddle, then reached down for Mary.

She took his hand and he pulled her into the saddle behind him, then she wrapped her arms around his waist before he turned the red horse south and headed back for Arizona City.

Mary was more than just content as she held onto Will. She was relieved, happy, and felt protected. Will had kept his promise to keep her safe, and she understood that she mattered to him after all.

As they rode, Mary said, "My father wasn't going to sell me to be married, Will. He was going to sell me to a man who runs a whore house. He was going to make me a whore!"

Will couldn't turn around but laid his right hand on Mary's hand to let her know that nothing bad would happen to her anymore.

Neither spoke again as they rode the three miles south and when they reached Arizona City, Will trotted the gelding to the livery and let Mary down before stepping down. He led the gelding into the livery as Otto followed.

"Lou! I'm back," he shouted.

Lou stepped out from one of the stalls and saw Will with Mary and Otto.

"I see you got her back. Did that feller give you a hard time?" he asked.

"He had a knife against Mary's throat. Remember what I told you about Otto, that he protects his friends? Well, I didn't even have to pull my pistol. Otto took care of him. He's out on the desert now. He's still alive, but I don't think he'll be that way very long."

"Who was he?"

"Believe it or not, he was Mary's father, or her stepfather, really. He was chasing her so he could sell her to a whore house."

Lou's mouth dropped open, then he said, "What a first-class bastard! I woulda shot him if I was you."

"Nope. This was better, Lou. He'll suffer for a while before he has to answer to God for what he did and what he was going to do."

"I sure as hell hope so."

"Hell is the word, Lou," Will said.

Lou walked up to Otto and rubbed his head as he smiled and said, "I think he's just earned double rations, but he probably would settle for some water right now."

Lou clapped his hands and said, "Come on, Otto."

Otto glanced up at Will, who nodded, then Otto followed the liveryman.

Will left the gelding in a stall, patted him on his neck, and thanked him for the job he did, then he turned and took Mary's hand almost without thinking.

"Let's get that shopping done, Mary," he said as he smiled at her.

She smiled back and clamped onto his right arm as they left the barn.

_____

In Gila City, Maria was wondering where Joe was. He didn't usually stay out this long, but she didn't go looking for him, either. She'd just enjoy the peace in the house and decided to fix herself a nice lunch.

_____

Mary bought herself two dresses, the necessary underpinnings, and a riding skirt and blouse. She asked Will if she could buy a Stetson like his and Will smiled at the question, then helped her to pick one out before he picked up a large travel bag.

He paid the bill and they left the store with Will carrying the bags while Mary just hung onto his arm.

"What now?" she asked.

"We go to the hotel, get a couple of rooms and then I begin my search."

"Why two rooms?" she asked in honest innocence.

"Because, Miss Fleming, we are not married. You are sixteen, and it would be frowned upon. We get the rooms and you can take a bath and get changed. I'm going to go to the saloon. That's my best bet to find Oscar Charlton. If that doesn't work, I'll try the sheriff."

"Alright," she replied as she blushed slightly, yet felt a bit of disappointment as well.

They walked diagonally across the street to the hotel. It wasn't an imposing structure, but it seemed clean. They entered with Will carrying her bag of clothes and the travel bag.

"I'd like two rooms, please," he said to the desk clerk, who looked at Mary.

"I'm sorry, sir. We'll let you have a room, but we don't allow Indians or half-breeds into the hotel."

"Excuse me?" Will asked with raised eyebrows.

"It's hotel policy. You can find accommodations for the young lady at Miguel's cantina down the main street on the left."

"Where did your parents come from?" Will asked suddenly.

He seemed to take affront as he replied, "My father was German, and my mother was Dutch if you must know."

"So, how come they let a half-breed work in their hotel?" he said as he picked up the bags, and a grinning Mary took his arm before they turned, then walked from the desk, crossed the lobby, and exited the hotel.

They found Miguel's Cantina, and Will preceded Mary into the establishment and found a woman behind the bar, which was different.

"Ma'am, I was told at the hotel that you have rooms to rent."

"I do."

"Could I have two rooms for the night?"

"I only have one left, senor."

"Alright. How much is it?"

"Two dollars."

Will handed her the two dollars, but no key was offered.

She didn't seem to mind that he was with Mary as she said, "It is the second door on the left up those stairs. The bath is at the end of the hallway."

He and Mary ascended the stairs, and when Will opened the door, they found that it wasn't bad at all. The bed looked clean and it was bright inside.

"I like it, Will," Mary said with a smile.

"It's better than I expected," he said, then added, "I'm going to go and do some quick questioning and I should be back in about an hour. I'm going to leave you my Colt. Okay?"

"Thank you, Will. It'll make me feel better."

He smiled at her but felt naked without his pistol. He'd swing by the livery and get another one out of their arms cache.

He left the room, closing the door behind him, then stepped down the stairs and was going to leave, but turned to the woman behind the bar.

"Excuse me, ma'am, but I was wondering if you know a man named Oscar Charlton."

"I have heard the name, but he doesn't come here. You would probably be better looking for him at the saloon."

Will felt his stomach flip as he said, "Thank you very much," before he turned and left the cantina.

Will was excited more than he'd been in years. No one had identified his name since the poker game at that trading post, and she heard his name and made it sound as if he lived here. Now, all he had to do was to find him and that meant he'd find his mother. He thought about running back upstairs and sharing the news with Mary but was too excited and decided he'd tell her when he had more information.

He left the cantina and thought about heading for one of the three saloons in town because if Oscar followed his past behavior, he'd be playing poker in one of them. But then he changed direction when he remembered he needed to replace the pistol he'd given Mary.

———

Three and a half miles north of Arizona City, Henry Walton looked down at Joe's body.

"Will you look at that, John? His right arm looks like it was plumb torn off by a wild animal. Lookit all that blood all over the place and them big paw prints. It's kinda spooky, ain't it?"

John Hitchcock stared down and said, "Sure 'nuff. What do we do with him?"

"We go through his pockets, take the mule and drag him off the road so the coyotes can finish him off. I ain't gonna bury him in this heat. Besides whatever tried to eat him might still be around."

John nervously scanned the horizons, then asked, "What would do that? It's not a coyote. Looks like a mountain lion or a wolf."

"I'm guessin' it was a wolf."

John shuddered before they dragged Joe's body away from the road a couple of hundred yards and went through his pockets finding only $1.27. The mule and saddle were worth having made the stop though. Finding the nice knife a few feet away was a bonus.

———

Mary lay in the cool bath. When she had disrobed, she discovered to her delight that her ribs were no longer showing. She was still thin, but she was no longer skinny. She found bumps and curves that weren't there after just a single week of heavy eating. She knew she had a way to go to impress Will, but she wanted to do it so badly. She had to try to convince him that she was a young woman and not just a girl. She wanted to grow up quickly but knew that it wasn't going to happen overnight. But she also knew that Will wasn't going to leave her. She felt warm with the thought, despite the cold bathwater.

———

Will reached the livery and retrieved one of the gunbelts, strapped it on, and felt better. It still had all its cartridge loops filled, too. He walked out into the Arizona dry sauna and headed down the street to the first bar, named Hobson's Saloon, and walked through the batwing doors.

The smell made his stomach flip, and not from excitement. He hoped that steak he'd eaten a couple of hours ago stayed put as he adjusted to the odors and walked to the long bar. There weren't very many customers at this hour.

"Excuse me," he said to the barkeep, "do you know a man named Oscar Charlton?"

"Nope. Not that it means much. I've only been here a few weeks."

"Thanks anyway," Will said as he turned, then crossed the floor heading for the doors.

After he left the saloon, he stopped out on the boardwalk, took a deep breath, and was grateful he didn't have to spend any more time inside. He turned left and had to walk four blocks to the Southwest Saloon, stepped inside, and was met with the similar, but not as intense, fragrance of eau de saloon.

He stepped up to the nicer, polished oak bar, motioned to the bartender, and when he was close, asked, "Howdy, you don't know a man named Oscar Charlton, do you?"

"Who's askin'?"

"Names Will Houston. I just got into town. I'm looking for his wife, Pearl. I grew up thinking she was my older sister until I found out that she's my mother and I've been looking for her for almost two years now."

The bartender's attitude changed. Maybe he had a similar story, or maybe he just was worried that Will was a law officer.

"Oscar comes in about four or five times a week. Usually around seven."

"What does he look like? I only saw him when I was six years old."

"A little shorter than you. Dark hair, with a heavy mustache. Dark eyes. Wears a flat hat and plays poker every night he's here."

"Thanks a lot. I'll be back at seven."

"Good luck with your search. Hope you find your ma."

Will smiled, then waved and left the saloon. He would know where his mother was in just a few hours, so once outside, he practically bounced along the boardwalk as he headed back to Miguel's to tell Mary.

————

Mary had finished her bath and was dressing in one of her new dresses. She wanted to look nice for Will and toyed with the idea of stuffing something into her dress to make her more filled out and womanly but thought it might look worse. Besides, she was sure that Will would wonder how she suddenly grew breasts in just a few hours.

She finished dressing, brushed her hair, then looked at herself in the mirror. As hard as she could imagine, she still looked sixteen, maybe even younger. It was a depressing revelation and one that she had hoped to avoid seeing. She put the shirt and pants in the travel bag with her other dress, the riding skirt, blouse and the pistol, then left the room and closed the door. She had decided not to wait for Will in the room. She'd wait outside so she could watch his eyes when he first saw her in a dress, then almost giggled when she remembered what she was wearing when he first laid eyes on her. She stepped down the stairs and headed for the door.

When she passed a table, a hand reached out and grabbed her by the wrist.

"Hello, senorita. Are you new here?" asked a smiling, swarthy vaquero as he pulled her closer.

Mary was more than surprised as she replied, "No. Leave me alone. I'm just staying here with my boyfriend. He'll be back here soon."

"You ain't got no boyfriend, girlie. You don't have much else, either, but I could overlook that. You have a pretty face, though," he said as grinned at her and ran his free hand across her behind.

Mary looked at the man and said, "Let me go!", but he had her wrist held tightly.

Will had just entered the door and saw Mary being pulled toward a large man's lap and could see his hand resting where it shouldn't be and the panic in her eyes until she saw Will and the fear flew from her eyes.

She shouted, "Will! This man thinks I'm a working girl!"

Will unhooked his hammer loop and pulled his Colt, then cocked the hammer four feet behind the man.

The vaquero froze but quickly released Mary.

Will growled, "Now, mister, where I come from, we don't grab women. It leads to consequences and none of them are good. Now, I'd like you to apologize to Mary for your unacceptable behavior, and don't make me bring Otto in here."

The man licked his lips. He knew that Colt was cocked and would take his head off at that range, *but who the hell was Otto?*

He looked at Mary and said, "Senorita, I apologize for my rude behavior."

Will released the hammer of the Colt and slid it back into his holster before saying, "Mary, let's go and get some dinner."

He held out his hand and she clasped it tightly as they left the cantina. The vaquero wasn't angry at all but thanked his lucky stars that the man with that Colt seemed to have some measure of restraint. He turned his attentions to a more heavily endowed working girl on the other side of the cantina, still wondering who Otto was.

"Will, is it always going to be this way?" Mary asked as she held onto his arm in a death grip.

"Mary, it may get worse as you get older and start filling out. Of course, having to stay in a cantina didn't help. The good news is that we may not have to stay very long. I'm going to go to a saloon at seven o'clock. I learned that Oscar Charlton plays cards four or five times a night there. Can you believe it after all this time, Mary? I finally found the bastard that took my mother away all those years ago after finding nothing during all that time. Nothing!"

Mary smiled at Will's excitement and exclaimed, "That's wonderful news, Will! You're so close!"

"That's one of the reasons I'm going to buy you a big dinner."

"What's the other reason?" she asked with a grin.

"Because I like having you around," he answered.

He couldn't have given her a better reply. Mary practically floated along as they walked on the boardwalk to the restaurant. They passed through the open doors, found a table, and the waitress handed them menus, which was a first for both of them.

Mary felt ashamed that she couldn't read and looked up at Will.

He knew she was distressed by her inability to read and told the waitress, "We'll have two of the prime ribs."

"Very good, sir."

She took their menus and left the table.

Will looked into those giant brown eyes and said, "Don't worry, Mary. We'll fix that problem."

"I'm too old, Will."

"No, you're not. Age doesn't matter if you're smart, and you're very smart. I know that we'll have you reading like a scholar before you're seventeen."

"You think so?" she asked excitedly.

"I'm positive. I promise."

Mary felt incredibly thrilled by his promise. She may not have any control over her physical development, but she could develop other things, including her mind. But when he told her that he'd fix it before she turned seventeen also meant that he still planned on keeping her with him, and that was what had made his answer so wonderful.

The waitress brought their coffee, along with sugar and cream. Mary added both to her coffee and smiled at the taste. A little while later, she set their thick prime rib dinners on the table.

Mary stared at the thick cuts of beef with the juice everywhere and felt her mouth already exploding in anticipation. She had never tasted prime rib before and was expecting something totally different when Will had placed their order. She thought they'd be like the ribs she had eaten before, but this looked like steak.

When she put that first forkful of meat into her mouth, she knew it was even better than the steak she'd had earlier on the trip. She closed her eyes and savored the amazing flavor, but the tasty delights weren't done yet, either.

She noticed a dish of sour cream along with a crock of butter for their baked potatoes and watched as Will put both onto his potato. She dipped her spoon tentatively into the sour cream, gave it a taste test, then smiled and scooped a large dollop onto her potato along with a slab of butter.

Will smiled as he looked at her plate, knowing that there was a potato under the butter and sour cream somewhere.

Mary noticed his smile, smiled in return then took a big bite, closed her eyes again, and let the flavor sit on her tongue and make her taste buds pop. She opened her eyes, added some salt and pepper, took a second bite, and was in heaven.

Will had watched her with a constant smile on his face and found himself wanting to please Mary as much as he could. The only other two people that made him feel that way were both living in San Miguel and running a boarding house.

After they had finished their meal, the waitress collected the plates and asked if they would like dessert. So, trying to keep Mary in culinary heaven, Will asked for two apple pie ala modes. Mary had never heard of ala mode and asked Will about it.

"It's French. You'll see that it's just a fancy word for something else."

The waitress arrived with their desserts and Mary's already large brown eyes grew larger as she saw the ice cream atop big slices of apple pie.

Will poured more coffee for each of them as they ate their desserts. Mary had never had ice cream before and only had a vague memory of apple pie, but together they were incredible. The plates were empty, and the coffee was gone in minutes.

Will left three dollars for the two-dollar bill as he was so impressed with the food and the service, and because it had made Mary so happy.

As they left the restaurant, Mary held onto his arm tightly as they stepped onto the boardwalk. It had become so familiar and so comfortable for them both that it seemed natural now.

Mary was floating along beside Will and said, "Will, that was the best food I've ever had in my life. Everything was so perfect, from the coffee to the prime rib, the sour cream, and all the way to the dessert. Thank you so much."

"I was glad just watching you enjoy yourself more than I enjoyed my own food, Mary. You seemed to be very happy."

Mary laughed and said, "I guess you enjoyed our dinner together, then."

Will smiled down at her as they entered the cantina and went straight upstairs to their room. Will had already decided that he would sleep on the floor rather than dare to sleep with Mary. He didn't want to tell her why, though. She might not be rounded into a womanly shape, but he knew for certain what effect she'd have on him if he slept near her, and that couldn't happen.

Once in the room, Mary just flopped onto the bed, her arms above her head, so utterly happy and content.

Will looked down at her and said, "Mary, I'm going to go to the saloon now, so I want you to keep your pistol near. I'll knock four times before I come in, so you'll know it's me. I don't think anyone will bother you."

"I think they all got the message earlier, Will. How many times will you have to come to my rescue?"

He smiled as he replied, "As many times as it takes, Mary."

After Will turned, left the room, and closed the door, Mary hung the gunbelt over the bedpost and removed the hammer loop.

———

Will stepped down the stairs and crossed the floor of the cantina, turned left once he was outside, and headed for the Southwest Saloon. He guessed the time was close to six thirty.

He arrived at the saloon and entered the place, now expecting the odors. Either he was getting used to the smell, or the slightly cooler air kept it down somewhat. The lamps were lit, giving it a different, more civilized appearance. He walked up to the bar and ordered a beer. He wasn't really fond of the bitter taste, but he could drink it if he had to, and he needed to stay in the saloon until Oscar arrived.

He paid his nickel, walked to an empty table, and sat down, waiting for Oscar Charlton. Every time the doors swung to admit a new customer his heart skipped a beat. A lot of customers came through the doors over the next thirty minutes, but none were Oscar Charlton. Several card games had started, and Will wondered if the bartender's description was off, so he began scrutinizing the card players. He was so intent on examining each one that he almost missed Oscar Charlton when he came striding into the bar. When he did notice Oscar, he was surprised that he actually recognized him. He really hadn't changed much in fourteen years.

Will stood and headed his way as Charlton waved at the bartender and was stepping toward an ongoing poker game when Will reached him.

"Mr. Charlton, could I buy you a drink?" he asked.

Oscar turned and looked at him, asking, "Do I know you?"

"No, sir. Not for a long while."

"Well, that being said, I wouldn't mind a bit," he said as he smiled and led Will to the bar.

"I'm buying, bartender," Will said.

"Whiskey," Oscar said.

Will said, "I'll have another beer."

Oscar grinned at him and said, "A wise decision, my young friend. I don't think whiskey should be imbibed until one is at least thirty."

"Then I've got a long way to go. I'm only nineteen."

"So, what can I do for you?" Oscar asked as the bartender put their drinks in front of them and Will dropped a quarter on the bar, which was snapped up and a dime dropped in its place.

Will left the coin on the bar and replied, "I've been searching for your wife, Pearl, for almost two years now."

"Pearl? Really?" he said as he laughed, "I haven't seen her in six years. The last time I knew, she was working customers in North Fork. Why are you looking for her, anyway? A young man of your age could probably do a lot better."

Will shoved his beer toward the back of the bar, glared at Oscar, and said with a growl, "Because she's my mother."

Oscar's mouth dropped open and then he shocked Will when he just started laughing.

Will snarled, "You low-life bastard!" as he tightened his fist.

Will wanted to beat him to a pulp, but he heard the bartender pull two hammers back on his shotgun, so he just stomped from the bar, crossed the saloon floor, and exited through the swinging doors. He was seething with an anger that he thought was beyond him as he stepped out into the dusk.

But he knew that the rage wouldn't find his mother, and if he gave into it, he might hang. He walked angrily down the boardwalk and let reason take control of his mind and emotions. He needed to find his mother, and now at least, he had a location.

HUNTING PEARL

Pearl was in North Fork six years ago, and that meant he'd have to go another hundred and fifty miles north. Charlton had said that his mother was now a prostitute, and he didn't doubt for a moment that he was the one who had put her into that position. Once the trading post owner had told him that Oscar had offered his mother as collateral in a poker game, he almost expected he'd do something like this. But he also knew that six years in that business would more than likely kill her. She would be thirty-five now, so the odds of her surviving that kind of life wouldn't be good, and now he began to think he'd be searching for her gravesite.

The evening air was cooling but he didn't notice. He'd go and tell Mary what he had found, and they'd head north in the morning.

He walked quickly back to Miguel's cantina, stepped inside, passed through the noisy crowd, and climbed the stairs quickly to their room. He knocked four times and opened the door, then quickly closed it behind him.

He removed his gunbelt and hung it on the other bedpost and just sat on the bed next to Mary.

Mary could tell how upset he was and was sure he had bad news.

"What's wrong, Will?" she asked quietly.

He looked down at her and said softly, "I found Oscar, Mary. When I told him that I was looking for Pearl, he said that he had left her in North Fork six years ago and laughed. He laughed, Mary! He left her there to be a prostitute, and even after I told her that she was my mother, he laughed. I wanted to kill him, Mary! I wanted to kill him so badly, but the bartender had his shotgun ready, and I knew that if I even tried, I'd never get a chance to find her."

Mary swung her legs around the bed, sat beside him, and put her hand gently on his forearm.

She turned her big brown eyes up to him and asked softly, "Are we going there to find her now, Will?"

Will nodded and replied, "We'll leave in the morning, Mary."

"Good. I'm not comfortable here. At least not when you're gone."

"I'm here now," he said as he smiled at her.

She inhaled and asked, "Will, are you going to sleep in the bed with me?"

"No, Mary. I'll just stretch out on the floor. I'm not going to make you uncomfortable."

"I wouldn't be uncomfortable, Will. Really. It would make me feel more secure."

"I'll be right on the floor nearby, Mary. I really think it would be better."

Mary knew she had lost the argument and brought up a new issue.

"I forgot to buy a nightdress. All I have is my two dresses, a riding skirt and blouse, and a camisole."

"Can't you sleep in the camisole?"

"It won't bother you?"

"Not if it doesn't bother you."

"It won't. Can I get changed now?"

"You go ahead. I won't look, Mary," he said as he stood, walked to the window, and looked outside across the street.

"Alright," she said.

She pulled the camisole out of the bag and laid it on the bed, then quickly removed her dress and slipped the camisole over her head before she climbed into bed, leaving the quilt across her stomach because of the heat.

"I'm in bed, Will," she said softly.

Will remained standing and looking out the window, having found her simple statement to be more suggestive than he knew she had intended.

Will turned around, sat in the one chair in the room, pulled off his boots, and tossed his Stetson onto the dresser. He realized he had no pillow but didn't say anything as he laid down on the floor.

Mary knew he'd be uncomfortable but didn't say anything as she lay there looking at the ceiling.

Four feet away, Will was looking at the same spot on the ceiling.

Mary was saddened that Will still didn't regard her as a female worth his attention other than as a friend. If only she knew what he was thinking, she would have felt much differently.

Will was fighting back the thoughts of Mary as a man thinks of a woman. She was so close and yet so far away, and his brain was playing a mental game of tennis. She's only sixteen. But you're only nineteen. She's just a girl and you're a full-grown man. But you were only sixteen when you were first introduced into the world of sex. He just went back and forth. As a healthy, nineteen-year-old, the only times he didn't think of girls were when he was being shot at and when he was sleeping, and he wasn't too sure about the times that bullets were flying. Thin she may be, but she was no longer skinny, and she was very pretty, too. And then there were those big brown eyes; it was always the eyes. Will knew he was going to have a long night.

Mary finally fell asleep around nine, but Will didn't. He stayed awake as he tried to find distractions by doing math problems, trying to remember the presidents of the United States, and even trying to remember every town he had passed through on his way to Arizona City, and wished he'd stopped in North Fork rather than approaching from the east. But if he'd taken that route, he wouldn't have found Mary and she might even be dead now. He shuddered at the thought and returned to just thinking about Mary lying asleep in her camisole just forty-eight inches away.

It was almost midnight when he finally drifted off to sleep, still playing that game of tennis in his mind, and neither side was winning.

CHAPTER 3

Will woke first the next morning because it seemed as if every joint and muscle in his body was complaining about his sleeping arrangements. He just sat up, quietly slipped on his boots, snuck out of the room, and walked downstairs and out to the privy in back before quickly returning and walking down the hallway to the bathroom to clean up and then heading back to their room. As he was reaching for the doorknob, he stopped. *What if Mary was getting dressed?* He finally sat on the floor with his back against the wall, waiting for any noises from the room. He should have gotten his shaving kit before he left so he could have taken care of that daily chore.

Mary had awakened while Will was in the bathroom and had waited to see if he'd return. She was getting desperate to go to the privy, but she waited.

Outside the door, Will waited for her to move.

It was Mary who ended the waiting when she had no choice. She hurriedly pulled off her camisole and threw on her riding outfit, but not bothering with her boots. She yanked open the door and found Will looking up at her but didn't have time for niceties as she leapt over his extended legs, raced down the stairs and out the door, and barely made it to the privy.

Will understood the reason for Mary's hasty, barefooted departure, and apologized to her even though she was gone, then walked into the room, leaving the door open. He buckled on his gunbelt and put on his Stetson making him ready to go, deciding that he'd forgo shaving today. He sat on the chair and waited for her return.

149

Five minutes later, Mary entered the room much more composed than when she left, and when they looked at each other, there was a three-second pause before they both started laughing.

Mary was still giggling as she packed her things and then put on her new gunbelt. Will had thoughtfully punched a hole further along on the belt as he had with her old Colt's gunbelt. After she put on her new Stetson, they left the room with Will carrying the bags of clothes and the travel bag.

They exited the cantina and ambled over to the café for a breakfast that included eggs and bacon.

An hour after they left the cantina, they arrived at the livery, saddled the three horses and loaded Buster with his supplies, and soon were ready to leave for North Fork. Will had saved two strips of bacon for Otto and handed them to a grateful pooch, although when looking at him Will doubted if anyone would have the sand to call him a pooch to his face.

Before they rode out of Arizona City, Will steered them over to the gun shop and picked up his sawed-off shotgun, a heavy bag of ammunition, and his modified back scabbard. He'd try it on later, but for now, he put the ammunition and shotgun on Buster. Will joked that if lightning struck Buster, the whole territory would go up in smoke, which amused Mary but seemingly didn't go over well with the ammunition-laden gelding.

Will mounted the big red gelding and they headed north out of Arizona City to begin their long journey to North Fork, one hundred and fifty-seven long, hot miles north. But compared to the hundreds, if not thousands of miles he'd ridden since he began his search, Will thought this was nothing more than a short joy ride, and he hoped at the end, he'd find Pearl still alive and happy to see him.

Will set an easy pace as they started out, knowing it was going to be another scorcher, which was the rule in southern Arizona in June. Technically, it wasn't even summer yet.

Once they had settled into their pace, he turned and asked, "Mary, when we get to Gila City, did you want to see your mother?"

Mary perked up and asked, "Could we? She probably doesn't know where her husband is."

"It'll probably be a real heartbreaker for her," Will said wryly.

"You are joking, aren't you?"

Will smiled and replied, "Of course, I was joking. But what will your mother do now?"

"Another joke, right?"

"No, not this time. I mean, what will she do for money?"

"My mother was the main source of income for the house. She took in laundry and did sewing. Her husband took most of the money for his pleasure."

"I'm just glad that he's dead and can't hurt you or your mother anymore."

"I was losing my senses before I saw you, Will. I didn't know what would happen. I was terrified, and then I saw a dust cloud in the distance, and I knew you were coming. You'll never know how that made me feel."

"I felt horrible not finding you at first, but once I saw the mule ahead, I knew that we could save you and I knew that Otto would be critical."

"He really came through, didn't he?" she asked with a smile as she glanced down at the big dog as he trotted easily alongside.

"Again. First, he warned us about those outlaws and then he took out your father. He's become our guardian angel, Mary."

"A big, furry, scary guardian angel, but I like him."

————

In Gila City, Maria was fixing her breakfast. It was so pleasant not having Joe around. She sighed, knowing that he'd probably be back today with Mary and then she'd have to do something. She looked at her butcher knife again and thought that it might be time.

————

One hundred and eleven miles north of Gila City, Pearl Charlton lay on her bed, trying to let the aches go away. It had been a long night and one of her clients had been especially violent. She'd have these bruises for weeks, but luckily, none were on her face. While she was without her makeup, she looked almost innocent despite her thirty-five years, but her age meant that the bruises took longer to heal.

She knew that she probably only had another year or two in the business if nothing else seriously bad happened. She had some money saved up, but not as much as she should have had, and Saul had what little she did have.

She suspected that when he kicked her out of his establishment that he'd just keep her money and toss her out into the street. She knew it was coming as he'd recently dropped the price that customers paid for her, which also meant that she was stuck with the bad ones.

Saul still took three-quarters of her earnings, and she now only made fifty cents a customer and still had to pay for food, clothes, and other incidentals. She didn't know what would happen after that, but now she just lay on her bed and nursed her injuries.

Despite all the time and all of the pain, the one thing that always stayed with her and buoyed her spirits was when she thought of Will. He was all she had now, and all she'd ever had that was good. Everything else about her life had been one nightmare after another.

That bastard Oscar had treated her badly from almost the moment he'd wrestled her into the wagon, but the worst of that day was seeing Will standing there on the porch not knowing that she was his mother. Now almost every day, she wondered if he had discovered that fact, and even more often, tried to imagine what he looked like now that he was full grown.

She always started with the eyes, those blue eyes that she knew had caused him so many beatings before she'd gone. Pearl always imagined her son to be a tall, handsome young man with broad shoulders, but still keeping a level of innocence as he protected the endangered innocents from the bullies of the world.

She dreamed but knew that she'd never know. She had been luckier than most of the women that had worked here. She'd never gotten pregnant or had any of the serious diseases that took the lives of so many of the others. But regardless, she knew she could never go back. Despite understanding that what had happened to her wasn't her fault, at least not after the initial sin that had created Will, Pearl was simply too ashamed to even consider returning to San Miguel. *What would Will think of his mother who had lived most of her life as a whore?*

Technically, she wasn't a whore when she was with Oscar. They'd arrive in a town and he'd start gambling and when he lost, which was too often, she would be the payment for his bad hands. But when he'd lost in North Fork, the only way he could settle the debt was to leave her with Saul, and that's when she officially became a whore.

Oscar hadn't gotten another dime for her, but as he left town, he seemed positively jubilant to be on his own.

––––––

Mary and Will found a spot near the Gila River for a lunch break just after noon. They had made good time and it looked like they might make Gila City before six that evening. Mary's desire to see her mother had spurred them into a slightly faster pace than they initially set and Will's only concern was for Otto.

But after they had their quick lunch, they hit the road again and Otto seemed fine.

The heat waves were shimmering off the road as they continued, but their pace began to slow, as they both knew it would. They had to stop around two o'clock to give the horses and Otto some water and a breather but started again fifteen minutes later.

The sun was low on the horizon when the outline of Gila City rose through the dancing heat.

Will looked over at Mary and said, "Almost there, Mary. Are you excited about seeing your mother?"

"Very. I can't wait to tell her she's free of that bastard."

"Are you sure she won't be mad at me?" he asked, remembering Mary's comment about what her mother thought of white men.

"No, but she may give you a hug. Just a bit of warning, though. My mother isn't as thin as I am."

"Few people are, Mary."

"I mean, well, this is hard to describe, but my mother is fully figured."

"She's fat?"

Mary rolled her eyes and replied, "No. Her waist is narrow, but she's very well endowed."

Will blushed lightly and said, "Oh. I understand. Thanks for the warning."

"Is that important to men?"

"Honestly? I hate to admit it, but, yes, it is."

"So, you wouldn't care for a woman who wasn't that way?" she asked in a tone that had an undercurrent of disappointment.

Will understood her concern and replied, "I didn't say that. I just said it has an impact."

"Oh."

Mary hated being sixteen and being thin and hadn't realized that she had already gained three pounds on the journey. When you're starting at a hundred and two pounds and you're five foot and five inches tall, that's a noticeable difference. But she was right about one thing; she was still only sixteen, and even though she knew some girls younger than she was who were much more advanced in their physical maturity and even married and felt cursed.

They walked the horses into Gila City twenty minutes later and headed for the square to allow the horses and Otto to drink. After they had enough, Will and Mary kept the three horses heading toward her house at a walk with Mary leading the way. Will had never seen it, so he was curious.

Mary led him to a small adobe house that barely qualified as one, pulled up, then hopped down quickly as Will stepped down and took her mare's reins. He wrapped the two horse's reins around a small, broken fence to the right of the house and followed Mary, who was already at the doorway crying out for her mother, then quickly ran inside.

Maria was in the kitchen area, had heard the horses' approach, and assumed it was Joe returning with Mary. When she heard Mary's voice, she was elated and crushed at the same time, knowing what it would mean when her husband did return, but it didn't stop her from enthusiastically running to her daughter.

"Mary! You're safe!" she exclaimed as she wrapped her daughter in her arms.

"And so are you, Mama! Joe is gone. He's never going to hurt you again."

That startled Maria as she stepped back and held Mary by her shoulders with straightened arms.

"What do you mean, Mary? Didn't he find you and bring you back?"

"He found me, Mama. But Will got there and Otto attacked him. He's dead, Mama."

Maria was stunned in disbelief. *How was this possible?*

"Mary, who is Will, and who is Otto?" she asked after what Mary had just said registered.

Mary turned and noticed that neither was in the house with her before she shouted, "Will! Can you come in please?"

Will stepped through the door and found the small house neat but lacking in furniture.

He smiled at Maria and said, "Hello, Mrs. Fleming. I'm Will Houston. How are you?"

She stared at him with obvious distaste; another white man, and even if he had saved Mary, he probably took advantage of her daughter.

She viciously asked, *"You saved her? What did you do in the time before that? Did you bed her?"*

Will was stunned by the attack and couldn't answer for a few seconds as he stared into her angry brown eyes.

Mary wasn't quite as surprised because her mother had preached often about not trusting white men but thought that knowing Will had saved her twice would eliminate her prejudice. She'd obviously been mistaken in that belief.

Will finally replied, "No, ma'am. I didn't do anything to hurt Mary. Between me and Otto, we made sure that she wasn't going to get hurt."

"Who's Otto? You had another white man with you?" her mother exclaimed.

Will was getting annoyed, as he turned his head, and said loudly, "Otto! Come!"

Otto trotted into the house and sat next to Will, who looked back at Maria and said, "This is Otto. He saved us both once and Mary twice."

Maria glanced at the dog, but said nothing to Will before she turned to her daughter and asked, "Mary, have you eaten?"

Mary was taken aback by the almost bizarre question, but replied, "No, Mama. Not since lunch."

Will saw an opportunity to calm the waters and said "Mrs. Fleming, why don't we take you out to dinner. What do you say, Mary?"

Mary smiled at Will, then turned back to her mother and said, "Yes, Mama. You've worked too hard. You deserve a break."

Will then added, "We can explain what happened while we eat."

Maria still wasn't pleased with the idea but wanted to know what had really happened and wasn't sure that Mary would tell her because of her shame in being with the man. She finally nodded, then wordlessly took Mary's arm as Will just followed behind, knowing his place. They walked two blocks to a cantina that offered a wide variety of food.

After they placed their orders, it was Mary who started the narration when she told her mother of her abduction and assault, and how she had been left in the desert to die, but Will had arrived and taken care of her. She told how he had protected her from bandits, pawing men, and finally, her father.

Their order arrived sometime during Mary's explanation, and Will discovered that Mary's mother ate every bit voraciously as Mary had. He also noticed, without trying to notice, that Mary had, if anything, understated her mother's bosom. It was disconcerting, to say the least.

Maria hadn't asked Will one question about why he had helped Mary, and in fact, she barely acted as if he was there at all. But when they had finished eating, her mother asked a question that neither Will nor Mary had anticipated but should have.

Maria looked at her daughter and said, "Mary, I'm so happy to have you home. You'll be staying with me now, of course. Won't you?"

She glanced quickly at Will, then back to her mother, and replied, "Of course, Mama. I'll help you now."

Will was both hurt and relieved by Mary's reply. Now he'd be able to move faster and find Pearl, but he would miss Mary. He would miss her terribly, but he smiled at her just to let her know it was okay. He was already planning on returning after he found his mother.

"You are going to go and find your mother?" asked Maria sharply.

"Yes, ma'am."

"When will you be leaving?"

"In the morning, I suppose. I have another hundred miles or so to go."

"Good. It's better that you leave, and the sooner the better."

"So much for calmer waters," Will thought.

Will paid the check and they all stood, left the cantina, and walked quietly back to the house.

When they arrived, Will thought that it might be better to leave now and camp a few miles north of town, and he was sure that Mrs. Fleming wouldn't object.

After they went inside, Will looked at Mary as her mother stood close by, glaring at him, which would limit any fond farewells.

He ignored her as much as possible and said, "Mary, I think it'll be better if I leave now and camp north of town. I need to get all your dresses and other things out of the panniers. Do you want to help?"

"Alright," she answered quietly.

Mary already felt the growing sadness as she followed him out to the horses. Her decision to see her mother had meant she was losing Will, and she knew he'd never return.

They spent ten minutes taking all her things from the panniers, then she stood next to her horse and asked, "Will, what about the mare?"

"The mare, the Winchester, and the Colt are all yours, and so is the hundred dollars. It'll help, Mary."

She nodded and her eyes already misting as she fought to hold back her tears.

With the load settled, Will knew there was nothing keeping him here and he knew if he was going, he had to leave quickly.

HUNTING PEARL

"You take care, Mary," he said barely able to look at her.

He wanted to at least hug her, but her mother was watching like one of those vultures that he'd seen hovering over Mary when he'd first found her.

He turned quickly and mounted the gelding, waved, and set off trailing Buster with all his guns and ammunition. Mary was dying inside as she watched him disappear but was surprised that she didn't cry after all. She turned and walked into the house to her mother, who followed her inside and closed the door behind her, despite the horrendous heat.

Will set a faster pace than he had before; he needed to get away. It was as if he was escaping from prison, but a prison he didn't really want to leave. It all kept coming back to the same things. Mary was sixteen and should be at home, especially now that there was no longer a threat. And with that mother of hers, he knew he wasn't welcome.

He finally camped six miles out of Gila City but didn't make a fire. He just set out his blanket and unpacked Buster, unsaddled both horses, and led them to the river. He found some tall, thick grass and let the horses crop it until it was short, thin grass.

When they were hobbled, he took out the shotgun's back scabbard and put it on, adjusted the belts, and then slipped the sawed-off shotgun inside. It wasn't as much an encumbrance as he had expected. He tried pulling it out and replacing it a few times and grew accustomed to the action. The shortened barrels earned the shotgun the well-deserved name of scattergun. This thing would spray those pellets over a wide range. Fire this thing in a closed room and nothing would be standing when the smoke cleared.

It was too dark to try the thing tonight, but he sure wanted to shoot it first thing in the morning. He set it aside and he and

Otto shared some jerky, figuring that he'd make a regular breakfast in the morning.

Six miles south, Maria didn't have to be clairvoyant to know what was troubling her daughter. She thought she was in love with her rescuer and understood how that could have happened, and admitted that for a white boy, he was good looking. Here was a good-looking young man who had rescued her more than once and provided her with food and clothes, so it was probably only natural for her to think she was in love with him. But she was only sixteen and needed to meet more boys...boys of her own kind. She would get over that one soon enough after a few days.

Mary sat in the corner stewing. *Why had Will simply left without saying anything of significance?* Maybe he didn't care about her at all. She was just a thin girl, and he even said that he preferred women with bosoms. She didn't know if she was more disappointed with herself or with Will. She didn't know what to think anymore.

They had enjoyed themselves a lot when they weren't being threatened with death, then smiled at the thought as she took out the bag with her clothes and began to pull them out of the bag. She found her toothbrush and hairbrush, set the toothbrush down, and began to slide the brush through her hair. She sighed, laid the hairbrush down, reached into the bag, and pulled out the small sack of penny candy. She had completely forgotten about it as she pulled out a lemon drop and put it in her mouth. Then the tears came.

Maria heard Mary crying and was angry that she had succumbed to such weakness. She'll get over it and meet a nice boy soon...one of her own kind.

———

The sun was up and so was Will. He made a fire and cooked a quick breakfast with extra bacon for Otto, then after he had cleaned up, he began packing everything. He had the Spencer in one scabbard and a Winchester in the second. He had one Colt at his waist and two extra gunbelts with loaded Colts in the pannier. He had eight boxes of .44 cartridges and two boxes and a dozen loose cartridges for the Spencer. Now, he had the shotgun and two boxes of shells. He took out two shells and loaded them into the tubes, snapped the shotgun closed, and stepped fifty feet away from the horses. It still might spook them at this range, especially Buster.

He had the shotgun in his scabbard, then chose a stand of cactus about twenty feet away as a target. The cacti were about thirty feet across, so he'd get a good read on the coverage. He pulled the shotgun, cocked both hammers, and just pointed it at the doomed plants. He pulled the trigger and the shotgun lurched backward as the loud report echoed across the nearby river. The large cloud of gunpowder smoke cleared enough after a few seconds to allow Will a good look at the damage, and it was downright scary. The center half dozen cacti were ripped to shreds, and those fifteen feet from either side still suffered significant destruction. The shotgun was one nasty weapon.

He reloaded the shotgun and returned it to the scabbard. When he turned, he was surprised to see Otto leading Buster back into the camp by the reins. He must have been spooked enough by the sudden blast to break his weak hobbles. The gelding seemed unaffected as he stood there looking at Will. He was even more pleased with the red gelding, but it was Otto who really kept impressing him.

After reattaching the trail rope to Buster, he mounted the gelding and set out on the road, making good time. Three hours later, he passed a familiar location, so he turned in and let the horses and Otto drink at the seep that Mary had told him about the day he'd found her. He filled all four of his canteens and pressed on, and as he went by the location where he had turned in to find Mary, he regretted having to leave her with her mother. But it was where she belonged, at least for two more years. He etched the date in his mind. When he had found Mary, he had eventually talked her into admitting that she had turned sixteen two weeks earlier. So, in early May of 1882, she would be eighteen, and no matter where he was, he would return to Gila City for Mary, and her mother would have no legal way to keep her there.

But what if she had found someone else by then? The revelation stunned him as he tried to imagine that very real possibility. He could write to her, but then he realized he never had the chance to help her with her letters. It was the first promise he'd ever broken, and it may have been the most important. Besides, her mother would probably just intercept the letters and burn them anyway. He was just going to have to trust that she would wait. But she had a lot of growing up to do, and not just physically. She could change her entire view of him in two years; hell, it could be in just two months. Everything about the future was just like one long game of poker with many different outcomes.

He kept riding past the Mary place and figured he'd stop at Harvey Freeman's trading post and visit. It was only another five or six miles north.

After he had ridden two of those miles, he heard what sounded like gunfire in the distance. He looked around and didn't see any smoke anywhere. It had to be some distance away and seemed to be coming from the north. *Harvey's?* He picked up the pace and pulled the Spencer from its scabbard. He'd need the range first, then when he was closer, if necessary, he'd use the Winchester and began to wish he'd bought that '76.

Five minutes later, he saw the gun smoke. It was off to the northeast, so it was Harvey's place. There was sporadic gunfire from different weapons, and that only meant one thing…Apaches. They didn't like to waste ammunition because they had to steal it for whatever guns they could get. He listened as he rode and counted four distinctly different sounds, so there were at least four attackers, and probably at least double that.

He cut cross country, and when he got within a half mile, he pulled up and finally got a good look at the action. There were nine Apaches surrounding the trading post and six had rifles. They were moving closer, and he heard Harvey let loose with a Winchester without any results. Will guessed that he was just fighting a delaying action hoping help would arrive or the Apaches would leave. Well, help had arrived in the form of Will Houston, he figured. He hoped it would be enough to at least get the Apaches to change their minds and was already surprised that the Apaches hadn't seen him yet.

He got within hundred yards of the closest Apache. Why they hadn't seen him yet was a bit of a mystery. Maybe the sound of the gunfire masked his approach, but more than likely it was because they were concentrating on the trading post. Just because they were Apaches didn't make them immune from screwing up. Everyone could do that. He didn't take time to contemplate the reason as he cocked the Spencer and brought it level, aimed at one of the warriors, held his breath, and fired. He quickly cycled the lever, grateful that the spent brass ejected cleanly, and cocked the hammer again.

The warrior who had taken the bullet was down, but Will didn't take time to see where he had hit him. Anyplace on the human body that felt the impact of the giant .56 caliber round would be devastated.

The Apache to his left had heard the report from behind him and turned just in time to catch Will's second round high in the right side of his back, blowing through his ribs, lung, and shoulder, and severing his right brachial artery. Like the other warrior, he didn't scream with the hit, but simply dropped to the ground as his blood pulsed onto the sand.

Two may have been down, but now, all the remaining Apaches knew that Will was there, so he'd take one more shot with the Spencer before switching to the Winchester.

At least that was his thought before he realized he wouldn't get the opportunity. The remaining Apaches had all gone to ground, and he had no idea where they were. He didn't know what to do, so he started the gelding walking slowly toward the trading post, pulling a straining Buster who was desperately trying to go the other way. He quickly pulled his knife and cut Buster loose. He couldn't afford to have him yanking the rope and inhibiting his freedom of movement. After he felt Buster lurch away, he slipped his knife back into its sheath while he kept his eyes peeled for the hidden Apaches. There were seven out there at least, but there could have been more on the other side that he hadn't seen. He couldn't count their horses, either.

As the gelding stepped forward slowly, Will was hoping for one to pop up and take a shot, but these were Apaches. They may have screwed up before, but they wouldn't be likely to do it again. He knew that they didn't have to shoot him to kill him. He could ride right past them until he discovered a knife sticking out of his back. He stopped the gelding and stood in his stirrups to get a better view, but still saw nothing.

He may not have seen them, but he knew they were there. He was sweating heavily, partly because of the sweltering heat, but more because of the tension. Then it hit him, and he felt like an idiot for not thinking of it sooner. He'd already been so used to having that shotgun on his back that he forgot it was there.

HUNTING PEARL

He quickly slid the Winchester back into its scabbard, drew the shotgun, cocked both hammers, and aimed at the ground halfway between his horse and the trading post. Aiming was unnecessary as he simply squeezed the trigger, sending a wide spray of lead pellets over the desert landscape which did the trick. As some of the hidden warriors screamed in sudden pain, others suddenly sprang from their hiding places and dashed away toward the eastern side of the trading post.

Will quickly dropped the shotgun, grabbed his Winchester, and began firing at the fleeing Apaches. Only two finally made it to their horses, leapt onto their backs, and quickly raced away to the east.

After their dust cloud faded away, he wondered if any were either still behind him or to his sides. It was a good strategy to try to convince an attacker that the battle was over, then as the victor let down his guard, they would mount a surprise attack.

He quickly slid the Winchester back into the scabbard, stepped down, snatched his shotgun from the ground then reached into his saddlebags and found the box of shells. Keeping his eyes open, he began dropping shells into his pockets until the box was empty. After he let the box fall to the ground, he popped the shotgun open, ejecting the two spent shells, and slid two more into the bores before quickly snapping the gun closed and cocking the hammers.

Will carefully stepped back into the saddle and began walking the gelding slowly to the trading post watching warily for any signs of motion. A wounded Apache was not someone he wanted to run across.

He kept his horse walking wide of the trading post, and rode a complete circle around the building, noted that Harvey still had three horses in his corral, and none had been hit by any shots, the Apaches' or his.

After his slow circuit, he shouted, "Harvey! This is Will Houston! I think they're either dead or gone!"

He continued to scan the area even after he heard the front door squeal open and heard Harvey's bootsteps on the porch.

"Will? Am I glad to see you! You comin' in?"

"I don't trust those Apaches, Harvey. I just don't think they'd give up that fast."

"Don't worry about it. They come and attack me maybe once a month. Usually, they only send five or six. This time they sent ten."

"I only counted nine."

"I got one about twenty minutes ago. Lucky shot."

"I know that I got two with my Spencer and two more with my Winchester. Two ran off, but I'd be surprised if I got three with that one shotgun blast. I could understand one or two, but not three."

"What do you wanna do?"

"I'm going to try something. You take my horse."

Will stepped down as Harvey scampered to him and took the gelding's reins. After he was on the ground Will reached into his pockets and pulled out two new shells, his eyes never leaving the fields around the trading post as Harvey led the gelding away and tied him off to the hitching post.

Will began walking to the back, releasing the left hammer and aiming the shotgun in an untouched area. He squeezed the trigger, the right barrel spewing its deadly spray of lead pellets over a wide patch of ground, creating a pattern of small dust clouds that soon merged into one large cloud.

As soon as the shotgun had steadied itself after the shot, Will released the left hammer. There had been no reaction from the first blast, and he hadn't been surprised. He expected one after the second shot.

He then opened the shotgun, replaced the right tube's empty shell with a fresh one, then closed it, aimed into another unscathed area, and cocked the left hammer before he pulled the trigger. This time, when the pellets smashed into the earth, Will quickly yanked back the right hammer just as he heard the war cry of an Apache warrior when he appeared almost out of nowhere to his right.

The warrior was just fifteen feet away with his knife raised over his head to strike a killing blow when Will pulled the shotgun's trigger again. The Apache must have been shocked beyond belief when he saw that big muzzle bloom with gunsmoke and flame before he felt the massive strike of buckshot slam into his chest, face, and gut. He staggered backward for a few feet before he dropped onto the desert floor just twenty feet in front of Will, his blood pouring from his multiple fatal wounds.

Will still wasn't sure that they were all gone, so he quickly refilled both tubes, cocked both hammers, and continued his search around the trading post, counting dead Apaches as he made his perimeter check.

He was still on edge as he circled the area and found a mutilated Apache who must have been hit by the shotgun blasts. He had to give the Apaches credit, though. Most of them hadn't uttered any sounds when they'd taken the hits and he could tell that at least two hadn't died right away. Most men would have been wailing like babies.

He passed the two he had hit with the Spencer, then he found the one that had been taken down by Harvey's shot. That made four. He headed for the target area where he had leveled his first shotgun blast and found the fifth. Then he found his two Winchester kills, accounting for six and seven. One more to go, assuming that the two that rode away didn't come back. He still swiveled the shotgun in all directions as he searched but didn't have to search long.

He had just swung his shotgun to the north when he caught movement out of his peripheral vision to the east, and turned, but not quickly enough. The Apache warrior had his blade out and swinging to plunge it into his chest, but Will quickly raised his left forearm in time to block the thrust and felt the blade strike bone just below his elbow, making him drop the shotgun. As the shotgun fell to the hard ground the trigger struck a rock and both barrels went off; the pellets spewing away from the two antagonists. But the shotgun itself obeyed Sir Isaac Newton's Laws, and as the mass of lead exploded out of the muzzles, the sawed-off shotgun flew backward, its heavy stock slamming into the Apache's left ankle and throwing him off balance.

Will took advantage of the brief lull in the attack and kicked the Apache as hard as he could in the side with his right foot and felt the toes of his Western boot bury into his stomach. The Apache grunted as Will's blow struck home and staggered back six feet. Before his foot had even planted itself back on the ground, Will had flipped his hammer loop free, started his Colt out of his holster, cocking the hammer as it came free, and as it soon as it barely cleared leather, he fired.

The Apache was struck in the pelvis, just to the right of center. At that range, the bullet smashed into the large bone and both the lead bullet and the bone splintered, causing such massive damage that would have made it difficult for even a trained pathologist to recognize the tissues involved. The Indian spun, then fell face forward into the desert as his life's blood flowed onto the Arizona sand. Then he finally shuddered and died, making him the last of the attackers that Will had to find.

Will holstered his Colt, picked up the shotgun then staggered back to the trading post, turned the corner, and saw Harvey looking at him.

"Got a sewing kit Harvey?" he asked with a grin before dizziness overtook him and he collapsed to the dirt.

———

When his eyes finally opened again, he didn't see the smiling face of a beautiful woman like heroes always did in those dime novels, he saw the grinning face of Harvey Freeman.

"So, you come back here first, and now you come back to the land of the livin' again," he said as he snickered at his own joke.

"How long was I out, Harvey?" expecting to hear three days or some other astonishing figure.

"About an hour or so. I did the best I could. It coulda been worse, I think. The front edge of the blade must have raked across your elbow. If it hadn't hit bone, you woulda lost the arm. As it is, you won't be able to use that arm worth a hoot for a month or so."

"Never could use my left hand much for anything anyway. It was good for getting past five when you're counting, though."

Harvey snickered again, the said, "Can always go barefoot and use your toes."

Will just smiled weakly, then said, "Let's see if I can sit up."

Will slowly started to rise. He didn't feel that dizzy, so he must not have lost too much blood. He looked down at his elbow and saw Harvey's handiwork and was moderately impressed. It didn't look too bad. The scar itself was only an inch and a half long, but it must have bled a lot though because there was blood all over his left side.

Suddenly he realized that Otto hadn't been involved. *Why not?* Otto should have helped him out in his search.

"Where's Otto, my dog?"

"Oh, him. He went and ran down your pack horse after you cut him loose. He was nigh on two miles south when your dog caught up with him, I reckon. I only saw him when I went out to find you."

"I should have had him stay and help me find the Apaches. They're not too keen on dogs, but I guess it depends on the dog, too. A growling Otto would make any man lose control of his bladder."

"So, any luck in finding your mama?"

"Kind of. At least I know where she was left six years ago. Her husband left her in North Fork, Harvey. He sold her to a brothel, probably to pay off some gambling debt."

"And you're still gonna go and find her?"

"I have to, Harvey. I owe her that. If I can help her, I will."

"You're a good man, Will."

Will shrugged at the compliment, and asked, "Why do the Apaches keep raiding you if they've never taken the place?"

"I don't think it's a large band. They always hoped to catch me nappin', and almost got me a couple of times, too. But I think they may give it up now. This one cost them too many warriors."

"How are we going to get them buried, Harvey?"

"They're Apaches, so we don't have to. They'll be gone in a few hours. They always collect their dead if they can."

Will just wanted to sleep and found himself drifting off, so he slowly lowered himself to the bed and closed his eyes.

Harvey went outside and unsaddled Will's horses and left them in the corral, then carried the saddle and all the panniers into the back rooms of his trading post, but kept the Winchester '66 that Will had left him and stood outside as he watched the Apaches collect their dead.

Will slept until eight o'clock the next morning.

———

Mary woke that day in a despondent mood. She had spent most of yesterday waiting for Will to return, and when he hadn't, she began to realize that he wasn't coming back...ever.

She began her first full routine day by making breakfast for her and her mother. Maria was happy to see Mary returning to normal after her return. She had just moped around the house all day yesterday, looking outside continually. Maria still had no idea what she was going to do about the guns or the horse, though. She would see if Mary would let her sell them as she could use the money. But mostly, Maria thought about being free of Joe, knowing that she'd be able to find a good man now. She knew she possessed womanly features that many men desired, and she'd aim high.

First, she needed to get the word out that she was a widow and needed some money to buy some new clothes and other things to look like the classy woman that she knew she was.

———

When Will finally awakened, he got out of bed and went outside, with Otto tracking along behind him. Like Harvey had said, all the bodies were gone. His elbow hurt like the dickens, but he just walked out the back door, answered nature's call, then checked on his horses before he returned to the post. As he turned the corner, he noticed some folks in a wagon parked outside waiting for another member of the family who must be inside the post.

"Good morning," Will said as he approached the wagon.

"Howdy there, young feller. Looks like you had a falling out with someone," said the older man sitting on the driver's seat.

"Not much. Caught a blade in the elbow. It could have been worse."

"You get into a barroom brawl or something?"

"No, sir. Ran afoul of some Apaches yesterday."

Will continued to walk toward the trading post as he talked. It looked like a whole family was on the move. The wagon was stuffed with household goods and a big machine that he couldn't figure out.

The father figure in the driver's seat with his wife asked, "How many were there?"

"Ten of them altogether."

"How many of them did you get?"

"Eight."

"By yourself?"

"Harvey got one and I took out the rest."

"A boy like you killed seven Apaches? Sounds like a tall tale to me."

"Does to me, too," Will said with a smile, not taking offense.

He walked into the post and saw Harvey helping a young woman, maybe within a year of his age. She was very pretty with light brown hair and blue eyes like his.

Harvey saw him enter, and said, "There he is, Minnie. That's the young feller I was tellin' you about. Say, Will, come on over and say howdy to Minnie Crenshaw. She belongs to the folks out front."

"Good morning, ma'am," Will said as he stepped closer.

"Good morning, Mister Houston. Harvey has been telling me about your exploits. He says you've saved his life twice now."

"He probably saved mine by sewing this thing up," he said as he lifted his left elbow.

"Nonetheless, what you did was very impressive."

Will ignored the compliment and asked, "Where are you and your family headed?"

"To Gila City. My father is going to open a newspaper there. They don't have one in town yet. I do the writing. Father does the printing and my mother does the bookkeeping."

"Sounds like a complete operation. Well, good luck to you."

"He tells me you're on a quest to find your mother."

"Yes, ma'am. It's kind of personal, though."

"I understand. Will you ever be returning to Gila City?"

"I had planned to, but there's no telling what the future will hold. Right now, I've got to get myself to North Fork."

"Well, if you do make it back, please look me up."

"I'll do that, ma'am. Right now, I've got to get cleaned up. This shirt isn't even good enough for the rag bin, I'm afraid."

"Well, you be sure to come and visit me when you come to Gila City," she said as she gave him a dazzling smile.

"I will," he said, finding himself remarkably immune from her attention for some reason.

"Call me Minnie when you do come to visit," she added as she passed by.

The scent of lilacs followed her as she climbed onto the wagon seat. Her father snapped the reins and the team lurched forward setting the wagon moving toward Gila City. She continued to smile at him with her blue eyes locked on his until it disappeared from sight.

She was a handsome young woman with a fine figure, and normally, Will would have followed her like a lovesick puppy, but he just headed to the back to get changed. His lack of interest must be a result of the wound, he thought.

He decided to toss the shirt but was able to save the britches by soaking the pants in hot water and using lye soap to get out the blood stains. He changed into one of his new shirts and pair of pants and ten minutes later walked back into the post.

When he came out of his personal space in back, Harvey asked, "So, what did you think of Minnie Crenshaw?"

"She was a very pretty woman."

"She was that, for sure, and she seemed mighty interested in your story, and then I noticed she seemed mighty interested in you, too," he said with a grin.

Will ignored the jibe and said, "I think I'll be heading out in the morning, Harvey."

"I wouldn't recommend that, Will. You should hang around a few days until we're sure there's no infection."

Will hadn't thought of that possibility. Infection was the big bugaboo when it came to gunshot or knife wounds. It can be sewn closed and then it starts getting red, swells and all sorts of nasty stuff starts oozing out, usually resulting in more cutting. He shivered at the prospect.

"Alright. I'll hang around a few days. How many you figure?"

"Three or four. But I suspect I took care of the problem."

"How's that?"

"Whiskey. I doused that wound with whiskey before sewin' her up."

"You've got to be kidding me, Harvey. Whiskey?"

"During the war, lots of us carried a flask of liquor, usually moonshine, with us, so if we got shot, we'd splash it on the wound. Course, not all of it would be saved for that purpose.

Some of it would find its way down our gullets," he said with a snicker.

"And it helps?"

"Seems to. Must clean it good. So, we'll see how yours looks over the next few days."

"What can I do to keep busy?"

"You can help with the customers and stuff."

"How many customers do you have? I haven't seen many."

"They come in clumps. Folks don't usually travel alone. My real problem is that damned railroad will be coming soon. It'll skip right on by just on the other side of that road. I imagine pretty soon there won't be any purpose to this place at all and I'll have to shut 'er down. Damned progress!"

Will just nodded to the inevitable march of progress and began his three-day sentence of helping around the trading post. Otto helped pass the time keeping both Will and Harvey entertained.

———

For three days, he was bored out of his mind. His elbow didn't hurt as much as he thought it would and he was able to bend it some after two days. He still didn't put any pressure on it, though. It looked like Harvey's whiskey therapy was going to work as the wound wasn't as red as it was when it was first sewn shut.

On the morning of the fourth day, Will was ready to go. He was going stir crazy, so Harvey helped him pack his panniers. He only needed two now and loaded some bacon, beans, another ham, some onions, some cans of tomatoes, sugar, salt, and his ammunition. After the horses were saddled and Buster was loaded down, Will was ready to make the long ride to North Fork. He shook Harvey's hand, mounted, then waved and headed northwest to cut diagonally for the road north.

Once he had reached the roadway, Will decided to do something momentous and finally name the gelding. The horse had behaved admirably since he had acquired the animal, and only Otto had overshadowed him.

"Alright, my fine equine companion, what name shall I give you? Something short and not as goofy as Buster. Something with some elegance and meaning. Give me a few miles and I'll come up with something."

He tried to think about a name for the horse, but his mind still kept sliding back to thoughts of Mary. He really missed having her along and wondered how long he had to be gone before she forgot all about him. It had only been six days now and thought that she wouldn't have forgotten him yet and was sure that he wouldn't ever forget her but decided he should just set his wandering brain back to figuring out a name for the horse.

He was saying different words to see how they fit as they trotted northward. This one was too long, that one is too girly, and the last one is too odd. Otto didn't offer any assistance at all, so finally, he just gave up and christened him Rusty for his red coat.

"Sorry, Rusty. It's the best I can do," he confessed as he rubbed the gelding's powerful neck.

Rusty must have been pleased with his new moniker anyway because he didn't complain.

———

They had covered almost thirty miles by the time they took a break. There had been a bend in the river and Will took advantage of the closer proximity to get some water for the animals. He had a quick lunch and let the horses munch on some grass and gave Otto some jerky followed by a large piece of ham.

They hit the road again a half hour later. It wasn't as overbearingly hot as it had been on the days before, it was merely as hot as hell. He appreciated the break from the serious heat and finally made camp after covering almost fifty miles, or halfway to North Fork.

———

Maria's campaign to let prospective suitors know that she was now a grieving widow had worked and it didn't take long for visitors to begin arriving at her home. Mary may have been sixteen, but she wasn't noticed by the men who came to see Maria. She was still a beautiful woman with exceptional female features, most notably in the front.

Mary was happy to see her mother being admired and her favors pursued, but she could see a problem if it got serious. When her mother had been married to Joe, Mary would sleep out in the front room on a cot. When Joe brought one of his paid women to the house for the night, she would be relegated to the floor. Things were better now, but that would all change if she married again. That was unless she moved to her new husband's house, which was looking more likely as she noticed the quality of the men that sought her mother's hand. *Then what?*

Her mother had sold the mare and saddle for fifty dollars and Mary had let her sell the Winchester as well. Mary hadn't gotten any money from either sale but had decided from the beginning not to say anything about the hundred dollars that Will had given to her. She knew her mother would take all of it, and Mary felt if anyone should take it, it would be Will. Her mother asked if she could wear Mary's new dresses after she altered them, of course. Mary had agreed and soon found herself wearing the shirt and pants that Will had bought for her. Mary had to admit that the dresses looked better on her mother than they did on her, anyway. She filled them up, even after the alterations. She was allowed to keep her Stetson, though.

But each night, as she sat on her bunk in the darkened house, Mary would have one piece of penny candy from the bag, just about the last thing she had left from Will. And as she tasted the sweetness on her tongue, she'd close her eyes and see his smiling blue eyes and hug herself, imagining that she was in his arms again.

Then a big change came to Gila City when the first edition of the *Gila City Chronicle* was printed and distributed. There was finally a real newspaper right here in Gila City.

Mary couldn't read, so it didn't matter to her, she thought, but it did matter. It mattered a great deal.

Maria walked into the house with the first edition of the newspaper, then sat down and turned to Mary.

"Mary, what was the name of that boy who brought you here?" she asked.

"Will Houston, why?"

"There's a very long story in the paper about a Mister Houston that has everyone talking. It seems that he stopped an Apache raid on a trading post about thirty miles north of here."

Mary was startled from her complacency and asked anxiously, "What happened, Mama?"

"According to the newspaper, the post was under attack and he rode in and killed and drove off the Apaches. He was knifed in the attack by an Apache, too. They don't say if he lost his arm or not. It seems that he had also killed two robbers at the same post just a few weeks before the Apache raid. It's a very good story, but it sounds like a typical gringo exaggeration to make another hero."

"Who wrote it?"

Maria looked at the byline and said, "Miss Minnie Crenshaw, and according to the short biography, she's the daughter of the owner."

"Oh. I wonder if she saw Will."

Maria was a bit angry at herself for even bringing it up, but said, "Now, don't you go worrying about him. He's gone, Mary, and you should start seeing some local boys. I'm sure they'll be interested."

"I'm too thin, Mama."

Maria put her hands beneath her impressive chest and said, "You are my daughter, Mary. In a few years, you will be as blessed as I have been and fill out nicely."

Mary nodded but didn't care about that right now. That story about Will had her both thrilled and deeply worried. She'd go and see Miss Crenshaw tomorrow to ask about Will. The thought of him being stabbed by an Apache knife terrified her as she understood the dangers of infection all too well.

———

Will woke up later than he had expected and moved more quickly to make up the difference. He ate some ham and cold beans and let Otto have some ham and jerky again. He saddled the horses and got on the road just an hour or so after dawn and set a faster pace while it was cool. His shotgun was in place on his back sheath and he had the Winchester and Spencer in their respective scabbards. He felt that he could handle anything that he met on the road. His elbow was still sore but had improved to where he felt he could use it marginally.

He hoped to make it to North Fork today, but he wasn't going to kill Rusty or Buster to do it. He needed to take care of Otto, too. He was looking a little thinner after all the running, despite the respite at the trading post, and knew that he needed to feed him more. But soon, he hoped that his wandering days would be over when he found his mother in North Fork, hopefully alive and well.

He noticed that it wasn't heating up as fast as it had before and there was a layer of high clouds that seemed to help. He looked over at the mountains to the west and saw thicker clouds that way. He hoped that it meant rain because it would be most welcome if it reached this far east.

He saw something else interesting on the northern horizon. There was smoke on the northwest side of the road about two miles ahead and wondered what it was. It wasn't dense enough for a big fire, it was much more localized, but it was pretty dark, too. After another mile, he began to hear other noises, man-made noises, banging, and hammering. He hadn't a clue what it was until he heard a new sound that he did recognize when he heard a train whistle. The railroad that Harvey had anticipated and despised was on its way.

He finally saw the work crews laying the track and was awed by the speed of their work. They looked like worker ants just moving rails and ties into place and then hammering the spikes into the ties. The efficiency of the construction ballet impressed him, and it was only then that he noticed the bed that had already been graded. He turned in his saddle, then followed it south until he saw another crew in the distance. They had been too far from the road for him to notice and guessed that the railroad would arrive in Gila City inside of a month, maybe less. It also meant that the railroad was already in North Fork.

He turned back to the front and kept the horses moving north, getting closer to the track-laying crew, and soon spotted a trestle across a wide, shallow gorge. The road just dipped down into it and another fifty yards later, climbed the six feet back out. The train couldn't do that, so they had constructed the trestle.

He reached the gorge and rode down into it. It was still pleasantly cool which was almost mystical for what was now officially summer in Arizona. He smiled but was suddenly startled by a roaring sound, pulled Rusty to a stop, and looked for the train. He stood up in the stirrups to see where the train was as the roaring grew louder. *Where in tarnation was the smoke from the locomotive's smokestack?* Then he saw dust churning in the wide gorge about half a mile away to his left and felt his stomach twist into a knot. *It wasn't a train! It was a flash flood!*

He gave a kick to Rusty to get him moving, but Rusty only strained his legs and failed to move. Will didn't understand at first what the problem was for a few seconds as the roaring grew louder.

Then he realized the problem, whipped his head around, and saw the terror in the whites of Buster's eyes as he was pulling the trail rope taut to break away. If he wasn't so close to the north side of the gorge, Will would have just wheeled Rusty around and let Buster run, but the other side was too far away and there wasn't a chance of reaching it.

Will gave one more kick to Rusty's flanks and could feel his haunches bulge as he tried to run, but Buster was determined to run east down the gully and escape the approaching wall of water.

Will had no choice, so he grabbed his knife and sliced through the stretched trail rope. Once free of Buster's anchor, Rusty shot away, blasting the remaining yards to the edge of the gully. Will glanced back at the disappearing Buster as the loaded gelding raced down the gully's bed. Then he turned to his left and felt the taste of bile in his throat when he saw the incredibly fast-moving wall of destruction just before it reached the new trestle.

The dirty water was ripping and churning around the legs of the trestle less than a hundred yards away and Will knew that it was going to be close. Rusty seemed to know what was at stake and he was almost at the short rise when the initial surge hit. His hooves were losing traction as the thunderous wave roiled about them, but Rusty didn't panic. He dug in with his hind hooves and almost flew out of the water onto the dry ground. He kept going until Will brought him back down to a walk, and then pulled him to a stop and turned him back around to face the gully. Will suddenly panicked. *Where was Otto?*

He began to scan for his friend and began shouting, "Otto! Otto! Come!", over the fading roar of the floodwaters.

Will suddenly started laughing in relief when he spotted a very much alive Otto trudging along from the southeast. He wasn't even wet and must have already reached the far side when he and Rusty were fighting with Buster. Will dropped down and hugged the dog, and Otto reciprocated by licking Will's face. Will stood and looked at the water still boiling past, knowing that Buster was gone. The only things he'd miss in the packs were the two spare guns and all the ammunition. He had two boxes of .44 caliber ammunition and a box of cartridges for the Spencer, but the only rounds he had for the shotgun were in the tubes. He had no food and little clothing, but he still had over six hundred dollars in cash in his pockets and money belt. Overall, he wasn't in bad shape. It could have been much worse.

He patted Rusty on the neck and said, "Thanks, Rusty. You're a hell of a horse."

He climbed into the saddle and they continued their ride to North Fork with Otto trotting alongside as if none of them had just narrowly missed death.

———

Mary walked into the new location for *The Gila City Chronicle*. There weren't many people in the office, so she approached the pretty young woman at the desk.

"Excuse me, could you tell me where I could find Minnie Crenshaw?"

"I'm Minnie Crenshaw. How can I help you?"

"Oh. My name is Mary Fleming and I wanted to ask you about the story you wrote in the newspaper."

She laughed and said, "I think about every young woman in town has asked me about that story. Everyone wants to know what Will Houston looks like. It seems that our dashing young hero has attracted the attention of many of them."

"Oh. How was he?"

"He is very handsome. Fairly tall and very well built, an ideal hero, really."

"No, I know what he looks like. I was worried about his wound."

Her casual response about knowing what he looked like piqued Minnie's interest. There might be another story here.

"How do you know Mister Houston?"

"I met him a month ago. Is his wound bad?"

"It was sutured closed by Mister Freeman. I think it will heal well."

Mary sighed, said, "Thank you, Miss Crenshaw," then turned to leave.

Minnie quickly stood from behind her desk and said, "Could you wait a minute, Miss Fleming? You never did say how you knew Mr. Houston."

Mary knew she was talking to a newspaper reporter and that she had to watch what she said as she answered, "He was passing through Gila City and he helped me with my horse. He was very nice."

"Yes, he was. Did you know he was looking for his mother?"

"He mentioned it."

"Do you know where he'll go next?"

"No."

"Well, I'll find out. I'm very good at what I do."

"Good luck," Mary said as she left the office.

She was almost numb when she returned home. *What if that woman finds out what had happened to her? Could she print that?*

When she went to sleep that night, she had more than one problem. In addition to the newspaper scare, her mother was entertaining Mr. Jesus Fuentes. She was surprised that a man of his stature would even know someone like her mother, but she was sure that he definitely knew her now.

———

Will arrived in North Fork just after eight o'clock that evening. There was still daylight, but he was exhausted, so he rode Rusty to the livery and stepped down, walked Rusty inside, and arranged to have him cared for. He left his long guns, including the shotgun, with the liveryman as well. Leaving him only the Colt as he left the barn. He also left Otto there, asking the liveryman if he could feed the dog. Luckily, the man loved dogs and promised to take good care of Otto.

It was too late to buy anything, so he headed for the café, had a late dinner then crossed over to the hotel and got a room. He walked slowly to his room, and once inside, took off his Stetson, gunbelt, and kicked off his boots, then walked to the bed and flopped onto his back. As he lay there looking at the ceiling in the dim light, he wondered if that flash flood had been a warning for what he would find out tomorrow.

Maybe it was just the final misadventure that would happen to him on this long search, but Will just had a feeling that it wasn't.

CHAPTER 4

Will was out of the hotel just after seven o'clock and eating breakfast at the café. He felt better but needed a shave and had to replenish his missing wardrobe and other supplies. There was no point in trying to find Pearl this early, not in her line of work.

After he finished eating, he crossed the street to the barber shop and got a shave and a haircut. When he left, he absent-mindedly ran his hand across his newly cleaned face and neck as he walked to the mercantile to improve his wardrobe. He just bought a single shirt, one pair of pants and some underpants and socks. He needed to reduce his wardrobe to fit into his single set of saddlebags. He also bought another box of shells for the shotgun, a new toothbrush, tooth powder, a razor, a shave cup and brush, and some soap. He added some jerky, but more for Otto than himself.

His last purchase served two purposes; it would help fill the time gap before he could go to the saloon and would give his mind something to dwell on other than Mary. The selection wasn't great as there were only three books available and he didn't believe that McGuffey's Primer would help. He bought Ouida's *Under Two Flags*, a title that he'd never heard before. It had been a long time since he'd read just for enjoyment, and as he paid for his purchases, he realized that this was the first book he'd ever bought. He'd read other books that had been passed around among his friends but never bought one on his own. He promised himself that he would make it a habit in the future.

He left the store and walked to the livery to visit his canine friend.

Otto must have smelled him coming because he trotted out of the livery before he even called his name. Otto's tail was wagging as he padded up to Will, who crouched down and scratched his ear while giving him his expected jerky.

He stood and returned to his hotel room, while Otto returned to his temporary residence with the horses. Will changed into his new clothes and then stretched out on the bed, opened *Under Two Flags*, and began reading as the sun marched across the sky.

———

Less than four hundred yards away, Pearl had rolled from her bed after a fitful sleep, punctuated by bad dreams.

She sat for a minute on the edge of her bed, sighed, then slowly rose and began what she knew would be just another pitiful day in her sorry excuse for a life.

———

Minnie Crenshaw hadn't lied to Mary, she really was very good at what she did. She knew that there was more to Mary's story and it didn't take her very long to dig up the rumors about how she had gone off with Will Houston to Arizona City after there had been some incident north of Gila City. She just needed to piece it all together and create another sensational Will Houston story that would make her name and her future.

Her story of the Apache shootout at the trading post had already been picked up by some of the larger papers in Phoenix and Tucson, and she saw her future growing brighter almost by the hour. She had hitched her wagon to Will Houston, and she was going to ride it as long as she could. Minnie was not only good at her job, she was unapologetically ambitious as well.

HUNTING PEARL

———

Will had read right through lunch, then had to make up for the skipped meal with a big dinner. He had just finished his meal, dropped fifty cents on the table, and left the café to finally go and meet his mother, assuming she was still alive.

He hadn't asked about her yet because he wasn't sure if she was still there, still used her own name, or even if she was still alive. But it wasn't hard to figure out where she would be if she was still working. There were two saloons in town, and the bigger of the two was Chauncey's Saloon. The other was the North Fork Saloon. Imaginative bunch there, he thought.

He headed for Chauncey's first, and after entering, walked to the bar and ordered a beer, leaving a nickel on the bar.

When the beer arrived, he asked the bartender if Pearl worked there, hoping that she used her real name. A lot of the girls changed their plain names to something more exotic, but he thought that Pearl should have been good enough.

"None here by that name," he replied as he scooped up the coin.

"Maybe she goes by another name. She'd be around thirty-five years old or so."

"None of our girls are that old. Why would you want a whore that old?" he asked.

"Experience," Will replied before taking a sip of beer.

The bartender looked as if he was going to say something, then just shook his head and turned to wait on a newly arriving customer.

Will took just one more sip of the warm beer, then turned and ambled across the floor and through the batwing doors. He turned left and headed for the North Fork Saloon. His heart was already pounding, even though he knew that there was still a good chance he wouldn't find her there. When he'd asked the bartender if Pearl worked there, he hadn't recognized her name and said she would have worked at the North Fork, and that should have told him that she wasn't there either.

He stepped through the batwing doors and saw two working girls already threading around the tables looking for business. One was young, just a couple of years older than he was, but the other was decidedly more mature, and wasn't getting the same attention as the younger girl.

Will felt his heart thumping against his chest as he looked at who might be his mother. She was walking partly away from him, but her face looked familiar. He wasn't sure, but he understood that thirteen years, half of it spent in a brothel can have an impact on a woman's appearance. He needed to have her turn, so he could see her face, and especially her eyes.

She suddenly turned, glanced his way, then headed for a table on the left side of the room. In that brief glimpse, Will Houston was convinced that he was looking into the blue eyes of his mother.

His knees weakened, and he wanted to rush to her and pull her into his arms, hug her and never let her go, but he knew that would probably cause the bartender to pull his shotgun. Lower-class saloons like this one were usually run by thugs that kept a tight hold over their working girls. He smiled at the thought, realizing that even Sarah probably didn't know things like that.

So, he slowly walked to an unoccupied table and took a seat, removed his hat and held up a finger to the bartender, and mouthed, "beer". The bartender nodded, drew a glass of beer, brought it to his table, and took his nickel.

After he'd ordered the beer, he'd just watched Pearl as she worked the room which was surprisingly more crowded than the larger saloon down the street.

He didn't notice the beer arrive or the nickel leave as he just watched his mother. The young whore had taken a customer up the stairs, leaving Pearl as the only woman in the place. He hoped she didn't find a client before she reached his table.

Finally, she left the table next to his, glanced at him, smiled, and sashayed his way.

She stood close to him, her perfume drifting in waves over him as she said in a sultry voice, "Hello there, young man. Are you looking for a good time?"

"Maybe. What's your name?"

She replied, "I'm Polly. Are you new in town? I don't remember seeing you before, and I'm sure I would have remembered you."

Will at least now understood why the bartender at Chauncey's hadn't known her name as he replied, "No, I just got in yesterday. I'm looking for someone."

"Well, welcome to North Fork, and if you'd like to join me in my room, I'll make it a very enjoyable welcome. What's your name?"

He looked into her blue eyes, and softly answered, "Will."

Pearl's smiling countenance dropped away as his name and his blue eyes slammed into her memory and she whispered, "Will?"

"Yes, ma'am. Will Houston."

Pearl stared into his blue eyes, then her blue eyes rolled back into her head and she simply melted to the floor.

Will was surprised by her reaction and shot to his feet to help her. The barkeeper raced around his bar when he'd seen her fall and just as Will bent over his mother, he arrived and stood behind him. Luckily, he wasn't carrying his shotgun.

He looked over Will's shoulder and exclaimed, *"What did you do to her? Did you hit her?"*

Will shook his head and replied, "No, sir. I told her my name and she fainted."

"Why the hell would she faint just because she heard your name?" he demanded.

"I don't know. Do you want me to take her to her room?"

"You can do that, but you'd better leave fifty cents on the table."

Will pulled a Morgan silver dollar from his pocket and tossed it to the bartender and asked, "Which room is hers?"

"Second room on the right."

Will slipped his arms under Pearl, lifted her easily from the floor, then said, "You can keep the change if you'll put my hat back on my head."

The bartender could have cared less about Pearl, *but half a buck for just picking up a hat?* Now that was easy money.

He grabbed Will's Stetson from the table, popped it onto his head, and returned to his bar as Will carried his mother across the floor while most of the other patrons watched and wondered what he was going to do with an unconscious old whore. But by the time he reached the top of the stairs, they had all returned to their poker games, conversation, or just plain old elbow exercising.

When he reached the second door on the right, he managed to open the door, then had to turn to get her into the room without banging her head, before he gently laid her on her bed and closed the door.

He sat on the bed beside her, took off his hat, and set it on the bed as he gazed at his mother's face and was pleased that she was still a handsome woman. She didn't bear too many scars of all of the pain that she must have endured since she had been taken away by Oscar Charlton thirteen years ago.

He then rose, walked to a pitcher of water on the dresser, stuck his right hand inside, then returned with his dripping fingers, sat back on the bed, and stroked across her forehead, creating small rivulets of water that drained across her face.

Suddenly, her eyelids fluttered, then her eyes focused, and saw her son's smiling face just inches away from her.

"Will? Is that really you?"

"Yes, it's really me," he replied softly.

Pearl didn't know how to react. *Did he know now?* He had to know by now or he wouldn't be here.

So, she put her hand to his handsome face and traced the side of his cheek as she asked quietly, "Will, do you know?"

Will smiled and replied, "Yes, Mama, I know."

Pearl closed her eyes and tears gushed from her eyes as she began to sob in an incredible release of joy. Her son, her beloved, long-lost son, had found her and knew that she was his mother.

Will just sat next to her and watched her cry, thinking that now, all he had to do was walk out of the saloon with her on his arm, take her back to the hotel, get her a room, and then leave North Fork tomorrow to return to San Miguel.

He could not have been more wrong.

Pearl continued to weep for another minute before her tears slowed and then stopped before she wiped her face dry as she slipped into the reality of her situation.

As hard as her life had been, this was the worst. She wanted to reach over and take her son into her arms and hold him close and tell him how much she missed him, *but she was a whore!* A woman who sells herself to any man who walks through those batwing doors. She wasn't a mother anymore. She was nothing more than a cheap, old whore, and she knew that she would have to send him away, as heart-breaking as it would be for her.

Now that she had calmed down, Will said, "Mama, I've been looking for you for more almost two years now. I've traveled for hundreds of miles all over New Mexico and Arizona Territories and didn't think I'd ever find you. But now I have, and I'm going to take you home now. Home to your mother and your sister where you belong."

The thought of seeing her mother, Emma, and her sister, Sarah, thrilled Pearl, but it also made it even less possible for her to leave.

She looked into his blue eyes, wishing she didn't have to say what she was about to say, but said, "Will, my son, my wonderful, wonderful son, I'm so sorry you had to find me here of all places. I'm so ashamed of what I've become, but it doesn't matter anymore. I am what I am now and as much as it will hurt us both, you've got to leave now. This is where I belong. I'm not your mother anymore, I'm just an old whore."

Will was stunned. This wasn't at all what he expected, but he wasn't about to give up; not now, not ever.

He shook his head and said, "No, Mama. You're still my mother, and you will always be my mother. It wasn't your fault that you're here doing what you do to survive. It's the fault of that bastard that took you away thirteen years ago. You don't belong here. You belong with your family, and you are going to leave with me."

Pearl dropped her eyes, shook her head, and said, "No, Will, I'm too ashamed."

Will looked at his mother and asked, "Mama, do you know how I found you? I was down in Arizona City and found out that Oscar Charlton lived there and when I found him in a saloon, I told him that I was looking for you. He laughed and told me that he'd dumped you at a brothel in North Fork and when he asked me why I was searching, I told him you were my mother.

"And what did he do after I gave him that answer? Did he apologize or even act afraid as he should have? No, Mama, he just laughed louder. Do you understand? He thought of you as nothing more than what you are now. If you stay here, you'll make that bastard happy. Come with me and don't let him win."

Will had no idea that he had unwittingly chosen the one argument that could have been used to change Pearl's mind to let her get past her overwhelming shame. She hated Oscar Charlton with every fiber within her and the thought of him gloating over her staying a whore was repugnant.

But that wasn't the problem now. She knew that despite her age and probable ejection within two years, she was still worth money to Saul, and he wasn't about to let her leave. And what made it truly impossible was that he had the muscle to prevent that from happening, and she wasn't about to let Will get hurt if he tried. He looked so big and strong, but she still saw the six-year-old Will's eyes when he looked at her and didn't want to risk losing her son in a vain attempt to try and free her from the North Fork Saloon.

She lifted her head, looked at Will, then said, "You're right, Will, I can't let him win, but I still can't leave, even if I wanted to."

Will was happy he'd at least convinced her to leave but didn't know what could prevent her from going, so he asked, "Why not, Mama?"

"I can't leave. It's not possible. Please, Will, I'm begging you to just leave me here and return to San Miguel."

Will looked at his mother's face, his eyes boring into her as he said, "No, Mama, I'm not leaving without you. You're coming with me right now. You don't need to bring anything with you."

"No, Will. I have to stay here. Please leave. It's dangerous for you to do anything."

Will asked, "Why is it dangerous?"

Pearl sighed and replied, "Saul, the saloon owner is a horrible, mean man and he has an even harder man that does all of his dirty work named Tom. The man has no conscience and is good with his pistol. I've seen him work, Will. He's very dangerous and would kill you just for looking at him. Now that I've seen you, I don't want to lose you. Please just leave. For my sake, not yours."

"Mama, in the past month, I've shot and killed four bad men in two gunfights, and ten Apaches in two others. I'm not that little boy that watched you being taken away thirteen years ago. I can handle myself now. Let me be the judge of whether or not I can deal with Saul and Tom. I'll make you one promise. I won't take an unnecessary risk, but I will take you away from here. Okay?"

Pearl looked deep into his eyes again, and once she passed the initial six-year-old Will memory, she saw the determination, fire, and strength in those eyes. The same look that she had imagined when she dreamt of what she hoped her son would grow into. Now, he had become that man, if not more, and a smile began to form across her lips as she let pride in her son push her concerns to the back of her mind.

She then nodded and said, "Alright, Will. I'll still have to work, so they won't know that you're anything more than another customer. Can you live with that?"

Will smiled at her and said, "I've known for a while what you had forced on you, and to me, you were always just my mother. I'm just so happy that I found you at all, Mama."

Pearl smiled, feeling tears welling in her eyes again as she asked softly, "Can you give me a hug now, Will?"

Will smiled back, kissed her softly on her forehead, enveloped her in his arms, and held her close as she sobbed.

Mother and son stayed like that for two minutes, each thinking private thoughts.

Pearl was thinking about what her mother and Sarah's reactions would be if she returned to San Miguel while Will was already trying to come up with a plan to free her from her bordello prison.

Finally, they parted slightly, Pearl wiped the tears from her face and giggled slightly as she said, "I suppose I'm going to have to fix my face before I go back downstairs."

Will smiled at her and said, "Mama, you're the most beautiful woman I've ever seen, and I'm sure you're even prettier without your makeup."

Pearl knew that was a son's voice speaking, but it didn't matter. It was her son's voice speaking to her and that was more than enough to make her happy.

Then she said, "Saul is a big man with thick black hair and big, bushy eyebrows that look like they're just one big eyebrow. Tom is even bigger. His size alone will let you know who he is."

Will was about to ask her more questions when there was pounding on the door.

Pearl shouted, "Go away, Saul! I'm almost done!"

A booming voice from the other side of the door shouted back, "He'd better be done now. You got another customer waiting."

Will looked at his mother, then she quickly stood and walked to her dressing table, sat down and began repairing her makeup.

Will hadn't realized that he'd been in her room that long, but he stood, grabbed his hat, and looked at his mother once more as she glanced at him in the mirror and smiled.

He then opened the door and found Saul still standing there, just glaring at him. He suspected that there was no customer for his mother and that Saul had been told of Pearl's collapse and that she had been carried to her room by some stranger. He'd probably been concerned about losing his property and had come to the room and stopped outside to listen to what was happening in the room.

The question that was foremost in his mind as he walked past the shorter, but heavier man was how much he had heard.

He didn't look back as he walked down the steps, crossed the crowded saloon floor, and left the establishment to return to his hotel room. He thought about just retrieving his shotgun and going back to take his mother from the place but didn't think he'd make it very far past the doors if he tried. Frontal attacks rarely worked, as he recalled the three men who attacked him and Mary south of Gila City.

––––––––

After he'd gone, Saul stalked into Pearl's room and slammed the door behind him.

"What was that all about, Polly? You fainting and getting that young feller to carry you up here?"

Like Will, Pearl wasn't sure of what Saul had heard, but she quickly improvised.

"Would you believe that he thought I was his mother?"

Saul stared at Pearl, then broke into a belly laugh and exclaimed, "You're kidding!"

"No. He really did. He didn't even bed me, he just wanted to hug me and tell me how he was going to rescue me from here. I played along for a while, but it got boring, so I finally asked him to leave, so my poor little lost boy didn't get hurt. He said he'd still save me though, so I warned him about you and Tom. I don't think he'll be back. He'll just go back to his hotel room and probably leave town."

Saul was still chortling as he walked from the room and back downstairs to his office.

Pearl exhaled sharply, hoping that he believed her story.

By the time Saul reached his office and took his seat behind his desk, he began to think about what he had heard and what Pearl had told him. Her story matched the scraps of dialogue that had filtered through the door, but like most men in his line of work, he was suspicious of everyone and would do what he thought was necessary to protect his livelihood.

He'd talk to Tom in the morning and have him pay this kid a visit. He might leave town tomorrow and he might not, but if Tom stopped to say hello, he was sure he'd be leaving, one way or the other.

———

Will lay on his bed just wearing his underpants in the heat, as he tried to come up with a plan to save his mother. He knew that whatever he did would require the services of his good friend, Otto, and he'd want to have his shotgun with him, too. It was just a matter of how he'd get it done and what the local law was like.

It wasn't until he was almost drifting asleep that he was satisfied that he had a good idea of what he would do.

———

Will was at the livery early in the morning right after an early breakfast to retrieve his shotgun and his friend. The shotgun didn't act as if it cared when he showed up, but Otto was bouncing all around him, despite having already been given some ham by the grinning liveryman, who was actually sad to lose the big dog.

Will slid the shotgun into his back scabbard, then walked with the Colt on his hip back to the hotel with Otto trotting alongside. Both he and the dog kept scanning the busy roadway for any threats, most noticeably in the form of a really big man.

His plan assumed that Saul would send the mysterious Tom to find him, so he'd just wait in front of the hotel until the unidentified giant arrived to do the saloon owner's bidding. Will found he was more curious to see just how big Tom was even more than he was worried about having to face him. Maybe he'd be more afraid if he didn't have Otto.

He reached the hotel just two minutes after leaving the livery and took a seat in one of the four rocking chairs on the boardwalk that the hotel conveniently provided for its guests. Will soon was rocking gently with his shotgun leaning against the hotel behind the rocking chair and Otto at his feet, relaxing. He would occasionally rub Otto's neck or back to keep him content as he kept his eyes across the street, mostly toward the North Fork Saloon about three hundred yards to his right.

While Will was rocking, in the saloon, Saul was talking to Tom.

The more he thought about it after shutting down last night, he began to wonder if Polly was lying to him. He thought about going upstairs and beating the truth out of her but decided that he didn't want to risk the lost income if he didn't have to and that Tom would handle the problem anyway.

He was giving instructions to Tom Pendergrass about what he wanted done with that kid. If he wasn't in his room, he wanted Tom to go and find him and then rough him up as much as he wanted, but he wanted the kid out of North Fork before lunchtime.

Tom smiled. This was what he did and enjoyed these kinds of jobs more than most. Tom was a very big man, over six foot five and almost two hundred and sixty pounds. He was thirty-six but still in good shape and was more than willing to show the troublemakers just how strong he was. The thought of taking on some kid would be child's play, then he snickered at his use of the word *play*. Tom thought of himself as an unrecognized genius who just happened to be big.

He acknowledged Saul's instructions and left to carry them out. As far as he was concerned, getting the kid out of town meant getting him out of the habit of breathing.

As Tom was leaving Saul's office, Otto was leaving, too. Well-trained canine that he was, Otto stood, left the boardwalk, and trotted behind the hotel to take care of business.

Tom stalked from the saloon, stopped on the boardwalk, and looked across the street to the hotel. He spotted what looked like his target sitting in a rocker in front of the hotel, and was downright surprised, but pleased. He'd have to drag him out of the chair and into the alley to do his job, but no one would complain. They all knew better, even that wimp of a town marshal, Hal Jacobsen. Even if he wasn't a wimp, he was getting a kickback from the North Fork and Chauncey's and wasn't going to say anything.

He stepped across the street, growling at a wagon driver who cut it too close.

Will saw him coming and thought of grabbing his shotgun but held off to see what would happen. He sure was a huge bear of a man, though.

Tom crossed the street, stepped onto the boardwalk with a loud protesting squeak from the boards, came to a stop in front of Will, and sized him up.

"You the kid that carried Polly to her room last night?" he asked.

"Yup. You here to thank me for helping her out?" Will asked in reply as he continued to rock.

"Hell, no. I hear that you think she's your mama, boy. So, what are you doing out here? Shouldn't you be over at the saloon sucking on your mama's teat?" he asked as he guffawed.

Will knew that the big man was trying to goad him into a fist fight that he knew he would lose, so he acted as if Tom didn't exist, which was a difficult thing to do considering his size. He knew that if he ignored the monster, it would probably infuriate the big man, and he was right.

Tom didn't like the absence of a reaction because it showed a lack of respect.

He took one, long, menacing step closer to Will and snarled, "Didn't you hear me, boy?"

Will looked up at him after another few seconds of strained silence, tilted his head, and asked, "Why would I listen to a big blowhard like you?"

Will misjudged the man and had expected another insult, so he was surprised when the giant suddenly grabbed his left arm, not realizing that the big man could move that quickly. He was jerked from the chair and felt himself being pulled down the boardwalk and into the alley as his feet flailed behind him trying to gain a foothold.

But he then realized that he was being dragged to the one place where he needed to be and that the big oaf dragging him would soon discover the reason why it was more of a refuge for Will rather than a place of punishment. He suddenly stopped struggling and let himself be pulled along placidly, which should have been a clue to Tom that something was wrong.

But Tom didn't care about anything as he was enjoying the moment. To him, this was better than drinking or whoring. Pounding another human being to near death was what excited him.

He was far enough into the alley and dumped Will to the ground as he said, "Now, boy, you're gonna find out what it means to get on Saul's bad side."

Will grinned up at him as he said, "Sorry, fat man. You lose."

Tom had his fist closed and ready as he glared down at him and snapped, "Fat man...who are you call..."

Then he halted in mid-sentence as a deep, terrifying growl at his back interrupted him, sending a chill down his spine and tickling the hair on the back of his neck.

Then, before he could turn to see what was scaring him more than he'd ever been frightened before, he felt sharp teeth clomp onto his right calf, then he screamed as Otto ripped into his muscle.

Will didn't want the attention, so he quickly stood, pulled his Colt, and smashed it against Tom's head, silencing the scream and dropping him to the ground as Otto quickly released his jaws.

Tom's right calf was a mess. It wasn't as bad as Joe's forearm had been, but it wasn't pretty. There was a lot more meat on Tom's calf than on Joe's arm.

Will pulled Tom's gunbelt and left the back of the alley, circled around the other side of the hotel with Otto trailing, and waited until the concerned citizens began congregating in the alley where Tom Pendergrass lay unconscious on the ground. He and Otto walked calmly across the hotel porch to the rocking chair and Will picked up his shotgun, knowing it was time to pay Saul a visit.

He crossed the street with the shotgun in his hands as Otto trotted behind him and entered the nearly empty saloon. The bartender spotted Will with his shotgun but quickly looked down at the more terrifying sight of the big dog as his eyes grew wide. He had seen Tom leave and there was no doubt he had gone to beat up the kid, yet here was the kid with a shotgun in his hands and a big, terrifying dog, and no Tom.

Will strode to the bar, stared at the obviously worried bartender, and asked, "Where can I find Saul. It's time I had a talk with him."

He shook his head and replied, "I don't know."

Will glared at him and growled, "You'd better know really fast, mister. My furry friend Otto over here is getting hungry, because Tom wasn't that tasty, or so he tells me."

The bartender took one look at the menacing German shepherd, who was staring at him as if he were a big steak. His fangs weren't bared, but the barkeep knew they were there.

He kept his eyes on Otto as he stammered, "He's...he's in his office. First door on the right."

"Give me your shotgun," Will ordered, and the bartender handed him the scattergun without argument as he continued to watch Otto.

Will cracked it open, pulled the two shells, and then turned and headed for the office with one loaded, short-barreled shotgun and the now unloaded one. Just outside the door, he set the empty shotgun on the floor.

He then swung the office door open and walked inside with Otto right behind him.

Saul looked up from the newspaper he was reading and gaped. *The kid? Where was Tom?*

Will didn't want to waste any time as he pulled both hammers back, pointed the gun at Saul then in a normal voice, said, "Otto."

Otto took two steps around Will's legs, saw the man who smelled frightened, then growled and bared those fangs that the bartender hadn't seen. Will saw complete terror in Saul's eyes and thought he might pee his pants as he stared wide-eyed at the threatening dog, and maybe he already had.

Will then said, "Saul, you've got my mother upstairs. You've probably been taking more of her money than she did for six years now. I'm going to take her home now. If you object, you can do that, but it will displease my friend, Otto, and he already doesn't like you. Are you going to object?"

Saul knew he could get at the most maybe two more years out of Polly and her popularity was already waning. He suddenly didn't care about the old whore at all.

He shook his head, unable to speak.

"Now, your friend that you sent to rough me up is sitting in the alley next to the hotel. He's alive but won't be much use to you for a while with his leg all torn up because Otto ripped his calf to shreds. If you try to stop me from leaving or try to hurt my mother, I will kill you, but only after Otto has had his way with you. He's already killed one man who hurt a woman I cared for. Don't make it two. Now, how much money do you owe her?"

"I don't know," Saul said weakly.

"How much does she charge per client?"

"Fifty cents."

Will was outraged, as he snapped, "Fifty cents! You cheap bastard! That's not going to work. I think it should be two dollars, and I'll use that as a starting point.

"Now, let's do the math together, shall we? I'll be generous. Two clients a night, that's four dollars a day. She didn't work seven days a week, so we'll make it six. That's six nights, times fifty-two weeks that's three hundred and twelve days a year or roughly twelve hundred dollars a year or seventy-two hundred dollars for the six years you've kept her here. I'll give you a break and say that's only seven thousand. I assume you kept the majority of her money, but again, I'll be generous and assume you only took half, which means that you owe my mother thirty-five hundred dollars. How much do you have here?"

Saul was shaken more by Otto than the amount of money that Will was demanding but still tried to bluff his way out of the situation when he replied, "Not that much. Really. I only keep a few hundred dollars here."

"You're lying, Saul. Sorry, Otto doesn't like liars at all. Otto!"

Otto took two steps forward and growled even louder.

Saul's eyes flew wide as he shouted, "Wait! Wait! I may have some more. Let me check."

"By the way, Saul, if anything other than money comes out of that box, this shotgun goes off and you'll have to be carted out of here in a wheelbarrow."

Saul licked his upper lip. There was a pistol in his drawer but knew he had zero chance of getting to use it. Between the snarling dog and the cocked shotgun, he'd die for sure. He pulled out his cash box, opened it, and handed it all to Will.

"There's only about three thousand dollars in the box. That's all I have here."

"That'll do," he said, as he scooped out all of the bills and began stuffing them into his pockets, as he continued, saying, "Now, I'm going to go and get my mother. If you want to chase after me or go and tell the sheriff, go ahead. I'm in a vicious mood. You're coming out of this pretty good, Saul. My mother is tired and won't give you much more service anyway. The money is probably less than you make in a month. Now, where is my mother?"

"She's up in her room."

"Stay there and live, Saul."

Will didn't have to back out, but just turned and walked out of the room as Otto covered his exit. Even after Otto finally left, Saul followed Will's instructions. Aside from the fact that everything the kid had said was true, he didn't think he'd be able to shoot both the kid and the dog with the pistol. He didn't want to lose his dignity either, as he sat in his own body waste that was more than just number one, while he listened to Will's footsteps go up the stairs.

Will left Otto downstairs to keep an eye on things while he went to bring his mother out of this place.

He rapped on her door, didn't get an answer, then slowly opened it and saw his mother looking at the door with frightened eyes until she saw his face and broke into a smile.

She stood and asked, "Will? What happened? I heard shouting outside."

He had the shotgun held outside the door as he replied, "We're going home, Mama. You've been fired by Saul."

"What? Why?" she asked in confusion.

"Because we told him to. Otto makes a convincing argument."

She was still confused when he mentioned Otto, but said, "But he has my money. I have over three hundred dollars that he owes me."

"No, you have three thousand dollars due to you and it's in my pockets already. Let's go, Mama."

She looked at her son and couldn't believe what he was telling her, but stood and looked around her room quickly, realizing there was nothing here for her.

Then, instantly, her concerns vanished, and her mood soared. Inside, she was dancing, but couldn't understand how this was happening. *He was only nineteen!*

"Okay, Will," she finally replied as a big smile grew on her face.

He finally stepped completely into the room with the shotgun in his right hand and offered her his still sore left arm, and Pearl felt as if she was going to cry just from pride in her son as she put her hand on his forearm, luckily not grabbing his knife wound.

They walked down the stairs and she saw a German shepherd staring at the bartender and hesitated.

Will saw her eyes stop on Otto, smiled, and said, "Mama, that's my best friend, Otto. He's the reason that Saul was so willing to let you leave."

Pearl relaxed, then they resumed stepping down the stairs, and when they reached the floor, Otto glanced at Will and then quickly returned to watching the bartender.

Will walked outside with his mother on his arm, and no one noticed as any passersby were all across the street looking at Tom, who was still unconscious and bleeding. No one had called for the doctor because Tom was not a popular citizen of North Fork and they were all probably hoping he'd bleed to death.

Will slipped his shotgun into his back scabbard, then steered his mother to the dry goods store and walked inside.

"Mama, pick out some nice clothes and a travel bag. Then, we'll go across the street and you can get changed. We'll take the next train. Do you know when it leaves?"

"The northbound train leaves around two o'clock."

"Okay, we'll need to hurry to make it on time."

Pearl smiled and picked out two dresses and the necessary underclothes and some other things that she'd need over the next few days. Will picked up a travel bag and they walked up front. The proprietor looked at Pearl with disdain, but Will ignored it and paid for the order. He didn't care what anyone in North Fork thought about his mother. Neither he nor his mother would ever set foot in the town after they got on the train.

They left the store and crossed over to the hotel and as they passed the front desk, the clerk looked at them and was going to say something, but Will glared at him and he decided that it would probably be wise not to comment. He opened the door to his room, put his things into his saddlebags, then left the travel bag for his mother, hoping that she didn't take the revealing dress that she was wearing.

He hung his saddlebags over his shoulder and said, "I'll be in the lobby when you're finished changing, Mama."

She smiled warmly at her son and said, "Thank you, Will."

He closed the door and walked out to the front of the hotel and scanned the street, noticing that Otto was sitting in front of the North Fork Saloon, making sure that no one exited. Otto was a tactical genius.

He returned to the lobby to wait for his mother, and Pearl came back out just a few minutes later, carrying the travel bag. She looked transformed after she had wiped her face of the makeup and lipstick. Maybe she'd used her old dress to wipe it off. She looked like a handsome, mature woman; she looked like his mother.

She smiled at Will as she drew near him and he said, "Let's go and get my horse, Mama, and then we'll get our tickets."

She took his offered right arm and he took the travel bag in his left hand, knowing how close her grip had been to his knife wound earlier.

When they stepped outside, Otto trotted up next to him, his watchdog duties complete. They walked to the train station, then approached the ticket window.

Will said, "I'll need two tickets to San Miguel, New Mexico."

The ticket agent had to look at his schedule to see if the train even went there before turning back and saying, "$63.40."

"I'll need transport for my horse as well. I also have a dog."

"They both can ride in the stock car. Is the dog well-behaved?"

"He's very well disciplined, but I wouldn't make him mad."

The ticket master just said, "Your new total is $81.20."

Will paid the fares and was given two tickets and a tag for Rusty and another for Otto. How he would put it on was answered when the ticket agent gave him a cord for Otto's neck.

The train was scheduled to leave at 1:40 and would arrive at San Miguel at 7:50 tomorrow morning. It was 12:10 according to the railway clock, so he thought there was enough time to have a hot, departing meal.

"Mama, would you like some lunch?"

"I'd love some lunch, Will."

He escorted his mother down the street and into the diner while Otto set up a station outside. No one seemed to recognize her in her new role as Will's mother as they ordered their lunch and enjoyed their first meal as mother and son. She didn't ask him much but would save that for the long train ride. As they ate, she just gazed at her son with a smile almost constantly on her face.

He paid for the meal, and they left the diner, picking up Otto as they left after Will handed him a large piece of chicken breast meat that he'd cut out for him. As they passed the hotel, the sheriff watched him leave. He had been told by Saul to just let him go as he had no intention of dealing with him again. He had been deathly afraid of dogs before, but now he'd have nightmares about them.

They arrived at the livery and the liveryman quickly saddled Rusty, then before they left, the liveryman rubbed Otto's head, gave him a piece of unidentifiable meat, and shook Will's hand before Will led Rusty to the stock holding corral. He put the tag on the tall gelding and told the stock manager that he would handle getting Otto onto the stock car.

"Mister, how good is that dog?" he asked.

"If I tell him to stay, he'll stay until hell freezes over. Why?"

"We don't have a lot of passengers, so just bring him on the train. Nobody will care if he's just lying there."

"Thanks, I appreciate it."

The train arrived on time and Will, Pearl, and Otto climbed on board and twenty minutes later, were leaving North Fork on their way home.

————

John Hitchcock and Henry Walton were eight miles south of North Fork and were in a great mood. It was the best find in all of their days of scavenging.

"I'll bet we can get forty dollars just for the guns, John."

John was so giddy that he laughed, then shouted, "Hell, I bet we can get sixty! We can probably get another fifty for the pack horse and saddle, too!"

Henry was still grinning when they spotted the train heading north and waved at the engineer as it passed. He waved back and gave them a long blast on the steam whistle in greeting.

Their hands were still in the air when their latest prize began bucking and trying to escape from the loud locomotive, almost yanking John's horse to the ground in panic.

"Dang it! That damned animal is the biggest coward I ever did see!"

————

Mary was protesting but knew she had no chance that her mother would change her mind.

"But, Mama, I can stay here. I'll be fine."

"Mary, Jesus has asked me to marry him and I've agreed. He lives in a very nice hacienda in town and he has the ranch, so why would you want to live here? Besides, he has a son that you would like. He is a handsome young man. What more could a girl ask for?"

"Why can't I stay here, Mama? It doesn't bother anyone, and it won't cost anything."

Maria sighed and replied, "Because, Mary I intend to sell it as soon as I am married to Jesus. We're going to be married next week on the first day of July. You aren't going to spoil this beautiful thing, are you, Mary?"

"No, Mama," she answered quietly.

"Good. Then it's decided. After the wedding, we'll both move into his nice hacienda."

"Yes, Mama."

Her mother was leaving shortly to go out with Mr. Fuentes again. *What had come over her mother?* She was always so nice to Mary when they had nothing, but once she was free of Joe Fleming, she was so different. Maybe it was because she knew it would be her last chance for a better life. Whatever the reason, it was very disconcerting. She was back home and should feel comfortable again after her father's death, but she felt so alone and out of place. Her biggest question was why Will hadn't come back for her. *Why did you leave me, Will?*

———

Will and Pearl had talked almost non-stop since the train left North Fork. Pearl was still in awe of the confident young man sitting beside her and had asked him how he had been able to not only get her out of her situation but get over three thousand dollars from Saul. He had given all credit to his dog, Otto, but she knew better. It had taken an extraordinary amount of courage to do what he had done. She had known so many men over the last six years, but none could hold a candle to her own son. Her son…just the sound of it generated a warm glow in her soul. Even the son she imagined had paled when compared to the reality of Will Houston.

Yet she felt incredibly cheated because she hadn't watched him grow up from that small boy who had been separated from her thirteen years ago. As miserable as her life had been, the worst, by far, was not being a mother to her son.

After he had concluded the stories of his search for her, leaving out none of the gory details, as she had requested, he ended the tale by having to show her his knife wound.

"Those stitches need to come out soon," she said.

"Yes, Mama. I'll get them taken out tomorrow."

"So, Will, what are you going to do about Mary?" she asked.

"I'm not sure, Mama. I was surprised she had agreed so quickly to stay with her mother. It wasn't a very pleasant house."

Pearl smiled and said, "You spent almost two years of your young life trying to find me, and then risked death to get me away. Why did you do that?"

"I had to find you, Mama."

"And Mary had to provide comfort to her mother. Don't give up on Mary, Will. Any woman who would do the things you told me is worth going after."

"But she's only sixteen, Mama."

"The legal age for marriage in Arizona is fifteen, Will."

"It is?" he asked in surprise.

"Actually, I've seen girls as young as thirteen get married, but they have to have their parents' consent. Sadly, most of them that are getting married that young are really being sold to their future husbands."

"Mama, why did you marry Oscar Charlton? I still remember the day you were riding off. You were crying."

Pearl took in a deep breath and replied, "Yes, I was crying. Oscar was an ultimatum from your father. He wanted me out of the house and threatened to hurt you if I didn't marry him. It was only after we were wed that he made it plain that you would stay in San Miguel.

"I tried so hard to argue with Oscar to bring you along, but he refused. He said I could get my things, but not my son. It broke my heart, Will, but your grandfather, who you believed was your father, gave me no choice. Ever since then, I've dreamt about you. I've imagined what you were like or what you were doing. For thirteen years, Will, you were always first in my mind and heart."

Will smiled at her and said, "I'm glad I found you, Mama."

"And I am beyond happy that you did, Will."

Pearl sighed and laid her head on her son's broad shoulder and began to think about seeing her mother and sister again soon. Will had filled in all that had happened to them after she'd gone and was happy that the bastard who had denied her the opportunity to share her life with her son was dead.

––––––

The train rolled on through the night, making its stops at watering and coaling stations as it crossed the desert landscape in the dark. They both made use of the rest facilities along the way and Otto simply lifted his leg or squatted whenever they left the train.

———

At 7:45 the next morning, the train was pulling into the San Miguel station as the sun was blazing and low in the eastern sky. Will looked out at San Miguel and noticed some new buildings and more houses too, but not too many changes in the long time that he had been gone.

Pearl saw many changes, including the train depot. She had never ridden on a train until Will escorted her onto this one. It was thrilling to be traveling at speeds of forty miles per hour for the first ten minutes. Then with the frequent stops and smoke being swirled into the passenger cars, it became mundane, if not annoying. But now she was back where she had started and was beginning to wonder about her reception. *Would her mother welcome her back*? Will seemed to think so. *But what would happen when her mother found out about her past? What then?*

As the train slowed to less than walking speed, Will turned to his mother, and said, "We're home, Mama."

Pearl smiled weakly and just nodded.

Will saw her concern, then leaned over and kissed her gently on the cheek.

She smiled as her eyes glistened and she finally recognized what was important. No matter what her mother and sister did, she knew that her son loved her and respected her, and that was all that mattered.

The train stopped and only four passengers were getting off while the train added water to its tank.

Will hung his saddlebags over his shoulder, picked up the travel bag, and stepped off the train first, holding his mother's hand. As she stepped down onto the platform, she experienced an odd sensation of going back in time. Otto trotted down behind them.

Will then said, "I'm going to get Rusty, Mama. I'll be right back."

Then he pointed at Otto and said, "Stay," as Otto sat.

Will left the travel bag and jogged over to the stock pen where he watched as Rusty was led off the car and into the corral. Will retrieved him and led him back to the platform. He was wearing his pistol, but the shotgun had been relegated to the inside of the bedroll, making Rusty one heavily armed horse.

He hooked the travel bag over the saddle horn, took Pearl's arm, and walked down the street, leading the big gelding with Otto walking beside his mother. Houston's Boarding House was only two blocks from the new train station and it only took three minutes to get there.

When they reached the house, Will tied off Rusty, took the travel bag down, and could see his mother's trepidation as they walked up the stairs to the door.

"It'll be alright, Mama. You'll see," he said in a soft, soothing voice.

Pearl nodded her head nervously but didn't say anything.

Will just opened the door without knocking and stepped inside.

Emma Houston heard the front door open and thought it was one of her eight guests. She was cleaning dishes from breakfast, but the footsteps were getting closer and she wondered who would be returning so soon. Usually, the boarding house was empty after breakfast.

Then she heard a voice she hadn't heard in almost two years and her heart leapt.

"Mama, I'm home!" shouted Will.

She dropped the plate on the wooden floor. It didn't break, but she didn't care one way or the other. Will was home. She lifted her skirts and trotted quickly out of the kitchen, turned into the hallway, saw Will, and then stopped suddenly. *Who was that with him? It looked like…*

Will answered her unspoken question when he announced with a giant smile, "Mama, I brought Pearl home."

Pearl didn't know what to do. She was frozen in place as she looked at her mother for the first time in more than a decade, but Emma knew exactly what to do. She ran forward and embraced her almost lost daughter. As the women hugged, they each began to sob uncontrollably in pure, unrestricted joy. Will and Otto were momentarily forgotten as mother and daughter stayed wrapped in each other's arms.

When they finally separated, Emma gazed into her daughter's face and said, "Pearl, I'm so happy you've come back home."

"Will brought me back, Mama. He searched for so long, then found me and forced Saul to let me go."

"Why did he have to force someone to let you go?" she asked as she finally glanced at Will, still not noticing the big dog that was sitting behind him.

"Oscar abandoned me in North Fork six years ago without any money. He had given me to a man named Saul as payment for a gambling debt. I was a prostitute, Mama. I had no place to go and thought I could never leave. Not until Will showed up," she said as she looked back at Will with a glowing face.

Emma looked at her grandson and said, "Will, how can we ever thank you enough?"

"Mama, I did it for myself. When I found out what had happened to her, I had to get her away from that place. I couldn't leave her there."

"Well, come into the kitchen. I'll feed you while you tell me what happened."

"Do you mind if Otto comes along? Without his help, I don't know if I could have gotten Mama out of there."

She finally spotted the German shepherd near the door. He was so quiet.

"Of course, he can. He seems like a good dog."

"He's much more than that. He's my best friend," he said as he slapped the side of his leg and Otto trotted up beside him.

They all went into the kitchen and while Emma prepared a quick late breakfast for Will and Pearl, Will began telling what happened in North Fork.

"I knew some of the things you had done before you got there, Will. That fight at the trading post with the Apaches for one." Emma said.

Will was surprised and asked, "How? I hadn't written in the last month or so. I've been a bit busy."

"I know. The Santa Fe paper is over there on the counter. I saved it."

Will stood and picked up the paper before sitting back down and read the lead story. It was a reprint from the new *Gila City Chronicle* and described in detail what he had done at Harvey's trading post, first with the two robbers, and then with the Apaches. What bothered him was that the writer had ended the story with the hint of future revelations about Will; specifically, about a young girl he had rescued in his travels. This wasn't good.

Pearl had heard all the stories from Will, so the stories themselves weren't new, but the fact that they had been spread across the Southwest was.

"Will, what are you going to do now?" asked Pearl.

"I'm not sure, now. This could change things. I don't like it much."

"Will, I know you just returned and need to settle in a little while, but I was hoping you'd come back so you could help me with a problem that's just come up," said Emma.

"Anything, Mama," he answered, not feeling the least bit awkward calling her mama with his mother sitting beside her.

"It's Sarah."

Max was startled. *He had forgotten about Sarah!*

"Where is Sarah?"

"She's married and living south of Santa Fe with her husband."

"When did she get married?" he asked, astounded at the news, although he knew he shouldn't have been surprised. She would have attracted many suitors when she came of age.

"About a year ago. She's living at her husband's ranch, the Double R, about six miles south of Santa Fe. Her husband's name is Ralph Rheingold."

"How did she meet someone that far away?"

"He was here visiting his cousin. He's a handsome young man and they seemed very happy. It's just that I had been getting almost weekly letters from her until a few months ago. Then, they stopped. I hate to ask you, but could you go and check on her?"

There wasn't any doubt in his answer as he quickly replied, "Of course, Mama. It'll give you both some time to talk. I'll leave in the morning. It's about fifty miles to Santa Fe, so I'll see if I can spot the ranch on the way in. If not, I'll have to go and ask directions. I should be back in a few days. Oh, and I forgot."

He reached in his pockets and began pulling out Pearl's cash. By the time he finished there was $3,127.00 on the table. Emma's eyes bulged at the sight.

Pearl smiled and said, "Will convinced Saul to pay me more money than he owed me."

"Otto was the convincer. I just added to his effect on Saul, and besides, he still made this much money off of you, Mama." Will said.

Emma still almost felt like he was talking to her when he addressed his mother, and it made her want to laugh.

Pearl looked at Will and said, "Will, you need some money for your trip."

"I have enough. I'll be fine," he said, knowing he still had over six hundred dollars in his money belt.

Will left his mother and his grandmother to talk while he returned to get Rusty into the barn, so he could prepare for his trip to Santa Fe and visit Sarah.

With all of the bad things he'd seen since he'd left San Miguel, he almost suspected that when he arrived at the ranch tomorrow, he'd find more mayhem.

At least he was better armed this time, he thought as he unsaddled Rusty while Otto sat beside him watching.

He was going to leave the Spencer and shotgun in the barn, but there was no one to watch over the weapons, so he put on his back scabbard, slid the sawed-off shotgun in place, then put his heavy saddlebags over his shoulder and took both carbines with him as he headed for the back of the boarding house.

Will entered the kitchen, interrupting what must have been a lively conversation between Emma and Pearl, as they both were smiling, and quickly looked at him as he entered.

Emma said, "Lord, Will! Do you have enough guns?"

"I needed them all, Mama. Can I put them someplace?"

"Your room is still the way you left it, Will."

"Thank you, Mama," he said as he walked through the kitchen and let them continue their extended reunion.

They had a lot of catching up to do, and he had told his mother just about everything that had happened to him since he left San Miguel, so there was no particular reason for him to be there.

He entered his room, and Otto trotted in and quickly established his spot when he laid down. Will set the two carbines against the near wall, left the saddlebags on the floor, and began disarming himself.

After he hung his hat on the bedpost, he pulled off his boots and stretched out on his bed, noticing that his feet hung off the end of the bed now. He didn't remember that happening before he left and wondered if he had really grown two inches since he rode out of San Miguel. Then he realized that he was going to be twenty in three months, so maybe he had grown after all.

He drifted off for a couple of hours until there was a tap on his door which startled him. Otto was already standing and looking at the door when he swung his legs around the bed.

Then he heard Emma ask, "Will, are you decent?"

Will snickered and replied, "I'm never decent, Mama, but I am dressed."

Emma was smiling as she opened the door and said, "I have lunch ready, Will."

Will nodded as he pulled on his boots but left all his hardware as he left the room with Otto trailing.

The guests could have lunch in the kitchen if they wished, but most were at work, so it was just him and his two mothers who sat down at the table.

As they ate, Emma said, "Pearl has been telling me about your adventures in Arizona, Will. After you check on Sarah, what will you do?"

Will took a bite of the stew that had been made from last night's leftovers and after he swallowed said, "I don't know yet, Mama. I need a little time to think."

"I was just curious if you already had plans, Will," she said as she looked at him.

Will glanced over at Pearl and wondered if this was another question about Mary. He continued to eat his stew as he dabbed some fresh bread into the gravy as he tried to think about tomorrow's trip to Santa Fe, but once he had Mary pop into his mind, it was hard to push her back out.

So, for the rest of the meal and even after he and Otto went out to the barn to check on Rusty, his thoughts revolved around the skinny girl he'd left in Gila City with her mother.

———

Mary was deep in thought as she lay in bed sucking on a peppermint candy. She knew she only had a few more days in this place she had called home for sixteen years. She wouldn't miss the house at all, but she did have one big concern. *What if Will returned. How would he find her? Would he return at all?*

Now, added to her concern about Jesus Flores was the recent arrival of his son into her life. Her mother had exaggerated when she called him handsome. Fernando Flores didn't come close to that level, and it was worse than his simply being less physically attractive. Despite his pock-marked face, he was a well-known womanizer. *And she was expected to live with them? What if she suddenly blossomed and became*

228

shapely? She knew that she was pretty in the face, but if she became womanly, it would be dangerous.

She was suddenly afraid of that happening when just two weeks ago when she was with Will, she prayed that it would. She felt like God was laughing at her because she thought she was starting to change. Maybe it was all the food she had been eating when she was with Will. She didn't know, but she noticed the changes. They weren't dramatic, but she still noticed.

Then there was that Minnie Crenshaw. Little Alfredo Sanchez had told her earlier that Minnie had been snooping around trying to find out about her, and that made her nervous. *Could Minnie put the rape by those two monsters in the newspaper?* She didn't know if they could write such a thing, even if it were true.

She sucked on the candy and let all these worrisome things roll through her head. All of them would go away if only Will would return and take her away from all this. *Will, where are you?*

———

CHAPTER 5

Will had Rusty saddled, his shotgun on his back, and the Winchester and Spencer in the scabbards. He had all four canteens full and his saddlebags contained ammunition for all his weapons and a clean shirt. He also had some jerky and smoked beef from the kitchen. He saw his mother and grandmother watching him prepare to leave and waved, getting the expected return waves. Emma had been amazed at the firepower he had with him, but Pearl was already accustomed to it.

He mounted Rusty and waved once more at his two mothers as he turned Rusty north toward Santa Fe as Otto trailed behind.

As she watched him leave, Emma said, "Pearl, I'm worried about Will. I shouldn't have asked him to do this."

Pearl had confidence in her son as she replied, "He'll be all right, Mama. If he could deal with men like Saul and Tom, he can do just about anything. Besides, it could be nothing."

Emma nodded, but it didn't help her disposition or lessen her worries.

After they left San Miguel, Will found that he was comfortable doing this. It was like he courted demanding situations and when he was put into a dangerous predicament, his mind cleared, and he found solutions quickly. It was a confidence booster, knowing that he wouldn't panic when bullets flew. Even when he had been momentarily blinded by that dust explosion, he still tried to fire at the blurry figure. Having Otto simply gave him more options than just guns. Otto had the unique ability to make even the hardest man turn to jelly.

He rode easily until noon, then stopped for a break at a small creek, not as rare here as it was in southern Arizona. As Rusty and Otto took advantage of the flowing water, Will pulled out some jerky for himself, then Otto quickly left the stream and trotted over to a grinning Will who handed Otto a piece, then tossed him three more. He was walking, after all.

After he was back in the saddle again, Will wondered what he would find when he did locate Sarah. He was getting annoyed with finding so many callous or violent husbands. If her husband, Ralph, was hurting her at all, he'd get a dose of Otto at least. But if he was, *should he take Sarah away from there?* He had no legal right to do anything about it and would have to play the hand he was dealt. He also began to spend some time just simply wondering how Sarah was. His now nineteen-year-old aunt, he thought to himself and laughed aloud.

They had already traveled almost thirty miles by the time the sun reached its zenith and he knew that the ranch could be on this road or another. This was the main road between San Miguel and Santa Fe, but there were smaller roads, trails really, that went south to the ranches and farms. He kept an eye out for ranch entrance signs as Rusty trotted along.

He made it all the way to Santa Fe without spotting the ranch, which meant the ranch wasn't on the main road. He walked Rusty to the central square trough and let him drink. After he and Otto had enough, he turned them toward the café, then when he arrived, he dismounted, tied off Rusty, then handed a pile of jerky to Otto, and went inside.

He took a table and the waitress arrived in short order.

She gave him her 'don't forget to tip' smile and asked, "What can I get for you?"

"Can I get a big steak and baked potato with some coffee?"

"I'll be back with your coffee in a moment."

She returned with his coffee a minute later and started pouring as he asked, "Excuse me, miss. Do you know where the Double R ranch is?"

"Yes. It's south about five or six miles."

"I just rode in from San Miguel and didn't see it."

"That's the southeast road. The south road leaves between the feed and grain store and the new county courthouse."

"Thank you."

He figured it was only four o'clock, so he'd have time today.

The waitress brought his steak, and it was enormous. He wouldn't be able to finish it, but luckily, he knew who would. He finished half the steak and all the potato and biscuits, then asked the waitress for a piece of butcher paper, so he could take the leftover steak to give to his dog. She probably thought he was going to eat it later himself, but it didn't matter. Otto would be pleased with the gift.

The waitress quickly brought him some butcher paper then he wrapped up the steak and left a nice tip with his bill. He smiled at the waitress as he left with his steak. Curiosity compelled her to wander to the window, and she was mildly surprised to see him hand the steak to a large, handsome German shepherd.

Otto wolfed down the steak as his ancestors had, and quickly caught up to Will who had mounted Rusty and was trotting toward the county courthouse, which turned out to be a very easily located building, as the bricks were still a deep red. He turned on the side street heading south which kept going after Santa Fe ended. Thirty minutes later, he spotted the Double R ranch sign and turned down the access road.

He thought it was a nice ranch as he kept Rusty walking toward the house and spotted some working hands nearby who eyed him up. He admitted to himself that he might be viewed as a threat with all his weapons.

He stopped when he was thirty feet from the house and shouted, "Hello, the house!", then waited for permission to set.

He didn't need to wait long for the door to open, and he hoped it would be Sarah, but instead was facing a heavy-set woman with graying hair and a stern look on her face.

"What do you want, mister?" she asked harshly.

"Just come to visit my sister, ma'am. My name's Will Houston."

"So, you're the brother, are you? I heard you were off killing folks in Arizona. Think you're famous, do you?"

Will was startled by her hostility, and after Mary's mother, wondered if all older women just disliked him.

Despite her unfriendly comments, he tried to change her opinion of him and cordially replied, "No, ma'am. Things just happened, that's all."

"Well, I suppose you can set. I'll tell her that you're here," she said as she scowled, then closed the door behind her.

Will stepped down, and as he was tying Rusty's reins, there was a loud crash when the door slammed against the side of the house as it was thrown open. He smiled as Sarah came dancing down the steps and threw herself at him. He caught her in his arms and hugged her.

Sarah gushed, "Will, you're back! I've missed you terribly."

"I've missed you, too, Aunt Sarah," Will said.

She pulled her head back, laughing as she drank in his much more mature face.

Will saw the same sweet sister he'd loved all of his life as he said, "You still look as pretty as ever, Sarah."

"You've changed a lot, Will. You look, I don't know, more manly and I like it. You seem to be well-armed, too."

"I needed every bit of them when I went looking for Pearl."

"Did you find her?"

"She's with mama right now. It took me a while, but I found her, Sarah. I'll tell you about it later, but she's home and she's happy. But I came here because Mama was worried about you. She hadn't gotten any letters from you in months."

Sarah's smile faded in surprise as she said, "But I've been writing them. She hasn't gotten any? Not even the one with the wonderful news that she's going to be a grandmother?"

"You're going to have a baby?" Will said with wide eyes and a giant grin.

She nodded vigorously and grinned back at him.

"Come and walk with me, Sarah. Can you do that?"

234

"Let's go," she said as she hooked her arm through his.

Will wasn't about to face that woman again, so he turned Sarah toward the access road and began walking.

"Before we go any further, Sarah, I have to remind you that your mother already has a grandson."

Sarah laughed again and said, "I keep forgetting that. You'll always be my brother."

"So, what will that make your baby?"

Sarah had to think about it before saying, "Um, I think he or she will be your cousin."

Will hugged her arm and said, "This is getting confusing, isn't it?"

"It is," she agreed.

Then, Will asked, "How are things with Ralph, Sarah?"

Sarah sighed and said, "Ralph is such a sweet man, Will. I think that's his problem. He lets his mother run everything. She dominates him and the household."

"How about you?"

"She ignores me. When she found out I was pregnant, she wasn't pleased either and that surprised me because I thought all mothers want a grandbaby. I think she was worried that Ralph would be pulled further away from her."

"Maybe that's where your letters went. You didn't mail them yourself, did you?"

"No. We have a box for outgoing letters and whenever anyone on the ranch is going into town or the postman comes out to drop off a letter, the box gets emptied."

"I think your mother-in-law is emptying your letters first. Can I help at all?"

"I wish you could, Will. But I don't see it improving in the future."

"Let me try at least, will you, Sarah?"

"Alright. It can't hurt. So, tell me, are all those stories true?"

"I read the article and they're pretty accurate. But there were a lot of stories that weren't in there that were at least as bad. Then there was Mary."

They continued to walk for another half hour while Will explained the rest of the stories, especially those involving Mary, to his aunt/sister. For some reason, he felt he should tell Sarah about Mary more than anyone else. He and Sarah had spent more time together than most siblings, but even she was astonished by some of his revelations. The story about freeing Pearl was the most telling.

Will had grown up enormously in those past two years. When he left, she cried for two days, knowing she would never see him again. She knew he was ill-equipped to deal with the trials that waited for him on the long trail. What she hadn't known was that he had the advantage of a slow introduction to the dangers as he made his way across the territories looking for his mother. As he kept dealing with ever-increasing threats, he learned and matured beyond his young age. But now, he was here with her and had vanquished them all and grown accordingly. She, like Pearl and Emma, was enormously proud of him.

When they finished their circuitous walk, they returned to the front porch and he asked, "Where is Ralph?"

"He's out on the southeastern pastures. He rides a palomino."

"I'll go and see him for a while. I'll be back," he said as he kissed Sarah on the cheek, smiled at her, then turned to his tall, red gelding.

He mounted Rusty and headed southeast. It was a big ranch. Will estimated it was eight full sections, almost five thousand acres, and kept riding until he saw figures in the distance then spotted the palomino right away. The man riding it was watching as his hands converted a heifer to a steer, but as Will drew closer, he turned to look at the approaching rider. Will noted that he was a handsome man of medium height and medium build with light brown hair and light eyes. He wasn't sure of the color in this light.

"Howdy, are you Ralph?" he asked when he was close enough to be heard.

"I am. Do I know you?"

"Not yet. The name's Will Houston. I'm Sarah's brother, or nephew, whichever you prefer."

His countenance changed as he broke into a grin.

"So, I finally get to meet her famous brother," he said as he trotted his palomino over to him and offered his hand, which Will shook.

"Got a minute, Ralph?" Will asked.

"Sure."

Will wheeled Rusty away from the ranch hands, and Ralph trotted his horse alongside.

After Will pulled Rusty to a stop, he turned and said, "Ralph, Sarah's mother asked me to stop by and see if she was okay. She hadn't gotten any letters from her in months."

He looked surprised and said, "That's odd. I know she's been writing."

"I know. I think your mother has been destroying them before they leave the house."

He looked stunned as he asked, "Why would you think that?"

"I met your mother. She seems to be a dominating person."

He laughed as he said, "She is quite intimidating, I'll admit that, but it's her house to run."

Will then threw him through a loop when he asked, "Don't you love Sarah?"

Ralph went from surprised to stunned, to shocked in one short conversation.

"Of course, I do. She's an incredible woman."

"And she's pregnant."

"I know and I couldn't be happier."

"The problem is that your mother doesn't seem to like the competition. Sarah said she was unhappy when she found out that she was going to have a baby."

"She was? I didn't know that. Why didn't Sarah tell me?"

"I think she's afraid you'd be angry at her for saying something bad about your mother."

"That's silly. Sarah always comes first."

"I can see that. The problem is what you said the first time, that the house belongs to your mother."

"But it's always belonged to her. When my father died, she ran the household for years."

"Is it your ranch or hers?"

"My father left me the ranch in his will and left a cash settlement for my mother."

"Then, your problem is that Sarah sees herself as a second-class member of the household. She can't say anything or do anything that would cause friction."

Ralph sat back and said, "I had never noticed, and it's my fault, too. I'd do anything for Sarah. Knowing that she's sad or worried bothers me a lot, but what can I do?"

"Rather than lay down the law and try to confront your mother, what I'd do is build a small house a couple of hundred yards from the main house and give it to your mother. It would be hard to convince her that it's better for all concerned, but you have to let her know that Sarah is your wife and the woman of the household now. It'll be hard, Ralph, and I don't envy you at all, but unless you want to drive a wedge between you and Sarah, something has to be done."

Ralph thought about it for a minute, then said, "You know, that may be the only solution. You're right, though. I'm not looking forward to it. I'd rather run down an ornery bull than try to argue with my mother, but it has to be done. Sarah deserves it."

"I wish you luck, Ralph. You've already had a measure of good luck, though. I thought I might have to use Otto over there as a persuader."

Ralph glanced at the calm, but still scary-looking dog.

"He could persuade anyone, I think."

They both laughed before Will said, "He already has a few times. He's a remarkable dog."

The hands were finished for the day, so Ralph and Will joined them as they all rode back to the ranch house.

As they stepped down near the barn and began to unsaddle their horses, Ralph asked, "Can you stay the night, Will? I need to hear some of these stories that are circulating around after that story in the paper."

"Sure. I don't feel like riding back to town now anyway."

The two men put up their horses and Will followed Ralph inside but had Otto stay on the porch rather than have him confront Ralph's mother, who would surely be annoyed by having a dog inside.

When they entered, Sarah looked quickly at Will, who winked at her a moment before she was trapped by Ralph and kissed. Sarah was pleasantly surprised, and Will noticed the disgruntled look on the mother's round face.

When he stepped back, Ralph smiled at his wife and said, "Sarah, Will is staying the night. I want to hear some of the stories."

Sarah was still surprised as she said, "He gave me the gist of them earlier, but I think there are a lot more there. Dinner is ready, and I made enough for everyone."

As they all sat down for dinner, Ralph peppered him with questions and Will didn't withhold anything. When he asked about Otto's two previous episodes where he had to persuade someone, Will even told him about Mary's father.

Will had been given a large chunk of freshly cooked beef for Otto, which he greatly appreciated.

After dinner and cleanup, they adjourned to the main room. Ralph's mother had remained remarkably silent during dinner and didn't join them in the main room. Where she went didn't matter to Will, and it apparently didn't to Ralph or Sarah either.

As they continued their talk in the nicely furnished main room, Will was pleased to note that Sarah and Ralph were sitting close to each other on the couch. He liked Ralph but didn't envy what he would have to do.

"So, what are you going to do when you get back to San Miguel, Will?" asked Sarah.

"That's a good question. I want to get back to Gila City soon, though. I have to talk to Mary."

"I thought as much. I hope it works out."

"At least this time, I can take the train."

The almost limitless stories kept going until well after normal bedtime, but they finally all found their beds around eleven o'clock.

———

The Gila City Chronicle printed the second Will Houston story that day, and it was more sensational than the first. Minnie had changed Mary's name to Maggie, but everyone knew who it was.

Mary's first knowledge of the story came from her mother when Maria stormed into the small house and found her daughter sweeping the floor.

"Did you see this?" she demanded as she held out the newspaper.

"No, Mama. I haven't."

"Is what this woman wrote true? You spent almost two weeks alone with that man? Why didn't you just come home to me the first day?"

"Mama! You know why! Your husband was going to sell me to be a whore! I was already afraid of him. Why are you doing this, Mama? When we were here just by ourselves, you cared about me. We shared things. You acted like my mother. Now, you act like you don't care about me anymore."

Maria calmed down but replied, "I have to look out for our future now. Jesus will provide for us. You shouldn't expect anything from a white man. Look at Joe."

"Will wasn't like him at all. He cared for me, Mama. He protected me and never even kissed me."

"It doesn't matter what he did. Everyone will suspect that you two spent those two weeks frolicking in beds or under the stars. After you had been found ruined, that's what most men would have done."

"That's not Will, Mama. He's not like most men. He's special."

"He's just another white man who wants to take advantage of you. Forget him. If Jesus will still take me as his wife after all this, you'll be moving into the house with us and if his son wants you, then you'll accept him."

"I'll run away first, Mama."

"You'll do no such thing!" she exclaimed, "You'll do as I say! I'm going to go and talk to Jesus about this newspaper."

She stormed out of the house, throwing the newspaper to the ground.

Mary picked it up and looked at the words. She couldn't read them, but she knew that those who could would know she had been raped and been with Will for two weeks and they'd think the worst of her and of Will.

She scrunched the paper in her right hand, stepped out of the house, and walked defiantly across the streets of Gila City. She reached *The Gila City Chronicle* office and almost yanked the door off the hinges.

Minnie Crenshaw was sitting at the desk writing when she heard the door being wrenched open and saw the clouded face of Mary Fleming.

"You wrote this!" Mary shouted, slamming the newspaper on Minnie's desk.

"Yes, I did. Everything is factual, and I took the noble step of not using your real name. You can forget about suing us for libel."

"I don't care about suing you. Everyone will think that Will and I were intimate, and we weren't."

Minnie's eyebrows rose as she asked, "How do I know that? Two young people alone on the road for two weeks together. It's very romantic."

"Romantic? Is being shot at, assaulted, grabbed, and absconded your idea of romantic? For two weeks, we had to avoid all that and more. You make it sound like all we did was…well, things."

Minnie laughed and said, "Well, that's your loss then, isn't it? If I had been in your shoes, I would have had him in my bed in a minute, but then, you don't have anything that would entice him, do you? I suggest, Miss Fleming, that you go back to your house and forget you ever met Will Houston. When I met him, I know I impressed him, and if he returns, he'll be calling on me, not you. How old are you, fifteen?"

"I'm sixteen, but that doesn't mean anything. Will loves me, not you."

"If he loved you, Miss Fleming. Why did he leave?"

"He had to find his mother. It's why he came here in the first place."

"What if I were to tell you that he found his mother in North Fork and took her back to San Miguel two days ago. Would that change your mind?"

Mary didn't have a response. *He found his mother?*

"You'll be able to read about it in the next edition of the paper, next Monday. I'm assuming you can read. You can read, can't you?" she asked as she smiled.

Mary didn't answer, but turned, hurried from the office, and streaked across the dirty streets. She had no skirt to pull up, and no petticoats to get dirty as she was wearing Will's shirt and pants.

She made it home and slammed the door behind her. It would get hotter in the house, but she didn't care. All she had was worry now: the story, her mother, the Fuentes boy, and now, Minnie Crenshaw. She was right about some of the things she said, and they all hurt deeply.

Minnie was prettier and had a full figure. She wasn't there when Minnie had met Will, so maybe he had been smitten with her. She let her fingers wander across her body noting the lack of almost anything feminine and then started to cry. *What did she have to offer Will?* Nothing. She couldn't even read the stories about him. She cried non-stop for ten minutes, then walked into the bedroom and sat on the bed. Across from the bed, sitting in the center of a small, crude table, was the half-full bag of hard candy. She reached inside and pulled out a lemon drop and put it in her mouth, wondering if all she would ever have from Will were memories and a few more pieces of sugary treats.

––––––

Across town, Jesus Fuentes was sitting with Maria and assured her that the newspaper story wouldn't change their wedding plans. They would be married on Tuesday, and she and Mary would move in that day. He said that his son, Fernando, was anxiously awaiting Mary's arrival.

Maria was ecstatic. She left the hacienda and raced home to tell the good news to Mary. The wedding was still on and Fernando was already interested in her.

––––––

Will was on the road south from Santa Fe by eight o'clock, using a shortcut directly east that Ralph had told him about, so he didn't have to return to Santa Fe. Ralph and Sarah had talked even later into the night when they were alone in their bedroom where he had explained Will's idea about the second house and told her he'd have it built within a month. He also apologized for allowing this to get this far and that she was in charge of the household, not his mother. He could tell, even in the darkened room that he now had a happy, contented wife, and she rewarded him with increased wifely attentions.

Before he left, as Sarah hugged Will goodbye and kissed him on his cheek, he could see the same, joyful Sarah that he remembered before he left San Miguel two years ago and was happy for her. He hoped that Ralph would follow through with his promises knowing that his mother would try to browbeat him into changing his mind. Sarah's letters would tell Emma if Ralph had withstood her attacks, but he'd done all he could that didn't involve putting a .44 through the cantankerous woman. He didn't doubt for a second that thunderclouds would be heard inside the Double R ranch house that morning, and he was glad he would be ten miles away when the storm struck.

He had more meat in his saddlebag for Otto and was happy to be able to keep him well fed for a change. They made good time heading back, and Will tried passing part of the time by launching into boisterous song, but after a serious objection from Otto, returned to just a mellow humming, which Otto allowed. After a short lunch/rest break, they pressed on, reaching San Miguel in the middle of the afternoon.

He rode Rusty to the boarding house corral, dismounted and unsaddled him, but temporarily left the guns in the barn before he put out more hay and some oats in Rusty's stall, then headed back to the house.

He entered through the front door and headed back to the private area, opened the door but didn't find anyone until he walked down the long hallway and found his mother and grandmother in the parlor with three men. Will recognized them all as prominent San Miguel citizens.

Emma looked up at him and said, "There you are, Will. Mayor Young has a proposition for you."

Will stepped closer and accepted the handshake from the mayor, suspecting that this had something to do with his newfound notoriety with guns.

"Will, we're all glad to see you back. The reason we're all here is that we have a problem that we hope you can help us with. City Marshal Winterbottom has decided to retire. Now, San Miguel is growing, and we can't be without a lawman. We were hoping you'd take the job."

Will thought about it and said, "I'm pretty young, Mayor."

"We know that, but we also read about what you've done. It seems like you have a way of handling bad situations."

"What does the job pay?" he asked.

"Well, we were only paying Joe Winterbottom fifty dollars a month, but like I said, the town is growing. We'd pay you sixty dollars a month, plus expenses and room and board. Joe's married, so he doesn't get room and board."

"It sounds like a generous offer. What are we looking at as far as timing goes? I need to take the train down to Gila City for a couple of days."

"That's not a problem at all. Joe will stay on the job until you return. How's that?"

"You mentioned room and board, but what happens if I get married?"

Emma and Pearl shared a smiling glance when he asked the question, each of them hoping it worked out for Will, but after hearing the stories, suspected that it wasn't going to be easy.

"Well, then we'd just pay you a flat eighty dollars a month. Is that acceptable?"

"That's fine, and I'll do what I can to keep the town safe."

The mayor grinned and said, "Thank you, Will," then he and the other men stood and after handshakes all around, the three men left the boarding house.

After the door closed, Will turned to his two smiling mothers and said, "Well, that was interesting," then asked, "How long were they waiting? I could have been gone another two or three hours."

"They only just arrived and didn't even know you were gone."

"That's not the only interesting thing that happened in your brief absence," Pearl said as she handed him a copy of the Santa Fe paper.

"Not again," he groaned as he accepted the newspaper.

He read the lengthy article that spanned two and a half pages and began fuming after the first page. By the time he finished reading, he almost had steam pouring from his ears.

"Will, how accurate is it?" Emma asked.

"Reasonably, but the implications are terrible. Especially for Mary. Minnie plays up the two weeks alone together like we were rutting every night. I never even kissed the girl."

"But you want to marry her?" asked Emma with raised eyebrows.

"Mama, when you meet Mary, you'll understand. She may be thin and only sixteen, but she's more of a woman than any other girls or women that I've met."

"But the facts are correct."

"All but one, and that one is a whopper. She writes that I killed Mary's father to save her and that's totally untrue. He was holding a knife to her throat and after I signaled for her to fall, she dropped, and Otto jumped on him, then grabbed his arm to get him to drop the knife. He really had to rip at the arm to get him to drop it, but he was alive when we left. Mama, the man was going to sell Mary to a whore house, but he would only get that much if she was intact, as he put it."

Pearl blanched at the similarity between her story and Mary's. The only differences were that Mary was younger and it was her father and not her husband that was going to sell her.

Pearl said, "Then walking away was the right thing to do."

"How'd they get this story here so fast? It says that it was only in the paper in Gila City yesterday."

"They telegraph the story at night at special rates, and the newspaper prints them at night. We get our papers delivered by noon the next day."

"Well, I think I'll head down there and see if I can help straighten this mess out for Mary. I need to go and find out how far the railroad has gone, too. I saw them laying track about thirty-five miles north of Gila City on the way here. I've heard that on flat land, they lay about five or six miles a day. It's already been a week, so I wonder if they've reached the town yet. It doesn't matter really. If they're close, I'll go to the end of the track and ride into town. I'll take Rusty with me."

"Will, what did you find out about Sarah?" asked Emma.

Will took a seat, smiled, and said, "It wasn't so bad, Mama. I didn't have to even threaten to shoot anyone or sic Otto on them."

Will then explained the situation and they both readily understood, having met controlling women in the past. They were pleased with the diplomatic solution he offered as both Emma and Sarah had been a bit concerned about his extensive armaments when he left. The fact that he had handled the delicate situation so well boded well for his future as a lawman.

But Will had withheld the part about the intercepted letters as a springboard for the best news from the visit.

He smiled at Emma and said, "When I asked her why she hadn't written to you, it turned out that the nasty mother-in-law had been burning her letters."

"That witch!" Emma exclaimed, avoiding the word she really wanted to use.

"Sarah was most annoyed because you hadn't received the big news that all mothers want to hear."

Emma's whole face exploded in joy as she shouted, "I'm going to be a grandmother!"

Will stood, spread his arms out wide, and said, "Remember me, Grandmother?"

Both of his mothers burst out laughing, fueled by all of the wonderful news they've been receiving almost non-stop since Will's return.

Will smiled at them, then left the house, walked to the train depot, and headed for the ticket window.

"Good afternoon, young man. What can I do for you?" asked the ticket agent when he appeared at the window.

"How far has the railroad progressed in southwestern Arizona?"

"Let me check. I get telegrams when they reach a new town, so I'll know how much to charge."

He rummaged through a stack of telegrams, checking dates.

"Looks like they passed through Gila City two days ago."

"How much for a ticket to Gila City for me and my horse?"

"$43.40"

"When's the next train?"

"Well, the next scheduled train isn't until tomorrow afternoon, but I have an express coming by early in the morning because there are some bigwigs heading down to end of track. Leaves here at 1:10 tomorrow morning and it'll get in at 3:40 in the afternoon. It's only stopping for about fifteen minutes, so you've got to be here on time."

"Okay, let me have a ticket and a tag for my horse."

Will handed him the money and received the ticket and tag.

"Thanks a lot," Will said as he pocketed the ticket.

He was going to go back to the house but stopped when he saw the Western Union office and thought it would be a good idea to let Mary know that he was coming. He knew that Mary couldn't read and was sure that her mother wouldn't pass it on to her, so he'd have to send it to someone he knew in Gila City. He only knew one other person in that town, and not very well, but he was sure that she knew him much better.

Unaware of the consequences it would create, he sent a very short telegram that read:

MINNIE CRENSHAW GILA CITY CHRONICLE GILA CITY ARIZONA

WILL BE ARRIVING ON TRAIN TOMORROW

WILL HOUSTON SAN MIGUEL NEW MEXICO

He paid the thirty cents and returned to the house. He had assumed that because Minnie had written the story about their relationship, she'd know where Mary lived and let her know he was coming just to get her reaction to another story. It was a bad assumption.

He told both of his mothers that he'd be leaving just after midnight and not to worry about getting up. It was another wrong assumption, but not a bad one.

––––––

He didn't even bother going to sleep, figuring he'd sleep a lot on the train, but about thirty minutes before midnight, he quietly walked out to the kitchen with his saddlebags over his shoulder and found both of them in the kitchen making him breakfast.

They smiled at him as he sat down, and they joined him at the table but only had cups of tea.

"Do you think her mother is going to let her come back with you, Will?" Pearl asked.

Will swallowed his scrambled eggs, then replied, "That's my biggest worry, Mama. I know that Mary really wanted me to take her with me, but she stayed just because her mother asked her. After watching the effect that Ralph's mother had on him, I hope that I can convince her to leave Gila City and her mother."

Emma asked, "What if she asks you to stay there rather than come back?"

Will sighed, then replied, "I don't know, Mama. I really don't know. I'll just have to see what happens when I get there."

Pearl laid her hand on his and said, "Well, you let us know, Will. You'll have three anxious women here praying that it all works out for you."

Will nodded, then finished the rest of his breakfast as he contemplated what might happen if Mary's mother put her foot down. *Who would Mary choose?*

After he polished off his second cup of coffee, he rose, and Pearl gave him a paper sack with two bacon and egg sandwiches for his lunch. He kissed them each on the cheek, pulled his hat from its peg and went outside. He decided not to pack his shotgun for the trip as it might spook some of the passengers. Nor would he bring Otto on this trip because he expected it to be short and non-violent, but he did give Otto an extended belly rub as a consolation.

He saddled Rusty, walked him to the depot, and once he arrived less than a minute later, hung the tag on his bridle and gave him over to the stock manager. It was only twelve-thirty when he finally sat on the platform, awaiting the special train. He had brought *Under Two Flags* with him to read on the way. He thought he'd have finished it by now but found Pearl had pushed it into the background.

As he thought of the book, he recalled his failed promise to teach Mary to read. He just hadn't expected to lose her so quickly, which was probably just one of the foibles of being young. It's like death or old age; young people just don't expect either to ever happen.

The train arrived a little early, the important railroad folks obviously anxious to get to the end of track, which should be at Arizona City by now. He was the only customer to get on the train at San Miguel, so he took his seat and instead of reading, just fell asleep as the express raced across the Southwest.

———

Minnie opened the door to the Chronicle and found a yellow telegram sheet on the floor, which wasn't uncommon, even in the first few days of the paper. She picked it up and set her purse and hat down on the desk, then opened the message and smiled.

So, Will Houston was coming back to Gila City, and he was coming back to see her, not that skinny girl. She decided to go and change into something more appealing and perhaps, make a stop by a certain small house on the way back.

She had only talked to Will Houston for a few short minutes, yet that little girl had been with him for more than two weeks, yet he had sent the telegram to her. Minnie recalled that when Mary had protested the story, she'd said that Will had never even kissed her. At the time, she didn't believe it, but now, it was in her interest to think that it was true. *Why would a man like Will Houston even think of kissing a little girl like Mary Fleming?*

———

Mary wasn't in any better frame of mind after dealing with Minnie and her mother. Her mother was making preparations for the wedding and wanted Mary to be there in one of her two new dresses, even though both had been altered to allow for Maria's more ample figure. It would make Mary seem even skinnier if that was even possible. She didn't really care much, because no one, specifically Will, would be there to see her, but it did gnaw at her a bit.

She finally just began cleaning the house again, still wearing the shirt and pants that Will had bought for her in Arizona City. She didn't wear the Stetson as much anymore as she had finally given up on Will's return.

It had been more than two weeks since he'd gone, but that didn't mean she'd give in to her mother's desire for her to marry Fernando. The man simply repulsed her. He had a bad case of acne and rotten teeth to boot, then made it worse by insisting on smiling every time he saw her. She shivered at the thought of even kissing the man.

She was still sweeping when there was a knock on the door, which she kept closed just to be alone. She put down the broom, walked across the room, swung the door open, and saw the loathsome, but admittedly pretty face of that witch from the newspaper, Minnie Crenshaw. What made it worse was that her choice of clothing not only enhanced her figure, it exaggerated certain features that Will had told her men admire.

Minnie smiled and said, "Hello, Mary. I just received a telegram that you might be interested in reading. It's from San Miguel, New Mexico. I believe you know the town?"

"It's from Will?" she asked quickly, her heart quickening.

"Yes, it is. He wanted me to know that he'd be arriving today on the train. Did you get a telegram, Mary?" she asked, then relished the moment when she saw the crushing disappointment in her big brown eyes.

She then continued, saying, "No? I thought you said he loved you. But I received the telegram, didn't I? I told you before, Mary, it takes a certain amount of feminine equipment to win a man, and you just don't have any. I'm sure you'll be at the depot in four hours to greet him. Won't you, Mary?"

She smiled at Mary, then turned on her heels and marched away from the house. As she had been talking, Mary had found herself staring at her cleavage, but hadn't said a word. It just wasn't fair.

She closed the door a lot more quietly than she wanted to, then walked slowly into her bedroom and took off her shirt. She tried to create her own cleavage by putting her hands on the sides of her chest and pushing. She could make some, but only if she squeezed a lot. She sniffled and put the shirt back on, knowing she would fail. It was no use. She was changing, but not fast enough. *Why couldn't she just go to sleep one night and magically the next morning be a full woman?* She sat on her bed, put her chin on her hands, and wept. *Should she go to the depot and watch Will kiss that woman? Could she bear the humiliation?* She wanted to crawl under the bed.

Then as she raised her head, she wiped her eyes, then saw the bag of candy through her still blurry vision. She took out a peppermint and when the unique flavor hit her mouth, she remembered the man who had bought them for her, and how he had looked into her eyes. Will wouldn't do this to her. She knew that he loved her. *But why had he sent that woman the telegram?*

She had so many questions but was only sure of one thing; she loved Will Houston with all her heart. She knew that she would have to be there, even if it meant having her heart broken into a thousand pieces.

———

Will was reading as the train entered Arizona where the tracks turned south and soon, he was passing through North Fork and wondered if Saul ever changed his pants and snickered at the thought.

A few minutes later, he saw the gully where he lost Buster. It was dry again, of course. The flash flood water didn't stay long after leaving death and destruction in its wake.

The train was just twenty minutes out of Gila City and Will was nervous. He hadn't seen Mary in three weeks and a lot could happen in three weeks. *What if she had already forgotten him or met someone else? Would he just bow out or fight for her?* He had so many questions but was certain of just one thing; he loved Mary with all of his heart.

The train was slowing as it arrived in town, but Will's heart was not.

———

On the platform, Minnie was waiting prominently in the center, a giant smile on her face as she anticipated Will's arrival.

Mary wasn't even on the platform. She was standing in the street waiting to see what happened and wasn't smiling at all.

The steam was being released from the iron engine as it passed the platform, then the passenger cars began to slide past. It was traveling at less than walking speed when Minnie saw Will hanging on the train's platform. He was even more handsome than she remembered, making her heart flutter a bit, which surprised her. Will was scanning the platform and spotted Minnie, *but where was Mary?*

Mary saw him looking around and noticed when his eyes stopped on Minnie and thought Minnie had been right. Will had returned to see her after all and the realization slammed into her like a runaway bull. She wheeled about and started slowly walking back to the house, her heart broken and her mind numb.

Will's continued scanning finally picked up the top of Mary's head as she strode away down the street. He leapt onto the platform as Minnie stepped forward to offer him a welcoming hug, but he shot past her with his saddlebags over his shoulder. He raced off the platform and hit the dirt at the same time his saddlebags did.

Mary didn't see him coming as she was so deep in her thought and was fifty feet from the platform when she was grabbed. She thought someone was going to molest her when she heard that incredibly wonderful voice.

"Mary! Where are you going?" Will asked.

She whipped around and was instantly enveloped into his arms. She clutched onto him as hard as she could, then as she looked up at him, the world stopped spinning and became completely silent when he leaned down and kissed her.

She was lost in an emotional tsunami when she felt his lips on hers. *He had come back for her! And he did love her!*

Minnie stood and watched the display. *What in God's name was wrong with him?* Mary was nothing compared to her. She left the platform and returned to her paper, already wondering how she could put that skinny girl in her place.

At the moment, Mary's place was in Will's arms. Neither wanted to let go but standing in the middle of the street does have consequences.

Will finally pulled Mary out of the street as he retrieved his saddlebags.

"Why were you leaving, Mary?" he asked as he bent over and plucked the saddlebags from the ground.

"Will, I was so afraid that you didn't want to see me. You sent a telegram to Minnie but not me."

Will suddenly realized his error in judgement and said, "Mary, I'm so sorry. I just didn't think right. I knew you'd have a problem with it, and I sent it to her because I didn't know anyone else in town. I read those stories that she wrote and figured she'd let you know."

"Will, she made it sound like you'd never want anyone like me when you could have a real woman like her."

"Mary, I love you and I want you to marry me. Will you do that for me?"

Mary heard it but didn't believe it. *So soon?*

"But Will, why would you marry me? I'm just a skinny girl."

"For the best of reasons, Mary. I love you and want to spend the rest of my life with you."

"I love you, too, Will, but I'm only sixteen. I still have to fill out."

"Then you can do it as my wife."

Mary wanted this so much, but everyone kept telling her that she wasn't a woman yet. She was just a skinny girl.

"Will, can we go to the house and talk?"

"Alright. But let me get Rusty."

He walked with her to the railroad corral where Rusty had been quickly unloaded, took the gelding's reins, then led him behind Mary as she walked, thinking about what Will had asked.

She had been so afraid of losing him to that Minnie woman just minutes ago, then overjoyed to know that he'd returned to see her after all. Then his sudden proposal had rocked her. She had hoped that if he returned, he'd just stay in Gila City, then they could get married when she was more physically mature.

She stopped at the house and waited while Will tied off Rusty.

He was completely confused about what had just happened. Mary was ecstatic to see him, but after he'd told her that he wanted to marry her, she had almost recoiled. He remembered back to when he had first found her. *Was that the problem?* She kept bringing up her age and her thin body. He just couldn't understand. Then he began to suspect that her mother's hatred of white men had begun to poison Mary's view of him. But she had told him that she loved him, *so what was the problem?*

He walked into the small house behind Mary and left the door open.

A distressed Mary found her seat on one of the two chairs in the front room before Will removed his hat and sat in the other.

He looked into those tormented brown eyes and asked, "Mary, what's the matter? I thought you would be happy."

"I am happy that you're back, Will. More than you'll ever know. But I can't get married yet. I just can't."

"Is it because of what happened before I found you, Mary?" he asked softly.

"No. I can live with that now. It's me, Will. Can't you see? I'm still a girl, not a woman."

"I don't see a child or a girl sitting before me, Mary. You may be thin, but you're still a woman."

She shook her head almost violently as she replied, "No, I'm not! I don't have any cleavage like Minnie or my mother. I don't even fill out these small pants. I'm just not ready for marriage yet. Can't you stay here and wait?"

Will felt some measure of relief that it still had come down to just her lack of curves and said, "No, Mary. I can't stay here. I don't have anything that I can do here. I've already accepted the position of city marshal in San Miguel and was hoping to bring you back as my wife. But if you won't marry me, will you still come with me? You could live with my mother and grandmother until you think you're ready."

The new solution appealed to Mary. *Why not leave?* She had nothing here and if she returned with him, she wouldn't have the specter of Fernando Fuentes hanging over her.

"Can I think about it? How long will you be here?" she asked.

Will saw light at the end of the tunnel and replied, "No more than three days, Mary. I promised them that I'd return and take over the job soon."

"Alright. My mother is getting married on Tuesday and wants me to move in with her to the Fuentes hacienda. He has two sons, and she said that Fernando is interested already."

The introduction of another, non-white suitor into the mix startled Will into asking, "Is that the reason for your indecision then, Mary? If you'd rather stay here and marry Fernando, then tell me."

Mary was stunned as she quickly replied, "No, no! He's hideous! The only reason I can't leave is because of what I told you and must stay for my mother's wedding. But your idea about moving in with your mother sounds like it might be a solution. I just need to think about it."

Her continued indecision bothered Will as he said, "Alright, Mary. I'll be at the hotel if you want to see me."

She nodded and watched as Will stood and picked up his hat. Mary was torn between her deep feelings for Will and the strong pull to go with him even now, but the sense of obligation she had for her mother kept her from giving in to her own desires.

Will smiled at Mary and wanted to give her a goodbye kiss but thought better of it. He believed that he had somehow already lost Mary. So, he just turned, walked out the open doorway, then mounted Rusty and rode for the hotel. He realized soon enough that he didn't even know where the hotel was but found it easily enough.

He walked Rusty to the livery and dropped him off, took his saddlebags, walked to the hotel and checked in. He went to his room and took off his Stetson, gunbelt, and boots, stretched out on the bed, and began to think about his bizarre arrival in Gila City. Of all of the possible scenarios he'd imagined, not one came close to this one.

He was going to go and have dinner when he remembered the two sandwiches made by his mother. His mother, the only thing that had turned out right for him on the entire trip was the one he had set out to do in the first place.

He wondered what he would do about Mary. When they were together on the trail, he thought he knew her so well. *Why the sudden fear?* She said it was because she was so thin and not a real woman. *Was that really it? Was that all there was to her hesitation?*

———

Mary was in worse shape as she remained sitting in the room in the oven-like house. *Why had she balked?* She loved Will fiercely but felt so inadequate. She had hoped so desperately that he'd return and now that he had, she had rejected his marriage proposal. *But his second offer?* That might work. *How long before she became a real woman? What if this was what she would always be?* The revelation startled her.

She always assumed that one day, she would develop the curves and softness of a woman and stop looking like a boy. *What if she never did? What good would going to San Miguel do if she stayed like this for ten years?* She tried to think if any other girls her age looked like she did and couldn't think of any. She even knew girls four years younger than she was who had more womanly features. She slipped deeper into depression at the thought of that possibility.

———

Minnie was seething as she sat behind her desk. She wanted that urchin humiliated and put in her place once and for all, and had an idea how to do it, too. In her investigations, she had found that Mrs. Fleming was dead set against her daughter marrying a white man, no doubt because of her late husband. She wondered if Maria Fleming knew about the display in the streets of Gila City. If she hadn't before, she would now.

Minnie grabbed her purse and hurriedly left the office.

Minnie knew Maria was going to marry Jesus Fuentes on Tuesday as her paper had already printed the announcement, so she walked calmly to the Fuentes hacienda.

When she arrived, she pulled the cord for an internal bell, and thirty seconds later, the housekeeper arrived and ushered her inside telling her that Mrs. Fleming was in the parlor and would see her momentarily.

Maria floated out of the parlor and saw Minnie Crenshaw waiting by the doorway. For a moment, she thought of letting the woman have a piece of her mind for those stories that humiliated her daughter and almost cost her the marriage but held off in case Jesus overheard the display of her hidden temper.

"What can I do for you, Miss Crenshaw?" Maria asked.

"Mrs. Fleming, I have some news that you may find interesting."

"And that is?" Maria asked with raised eyebrows.

"About an hour ago, your daughter and Mister Will Houston were seen kissing in the street outside the train depot. My impression was that he was asking her to run away with him. Now that would be scandalous, would it not?"

Maria's curiosity gave way to instant rage, and her dark eyes grew darker as she glared at Minnie and she asked, "Why are you telling me this?"

"I have my reasons."

Maria looked at the newspaperwoman then her anger gave way to a look of understanding before she said, "You want Mister Houston to yourself, don't you?"

"Perhaps. Or maybe I just want to write more stories about him."

"Whatever your reasons, I'll see that my daughter no longer stands in your way. What you do after that is up to you."

The flush of victory flowed through Minnie as she smiled, then said, "Thank you, Mrs. Fleming. And congratulations on your upcoming nuptials."

"Thank you. Good day."

Minnie nodded, then turned and left the house with stage one of her mission accomplished.

After she had gone, Maria sought Jesus for advice. He would know how to deal with the problem better than she would. After she explained the problem, he told her not to worry and that he would take care of it.

After Maria left, he called in Fernando and told him what he wanted him to do, directing him to take Mary to the ranch and have her stay in the main house with the housemaid until the gringo left Gila City.

Fernando smiled as he saw an advantage to this but assured his father that it would be done as he asked.

———

An hour later, Fernando had harnessed the family's buggy and driven to the Fleming house. He was armed in case that gringo was there and hoped that he was. He had great confidence in his ability with the pistol; a confidence that was unsupported by any genuine talent. He arrived at the house, climbed out, then left the buggy in place without looping the reins around the rickety fence before he stepped to the house and knocked on the door.

Mary heard the knock and a smile crossed her face as she thought that Will had returned to make his case again. She still was unsure of her answer but went to the door hoping that he had decided to stay in Gila City after all.

So, with hope in her heart and a smile on her lips, Mary swung the door wide, then froze when she saw Fernando Fuentes grinning at her with that horrible smile.

She then quickly asked, "What do you want, Fernando?"

"Your mother is at the ranch house and wants to talk to you about the wedding. She also has dinner prepared for you."

Mary wasn't quite sure, but it was her mother who had asked, so she closed the door behind her and walked with him to the waiting buggy, then climbed aboard as Fernando took the reins and turned the buggy south.

The Fuentes ranch outside of town was one of the biggest in the area. He ran almost three thousand head of cattle and employed over a dozen vaqueros. She had heard about the massive spread but had never been there. Her curiosity about seeing the Fuentes ranch pushed aside her concerns.

Fernando didn't say anything as the buggy left the city and headed east toward the ranch. The main house was six miles from town, and more importantly, there was a smaller hacienda that was currently unoccupied. It had been the original hacienda on the ranch, was still in good condition, and was even furnished. Even the bedroom, Fernando thought as he smiled.

The further they drove from Gila City, Mary's concerns began to overtake her curiosity but knowing that her mother was there kept them at bay.

They arrived at the ranch where Fernando drove to the small house, pulled the buggy to a stop, and said, "Your mother is here right now because she said it wouldn't be proper for her to be seen in the main house with my father."

It made sense to Mary, so she stepped out and walked to the small house as Fernando walked behind her. He then hopped in front of her and opened the door. When he followed her inside and closed the door, Mary felt the threat immediately and turned around to face him.

"Where is my mother, Fernando?" she demanded.

"Your mother asked my father to bring you here to keep you away from that gringo. He and your mother both understand what you do not. He is not right for you, Mary. But I, Fernando Fuentes, am going to make you happy that you are here, and you'll never think of him again."

She took two steps backward, then turned and ran to the farthest room with Fernando close behind. She entered the room, then grabbed the door and tried to close it quickly but Fernando was too close, and he easily pushed his way inside.

As Mary stared at Fernando's lust-filled eyes, she realized with horror that she had chosen the bedroom for her failed attempt to find refuge.

Will had finished his sandwiches and *Under Two Flags*, and now lay on the bed when he realized that he had never arranged to have the stitches removed He looked at them and saw that most had already fallen out, probably rubbed off from use. He pulled out his knife and used the point to cut the remaining threads. They stung as he slid them out of the skin but probably wouldn't have hurt if he had removed them when he should have.

With his wound forgotten, he stared at the ceiling overhead and wondered what to do about Mary. *What could he do about Mary?* The answer was simple enough: nothing. It was her decision to make, not his. He had made his case and failed unless she suddenly decided to return with him to San Miguel, but he was beginning to believe that her mother had much more influence over her than he did, and he could understand that. Maybe she was better off here after all.

He was so confused by what had happened he just couldn't think straight. He had envisioned his return vividly in his mind and it had almost worked exactly as he had hoped it would until he had asked her to marry him. Then the wheels fell off and the train plunged into the abyss. Nothing was working now, and he felt miserable.

Mary felt worse than miserable. She was humiliated, hurt, and ashamed. Fernando had taken her just as cruelly as those two men on the road north of Gila City.

He had simply ripped off her shirt, yanked off her boots and pants, and taken her. The entire rape had lasted less than five minutes. Then he had added insult to what he had done when he had grinned at her and asked her to thank him before he left the small house, locking the door behind him.

She laid there naked on the bed, stunned by what had happened. She hadn't even fought him as much as she had the other two men. It was as if she had resigned herself to her fate. Now, she wanted to cry but couldn't find the tears. She had her entire future with Will right in front of her and she had balked. She had turned him away, and now this had happened. What was worse was that she knew Fernando would be back again because he had told her so. He would be back again, and again, and again. Then, sooner or later, she would have no choice but to marry him.

But what if that wasn't even a possibility? What if he just decided to keep her as his private, skinny whore? She didn't know his father that well and was no longer sure that her mother would even care. *But what about Will? Would he still care?*

She finally rolled onto her side then curled into a tight ball as she succumbed to her tears and asked in a whisper, "Will, what have I done?"

———

The next morning as Will began his day, he decided that he needed to talk to Mary again. She was too precious to him to just let things work their way out. If he wouldn't fight for her, then maybe he was the problem.

So, after Will had breakfast at the café, he walked to the Fleming house to see if Mary was there. The door was partly open when he arrived, so he wasn't sure if she was home as he walked up to the door and stopped.

"Mary?" he called out quietly.

There was no response, so Will assumed she didn't want to talk to him. He sighed, then turned and left the house.

He was barely ten feet from the house when he saw little Felipe Gonzalez standing there just looking at him. Will smiled, remembering the sight of him racing away, taking the note to Mary's mother.

"Hello," Will said as he stepped closer to Felipe.

"Good morning, senor. You are looking for Miss Mary?"

"I was, but I think she's not talking to me."

"She is not inside the house."

"She isn't? But the door is open. Where is she?"

"Fernando Fuentes arrived with a buggy and took her away."

"She went with him?" Will asked, stunned by the news.

"Si, but I don't think she was happy when she went with him. She had a sad face."

"Where would he take her in a buggy?"

"Probably to the family ranchero. It is that way," he said as he pointed.

"Did they come back?"

"No, senor. Miss Mary does not like him. Nobody likes Fernando except Fernando."

"Is her mother there?"

"No, senor. Her mother is with Fernando's father in their hacienda in the city."

"Then why would she go with him?

Felipe shrugged, so Will asked, "Do you think I should go to the ranch and ask?"

"I think she would like that, senor, but I do not think Fernando would be happy to see you."

"I'll agree with you about that, son."

Will reached in his pocket and handed Felipe a silver dollar as his eyes grew wide.

"That is for being such a good friend to Miss Mary."

He grinned, then turned and shot away to show his friends more money than any of them had ever seen before. He knew how impressed they had been when he had those two nickels, but this was unimaginable wealth.

Felipe hadn't taken four fast strides before Will turned and began walking quickly to the livery where he saddled Rusty. He had his Spencer, Winchester, and his Colt and really wished he had Otto, but it was too late now. He was soon in the saddle and set Rusty to a medium trot as he left Gila City behind. It didn't take him long to find the trail and soon moved Rusty up to a fast trot.

———

At the ranch, Fernando was sitting in the kitchen of the main house having coffee. He had been quick with Mary that first time because he was too excited. She was thin, but it didn't matter, when his blood was boiling for women, he was always ready.

He did like what she had, though. It wasn't a lot, but it was nice. Thinking about her started heating his blood again, and he kept adding more heat as he pictured Mary naked. He was ready for another excursion to the small house and pleasure for both himself and Mary because he knew that she really enjoyed his lovemaking. *What woman wouldn't?*

———

Mary had pulled on her shirt and pants again and was searching the house for a weapon to defend herself against that bastard. After her initial sense of almost acceptance, she'd let her anger grow and decided that she was not going to let him take her again. She was tired of being the victim. She didn't want Fernando to touch her again without pain, even if it meant that he would kill her afterward.

There were no knives in the kitchen, but she kept looking, suspecting that Fernando would return later that night, not realizing he might arrive much earlier. *Where could she find something that she could use to protect herself?*

———

Will could see the ranch in the distance and knew that he was at a disadvantage, several disadvantages, in fact. He didn't know where Mary was, or if she was even there. If she was there, he didn't know if she was being held against her will or was there voluntarily, despite what the boy had told him.

Then, there was the layout of the ranch. He could see the main house, but it was unlikely that she would be there because there were too many servants. A barn, maybe? The bunkhouse would be out, the vaqueros would use that, and that in itself posed more problems. How many vaqueros on the large ranch, were they aware of Mary's presence, and would they protect

Fernando Fuentes if he had Mary held there as a prisoner? They might just shoot him for being a gringo.

The question about where Mary could be was answered when he turned down the access road and saw the small house. Unless Mary wasn't at the ranch at all, or she was there because she wanted to be, that's where she'd be held.

He was walking Rusty on the access road when he pulled his Winchester. He didn't need the range of the Spencer anymore.

––––––––

Fernando left the main house via the kitchen door, and as he came around the side, his blood was hot for Mary and his mind was racing, making him almost miss seeing the gringo walking his horse down the access road.

Will didn't miss seeing Fernando walk out of the house toward the small house, which made him sure that Mary was inside, although he still wasn't sure if she was there of her own accord. Either way, he made sure Fernando saw both him and the Winchester.

Fernando finally had spotted Will, and to his credit, or to his lust, he kept walking toward the small house, ignoring the approaching rider. He wasn't worried because he didn't think the gringo would shoot him with the rifle. He'd want to get within pistol range to make this personal. It was just another duel about a woman and Fernando had already had two of them.

Will seriously thought about shooting nearby to get him to pay attention, but he still wasn't sure if he had taken Mary hostage, despite the boy's assertion that Mary didn't like him. If he had known what Fernando had already done, he probably would have shot the bastard, but only after letting him know what was going to happen. But he held off as he walked Rusty within fifty yards of Fernando.

Fernando finally stopped walking, turned to face him, pulled his hammer loop off his Colt, and smiled.

"What an ugly smile," Will thought as he removed his hammer loop, then stopped Rusty and stepped down.

"What are you doing here, gringo?" he shouted.

"I've come to take Mary home," he yelled back as he began to walk closer, now less than thirty yards away.

"Mary came here because she wanted to be alone with me," he said as he grinned.

"From what I hear, not even the hog cows want to be alone with you, much less a real woman," Will answered loudly as he drew closer.

In the house, Mary could hear the exchange and was thrilled and panicked at the same time. She knew Will had come for her and she also knew of Fernando's reputation with the pistol. She ran to the front door and began banging loudly, wishing that there were glass windows in the old hacienda and not the heavy shutters.

Both men heard the noise and then Will had his answer about whether Mary was there by choice or not.

He said calmly from about twenty-five yards, "Fernando, why don't you unlock the door and let Mary out. If she says she wants to stay here, then I'll leave."

"I give you my word of honor, and that should be good enough for you, gringo. Go now and I won't kill you."

Will continued to close the gap as he stared at him and growled, "You have no honor, so your word means nothing, greaser."

"You insult me?" Fernando shouted.

"You've been calling me gringo for the past minute. That's an insult, but I let it go once or twice. Insult me again and I'll make it worse and end your womanizing by putting a .44 between your legs."

Fernando was glaring as he bragged, "I've killed two men with my pistols."

Will thought he was close enough, then stopped and replied, "I've killed three men with my pistols, two with my Spencer, three with the Winchester, and four with my shotgun. Two were killed by my dog, but I left him at home, so you'll die by lead."

Fernando's glare was replaced with a confident smile as he said, "You talk bravely for a man who is about to die."

"That's one of the many differences between us, Fernando. I don't care all that much if I live or die because I have nothing. You, on the other hand, will lose your ranch, your hacienda, and all of your money. You will die, and I'll let the vultures and coyotes pick at your body."

Despite himself, Fernando shivered at the thought, licked his upper lip, then said, "You've talked enough. It's time to die."

Will watched him carefully for a tell that would let him know when he was going to draw. He knew he wasn't the fastest draw, but he was accurate when he shot. They were sixty feet apart, beyond the normal distance for pistol fights, but not outside the range of the pistols themselves. He had to trust his accuracy but knew that if he killed Fernando, it would only make the situation worse because of where he was and what he was, so he decided that he'd shoot low, assuming that he even got a shot off.

Fernando also watched. The gringo wasn't as fidgety as the other two men he had killed, and if he'd been honest with himself, he would have admitted that neither of the other men was very good. The gringo was a hard read, but Fernando decided that it didn't matter. The distance was long, but he'd fan his revolver and probably get three shots off before his antagonist even pulled his trigger if he lived that long. He knew that he had already waited long enough and suddenly went for his Colt.

Will had seen the shoulder twitch and reached for his pistol at the same time. It was cocked and three-quarters of the way up when Fernando opened fire.

Fernando had been right about getting his pistol out and ready to fire first and fired his three shots before Will fired once, but his three shots were all wide right, and Will's one .44 hit him solidly in his left knee, shattering his patella into dozens of pieces before drilling through the joint, destroying tendons and cartilage before exiting the knee and slamming into the dirt.

Fernando dropped to the ground, screaming from the incredible pain. His pistol hit the dirt at the same dime as he rolled and shrieked, so Will raced to at least disarm the man before trying to help.

When he reached him, he kicked the fallen Colt away, then took a knee next to Fernando and ripped away his pants.

The cook and the housemaid came running from the hacienda at the shots and stopped on the large porch looking down at the Yankee standing over Fernando.

Will looked at them, as he put his Colt back into its holster and said loudly, "Get a cloth to stop the bleeding!"

The housemaid understood English and ran inside, then less than a minute later returned with two towels and handed one to Will, who had used his knife to cut away the bloody pants leg.

He dropped to his heels and began wrapping the towel around Fernando's knee then said, "Give me the key to the small house, Fernando."

Fernando didn't reply but continued to moan as he pulled the key from his pocket and dropped it onto the sand.

Will picked it up and handed it to the housemaid, saying, "Go and open the door and let Miss Fleming out of the house."

Mary had heard the taunts and then the shooting followed by the loud scream. She was terrified that Will had just been shot because of her and began pounding the door even louder.

The housemaid trotted to the house, inserted the key into the lock, and turned it. When Mary heard the click, she ripped the door open, nearly yanking the housemaid into the room.

She saw Will kneeling over Fernando near the big hacienda and felt an enormous amount of relief before the rage built up inside her shoving the relief aside. *No more!* She had been violated three times now and had been unable to have her revenge. This time, she wouldn't be deprived of delivering justice. She calmly stepped across the gap between the two houses, and when she was close to where Will was treating Fernando, she picked up Fernando's Colt that was laying in the dirt.

Will hadn't even heard Mary's approach over Fernando's loud groaning and his inspection of the damage his .44 had caused, but the housemaid and the cook watched in horror as Mary walked closer to the two men with the pistol in her hand, thinking she was going to shoot the Yankee.

Will caught movement out of the corner of his left eye, then heard the loud click of a Colt's hammer being pulled back. He quickly turned and saw Mary's intense look as she prepared to shoot Fernando. Will quickly slid in front of Fernando and put his hands out in front of him as he slowly rose to his feet.

He looked into her intense, hate-filled brown eyes and exclaimed, "Mary! Don't do this! It would be murder! You'd hang!"

Mary rasped in a cold, almost evil voice that Will had never thought she could possibly possess as she said, "He raped me, Will. He lied to get me into the house, and he raped me. I want to kill him for what he did."

"No, Mary! You can't! You have a future now. Don't throw it away over someone who needs a doctor and a dentist."

The small and weak joke about Fernando needing a dentist released some of the incredible hate she had, and she slowly lowered the pistol.

Fernando knew how close he had come to death and that the gringo had shielded him, making him feel like a coward.

Mary's arm continued to slowly move downward, then, as it reached the end of its arc, her fingers released the pistol and it fell to the ground but didn't go off. She just stared at the scene in front of her with distant eyes. She had been raped and now almost became a murderer. She hadn't received any justice for what had happened to her and knew that she never would. Yet having been so close to killing an unarmed man was worse. Those two extraordinarily intense realizations combined to smash through her mind's shields and threatened to take control of her conscious thoughts before her mind began to shrink into a protective shell; into an internal world where those horrible thoughts couldn't enter. Her mind sought peace and it was the only way.

Will knew that Fernando would never walk right again, but he'd live. But his only concern now was Mary. He stepped closer to her and put his fingers on her cheeks and saw her normally lively brown eyes slide into the same deathly appearance as one who had already stopped breathing.

"Mary? Are you all right, Mary?" he asked softly, knowing that she wasn't.

She continued to stare straight ahead, even after his touch, and Will was deeply alarmed. He had never seen anyone react like this before and it scared him.

In a louder, almost desperate voice, he said, "Mary! This is Will. Can you hear me?"

Mary heard something far away, but nothing that made sense. Her eyes were open, but she didn't see. Her mind needed to protect her from the outside world.

———

There was the thunder of hooves coming around the house as four vaqueros rode around the corner with Winchesters drawn.

Will quickly swiveled as the cook and housemaid looked at them as did Fernando, but Mary continued to stare straight ahead, unaware of anything.

"Drop the gunbelt, mister," said one of the vaqueros.

Will knew it really didn't matter now and replied, "No, I'm not going to disarm myself. Fernando and I had a fair shootout. He fired three times and missed. I fired once and didn't. Now, you can try my accuracy, but there's no need. Go and bring his father, Senor Fuentes, here. We need to talk."

They were confused at first when he didn't drop the gunbelt. The segundo then turned to one of the men and ordered him to ride to Gila City and tell the boss that Fernando has been shot and to come quickly with a doctor. The vaquero nodded and raced off to the northeast. A shortcut, no doubt, thought Will.

Will turned back to Mary, who still stood like a statue staring straight ahead looking right through him.

"Mary. Can you hear me?" he pleaded, but still received no response.

The vaqueros could see that Mary was deeply affected by something, so the segundo turned to the housemaid and asked her what had happened. She began talking as she pointed to Fernando, Mary, and then Will. Will understood most of it and was impressed that the maid wasn't lying. She said that Mary had told Will that Fernando had raped her, and she was about to shoot Fernando, but the white man had shielded him.

Then they all waited. Will spent most of his time trying to get Mary to come out of her trance but didn't go as far as slapping her. He just talked to her, including whispers of love into her ears, but nothing seemed to get through her mental fog.

Will took time for more than a couple of glances back at Fernando. His knee had gone numb, and Fernando was grateful for that, but it was shattered, and he knew he might even lose the leg, but he was still alive.

Forty-five minutes after the vaqueros had arrived, more hoofbeats announced the arrival of Jesus Fuentes. He saw the group clustered about his son, then leapt from the horse and ran to him. He took a knee near Fernando and asked him quickly what had happened.

As his son spoke, Jesus occasionally glanced up at Will and then asked Fernando a few more questions. Will knew he had asked him if he had raped Mary and Fernando tried to justify it with several different excuses, but even his father didn't accept the lies. Jesus loved women, but he never countenanced this. He looked at Mary's blank face, then stood and walked over to Will.

"How long has she been like this?" he asked Will.

"For almost an hour. I think she needs to lie down and get away from this scene."

"Take her to the main house. Lucia will watch over her."

Will put his hands softly on Mary's shoulders, turned her, and gently pushed her along; her legs and feet working mechanically on their own. When she reached the steps, Will thought he might have to lift her onto the wide porch, but she stepped up and Will navigated Mary into the large house and followed Lucia into a bedroom. He sat her down and then laid her gently onto the bed, resting her head on a pillow.

He looked at Lucia, the housemaid, and said, "Let me know if she comes out of this confused state. Could you do that, please?"

She nodded, and Will took one more look at Mary, then exhaled sharply, turned, and left the room.

As he entered the large parlor, three vaqueros carried Fernando into the house, then past Will before they brought him into another bedroom. Jesus followed them and went inside.

Will was numb as he left the house, then after crossing the porch, walked out to where Rusty still stood, immobile despite the gunfire.

"You're a keeper, Rusty," he said as he rubbed the horse's neck.

He led Rusty back to the ranch house and tied him off at the fancy hitchrail before taking a seat on the stairs to the big porch, wondering what Jesus' reaction would be.

But mostly he worried about Mary. *How much was she hurt by what had happened?* He remembered how she had responded after he had found her and how she had survived that experience and bounced back so quickly. Something about this one had really hit her hard, and he suspected that it was a combination of this incident and the others that had finally been too much for her mind to accept.

He heard more hoofbeats approaching, not racing but trotting fast. He looked up and saw a buggy coming toward the house, and it was being driven by Mary's mother. Will said nothing as she stepped out and approached where he was sitting then stopped. He then slowly raised his head as he looked at her, certain that it had been her mother who had put Mary into this whole situation.

She glared at him and then shouted, "What have you done to my daughter, you pig! Minnie Crenshaw warned me about you!"

And then she slapped him...hard. Will didn't even flinch as the red welt appeared on his cheek but just looked at the angry woman. She glared at him for another few seconds, then spat at

282

him, then continued onto the porch. He wiped his face and waited for Jesus to arrive. He could hear him talking to Maria in the parlor, but they were talking so fast that he only got the gist of it.

He truthfully told her that his son had abused Mary and she had tried to shoot Fernando, but the rest was lost to him. He always was impressed with how Spanish flowed, much more than English did. English and German were stop-and-go languages, but Italian, Spanish and Portuguese all flowed, so they could be spoken more quickly. He figured that it must have something to do with a lot of words ending in vowels.

He checked himself to keep his mind from wandering, then wondered what was taking Jesus so long. He saw another buggy coming rapidly down the access road and guessed correctly that it belonged to the doctor.

The doctor hurried past Will without acknowledgment and walked into the house.

Will figured nothing would happen soon, so he stood and started walking back down the access road. The heat didn't invade his thoughts at all as he wondered if there was anything he could do for Mary. He wasn't a doctor and she would need help. She would need someone she could trust to care for her, but there just wasn't anyone he could think of that would fall into that category. He reached the halfway point, turned around, and began walking back to the hacienda.

He was almost back to the house when Jesus walked out of the house and saw him.

Jesus Fuentes was a very imposing man. Will guessed his age at around fifty, with his gray streaks mixed among his thick head of black hair. He wore a full mustache that ended at the corners of his mouth. He wasn't overly large, but he had a presence about him.

He stepped over to Will and said, "I owe you an apology, senor. I was the one who told Fernando to bring Mary here after her mother asked me to pull her away from your influence. The woman from the newspaper told her of your arrival and meeting Mary, but all I asked of him was to bring her here.

"I didn't expect Fernando to do what he did, and I am ashamed for myself and my son. I, too, easily believed Maria when she said you would harm Mary, yet it was my own son who harmed her. You rescued her from further abuse, but what is done is done. I have read the stories in the paper, and they imply that you and Mary had relations. Is this true?"

"No, Mister Fuentes. I was furious when I read the story as I had never even kissed Mary until today when I met her at the depot. She was why I returned to ask her to marry me."

"She declined?"

"Yes, she refused me, but not because she didn't love me as I love her. Part of the problem was the debt that she felt she owed to her mother, but the bigger issue is that Mary is obsessed with her lack of, shall we say physical female qualities.

"She told me that she wanted to wait until she was a real woman before we married. It's a sad thing that we make wonderful women like Mary think they aren't real women because they don't have large breasts. Mary is only sixteen and yet she is more of a real woman than most others that I know."

"What you say is true, and I admit to being guilty of that sin myself. Tell me about the shootout."

"I saw Fernando come out from the house as he was walking to the small house, where I guessed Mary was being held. We had words, and both had our hammer loops off. We both pulled about the same time. Fernando was faster than I was, but also fanned his revolver, making him less accurate. He got off three shots before I fired once. I fired at his legs because I wanted him out of action, not dead."

"Why would you do that?"

"Because if I killed him, we wouldn't be having this conversation. You would have assumed that he was blameless, and I was guilty and probably would have had me killed without a second thought. I'm tired of all the violence I've encountered on this journey of mine to find my mother. I've killed a dozen men and wounded some. I started none of the fights, but still, I am tired. Now my Mary is hurt in her mind and very badly. I don't know how I can help."

"The doctor is helping Fernando now and will look at Mary soon. Fernando will never walk normally again, but he'll be able to ride, and I am grateful to you for sparing his life. Although I will tell you honestly, if I had known what he had done to Mary, I might have killed him myself. May I ask, did you find your mother?"

"I did. Her husband, who took her away from our ranch when I was six, eventually tired of her and abandoned her in North Fork with no money and had sold her to the owner of a brothel. She had been there six years when I found her. I persuaded the owner to release her, then took her home and she is now living in San Miguel with her mother."

"Men like that are not worthy of living."

"I agree. I found him in Arizona City. When I asked him where his wife was, he laughed and said he left her in North Fork. I should have stayed and beat him to a blubbering mess, but I was too anxious to find my mother. He's there still, I think."

"What is this man's name?"

"Oscar Charlton."

Jesus just nodded before asking, "What will you do about Mary now?"

"I'll wait until she comes out of her shock. I've already accepted the job of marshal in San Miguel, so I do have to return shortly."

"Will you still want to marry her?"

"I love Mary, Mister Fuentes. If I have to wait twenty years, I will."

"What if she becomes heavy with child because of what Fernando did?"

"If she's my wife, we'll raise the child as our own. We'll cherish the baby as all children should be treasured."

"If it is a son, would you let him come here to live with me?"

"You're asking too much, Mister Fuentes. If Mary has a baby, she will love the child so much it would break her heart to give him up, just as my mother's was broken when she lost me. So, no, Mr. Fuentes, any baby that Mary has will be ours. This all assumes Mary returns to us and will accept me as her husband."

"Good. If you had said I could take the child, I would have doubted your commitment to Mary. Why do you think she is the way she is now?"

"I think the horror of being raped before I found her, then again by your son followed by the sudden shock that she was going to murder Fernando all finally added to too much pain for her to accept. Even as I was trying to talk her out of her mindless state, I could see her eyes begin to fade even more. I just don't know how she will get better."

"We'll see what the doctor says. And I talked to Maria after I heard what she did to you. She blamed you for what happened but didn't know what Fernando had done. I'm not sure she's forgiven you, or ever will, but at least she won't shoot you."

"I'm not sure about that, sir," Will replied without a hint of humor.

"Let's go and see what the doctor says about Mary."

After entering Mary's new sickroom, they met with the doctor for almost twenty minutes, but he hadn't a clue what to do about Mary. She was functioning, but not talking or reacting to anyone. She was still just lying on the bed staring straight at the ceiling.

After listening to the doctor's depressing prognosis, Will sat down on the bed and looked at her.

He leaned forward to her ear and whispered, "I love you, Mary, and I'll always be here for you."

He sat back, then looked at the big brown eyes and saw no reaction at all as he wondered, "*Where are you, Mary?*"

He stood and turned to Jesus and asked, "Mister Fuentes, where will Mary stay?"

"The doctor recommends that we move her to my hacienda in the city, so he can monitor her more closely."

"Alright. I'm going to go back to my hotel room in Gila City."

Jesus nodded, as Will took one last glance at Mary, then turned, left the bedroom then walked past a glaring Maria as she sat in the parlor. Will wanted to slap her back and tell her that she's hating the wrong man, but he didn't see any advantage to it before he left the house.

He stepped off the porch, untied Rusty and stepped up, wheeled him around, and trotted from the ranch via the access road, keeping him at a walk. He needed time to think. The trouble was he didn't have the vaguest idea what he could do about anything. Mary may be lost to him. He should hate Fernando Fuentes, but he just didn't have the energy anymore.

But he knew that when he returned to Gila City, he needed to talk to another woman. Thirty minutes later rode up to the door of *The Gila City Chronicle* and stepped down. He tied Rusty's reins around the hitching post and walked into the office, opened the door, and spotted Minnie Crenshaw smiling at him from behind her desk.

She set down her pencil and said, "Well, if it isn't Arizona's biggest hero. How are you, Will?"

Will was beyond simple irritation as he said, "Miss Crenshaw, I just left the Fuentes ranch. Fernando Fuentes had been told to move Mary Fleming to the ranch by his father because you told Maria Fleming that I was trying to steal her daughter. As a result of that little trickery on your part, Mary Fleming was raped by Fernando Fuentes, I had to shoot Fernando to free her, so he'll never walk right again, and now Mary is in shock and withdrawn into herself. I hope you're proud of yourself."

Minnie tried to be defensive, but it didn't work as she said, "I just told her mother what had happened at the depot."

"I don't know what your game is but trust me on this. I am going to sue your paper for libel."

That scared Minnie more than the realization that she had caused harm to another woman and she quickly replied, "You can't sue us! We changed her name."

"It has nothing to do with that. You wrote that I had killed her father. You essentially accused me of murder. I did not and have witnesses that can testify to that fact. Oh, I can sue you, Miss Crenshaw. You'll lose your paper and every dime you have."

Minnie was speechless as Will turned and left, slamming the office door behind him, the glass continuing to shake for several seconds.

She quickly grabbed the copy of the story and found the paragraph in question. *How had she missed that?* She did say he killed her father. Granted, she had made it sound like the father was a monster and had kidnapped his daughter, but she didn't know that he had or had not killed the man. She knew she would lose any libel suit and then dropped the paper, stood, and quickly walked to her father's office.

Will arrived at the livery and left Rusty, then walked back to his hotel, entered his room, removed his gunbelt, and tossed it on the bed. He felt powerless to do anything anymore.

———

They moved Mary and Fernando to the hacienda in town later that day. Fernando didn't lose his leg, but the bullet had destroyed the knee joint. The doctor removed his kneecap and all of the fragments but was able to save the leg. He'd limp for the rest of his life, and Jesus still didn't know what other consequences would come from what Fernando had done.

Maria had already forgiven Fernando for his indiscretion, which Jesus found unbelievable, as he hadn't and never would.

Will had visited Mary after she'd been moved into town and saw that the doctor had inserted a tube through her nose and they were pouring a broth down the tube to give her nourishment, but she wouldn't chew any food. She didn't have any fat reserves and he knew that she would start losing what little weight she had soon. Mary was in danger of just wasting away in her bed and the thought was beyond depressing to him.

———

There were no changes over the next day. Will ate at the café and returned to his room in between, but no one gave him information about any change in Mary's condition, and he was getting frustrated and angry. He'd take Rusty for rides to keep busy, but knew he'd have to return to San Miguel soon and may have to let Mary go.

He checked with the ticket master at the end of that day and was told that the next train would leave tomorrow at 11:10.

———

He had his breakfast the next morning and then rode to the Fuentes hacienda, wanting to see Mary one more time before he left.

He pulled up in front of the large house and stepped down, hitched Rusty to the rail and climbed the steps to the porch, and soon reached the door. He used the knocker and the door was opened thirty seconds later by a housemaid.

"I'm here to see Mary, ma'am. Could you tell Mr. Fuentes?"

"You are Will Houston?" she asked.

He nodded before she waved him in and said, "Follow me."

She led him to a bedroom and stood aside as he entered.

He saw Mary just lying in the bed, unchanged from when he had last seen her. He stepped over and sat on the edge of her bed and looked into her lifeless brown eyes.

He spoke in a normal voice, saying, "Mary, I have to go back to San Miguel now. I feel helpless being unable to help you and wish I could change so many things. The one thing I'll never change is how much I love you, Mary. When you come back to us, just get on the train and come to San Miguel where I'll be waiting. I'll always wait for you, Mary, until the day I die."

He leaned forward and kissed her on her forehead, then he stood again, looked down at her, and said, "Otto will miss you, too."

He walked out of the door and saw Jesus walking toward him, then said, "Mister Fuentes, I have to leave now. If Mary's condition changes, send a telegram to me in San Miguel. They'll know where I'll be."

"There is something that the doctor says is very unusual. She sleeps normally, it seemed. Then, when she awakens, she just stares straight ahead as she had from the beginning."

"That's something. But she really needs food, Mr. Fuentes. She has no fat to use."

"I know. We are giving her all we can."

Will nodded as he smiled at Mister Fuentes.

Jesus could see the pain in Will's eyes and offered Will his hand. They shook hands before Will left Mary's room, returned to Rusty, then mounted and rode back to his hotel room to pack. When he finished his three minutes of preparation for departure, he left his room, dropped the key at the desk, then rode Rusty at a slow walk to the train station where he bought his ticket and tag. With everything done, Will just took a seat on the platform and waited for the train, his blue eyes almost as vacant as Mary's with the deep belief that he'd never see her again.

An hour later, he was on his way back to San Miguel.

————

As he had left the hacienda, deep in Mary's mind, the name Otto struck a chord.

"Otto. Otto," her mind kept hearing and repeating. He was a dog, a big dog who loved to eat meat, lots of meat.

When the nurse hired by Jesus arrived to feed her the broth, she was shocked to hear Mary's other worldly voice.

Mary whispered simply, "Meat."

She turned, ran from the room and told Mister Fuentes, who returned with her to Mary's bedside where she repeated the one word. He then left the room, had the cook slice some ham and the nurse carried it to her room. She slid a slice of ham before her lips, and Mary opened her mouth. When the nurse slowly slid it between her teeth, Mary closed her mouth, chewed and swallowed it as her eyes still stared straight ahead. The nurse was excited and began feeding more ham to Mary. Soon, she was eating other foods, but that was the only change in her behavior. She didn't say another word, but she was eating, and new hope filled the Fuentes household.

————

When Will returned the next morning to San Miguel, he retrieved Rusty from the stock pen and led him to the barn behind the boarding house. He unsaddled him and left his rifles in the barn, then entered the house and was almost knocked over by Otto. Will smiled for the first time in five days as his hands worked the thick fur around the dog's neck.

He entered the parlor, where Emma and Pearl noticed his somber expression.

"You're back, Will. What happened with Mary?" Pearl asked in concern.

Will exhaled, took a seat, and replied, "It'll take a while to explain."

"You have a telegram waiting for you," she said.

"*What did it say?*" he asked excitedly, hoping it was good news.

She handed him the telegram, which he snatched from his mother's hand expectantly.

It was short, but it said a lot, and it was good news, just not the wonderful news he had expected.

WILL HOUSTON SAN MIGUEL NEW MEXICO

MARY EATING
STILL NOT TALKING OR SEEING

JESUS FUENTES GILA CITY ARIZONA

"Is it good news, Will?" asked Emma.

"Sort of. Let me tell you the full story."

He explained what had happened in Gila City to his two mothers for more than half an hour. Both knew that Will felt troubled and powerless, but the telegram at least gave him some hope.

But even as he talked to them, Will knew that all he had was hope, but still had obligations to get on with his life. Mary was in God's hands now.

CHAPTER 6

Will was sworn in as town marshal the next day and was given a brief outline of his duties by Joe Winterbottom. It seemed pretty straightforward, so he took over the duties before noon. His first duty was to have lunch courtesy of the town.

After lunch, he checked the weapons that were available in the small jail. There was a shotgun there, but he decided to keep his sawed-off shotgun with him. He changed the loads to bird shot to minimize deaths but still hoped that he didn't need to use it at all.

He walked the town at least twice a day, and unlike his married predecessor, he would spend a lot of nights there as well, only returning to his room at the boarding house after midnight. Wherever he went in town, he'd have Otto alongside, which was better than having a deputy. Everyday citizens appreciated Otto's presence because he was very pleasant with children and regular folks, but if someone started trouble, his mere arrival squelched it quickly.

Will would practice with his Colt almost every day and spent some of his remaining funds on a new Colt, so he'd have one he could count on that wasn't having its rifling worn by so much practice.

In August, he received a large envelope from Gila City and thought it might be something to do with Mary, so he ripped it open anxiously, but only found a stack of legal documents. He had totally forgotten that he had sued *The Gila City Chronicle* for libel, yet here was a draft for two thousand dollars which required him to sign a waiver of liability for anything written in the story. It had only been an idle threat anyway because there were no real witnesses other than Mary, so he may as well cost them something. He signed the forms and put them in the included envelope, then mailed the legal document and deposited the draft in his account at the bank that he'd started with the cash from his money belt.

––––––

He got into his routine once he settled in as the marshal and the days passed, with each day pretty much the same as the previous day. He'd have breakfast of bacon, eggs, biscuits, and coffee early in the morning, then go to the office and check for messages or telegrams. He'd make one round between eight and nine o'clock, never going in the same direction or at the same time. Being predictable was bad in the law enforcement trade, but he didn't notice because it was so peaceful.

He'd have lunch and make another round in the early afternoon followed by shooting practice. Sometimes with one of the town's Winchesters, and sometimes with his Colt, but every afternoon he would be out on his target range firing a weapon.

After dinner, he'd go back to the office and check again for notes or telegrams, then make another round and then return to the jail. Every day was so routine and so much like the previous day that he almost lost track of time. But each night was just like the previous night too, as he spent the darkness thinking of Mary and wondering if he should go back and see her again. But the next morning, as the sun crept over the horizon, Will knew that his duty was here and that seeing Mary lying in the bed with her lifeless brown eyes would be more painful than helpful.

In October, he received another large envelope, only this one was from Arizona City. He was less enthusiastic this time as he cut the edge off with his knife and dumped its contents onto his desktop. It was just a copy of the local newspaper and had no idea why it was sent until he turned to the second page where he read a story of how a local gambler, Oscar Charlton, had been found dead in an alley outside the Southwest Saloon. He had been robbed, but Will doubted if that was the motive. He gave the paper to his mother that evening and explained what he believed had happened.

Pearl felt surprisingly little when she read about Oscar's death. She had almost forgotten what he looked like and the happiness and pride that she now enjoyed daily seeing her son providing protection for the entire town was all that mattered.

———

There were only a few incidents in San Miguel in those first few months. Most involved barroom fights that came to an immediate peaceful resolution when Will and Otto arrived. There was one almost shoot-out outside Porter's Feed and Grain that ended abruptly when Will aimed his scattergun in the direction of the two would-be protagonists.

Then there was a serious incident in early November when he had the first one that required him to fire at a man.

It was a Sunday, technically Will's day off, but he rarely stayed home for the entire day. But since his return, he did go to church every Sunday morning. He had started going to the Catholic church on Sundays because he knew that Mary was a Catholic. Ironically, it was St. Mary's parish. He didn't understand the Latin Mass, but he got the basic meanings of the ceremony. Mostly though, he'd use that opportunity to pray for his Mary. It was the only route he had available to help in her recovery.

He was in the back pew, as he always was when he heard gunfire, then quickly stood, ran from church, and didn't touch the three entrance steps as he headed toward the main street. A rider was shooting past as he reached the road...literally. He had seen the star on Will's chest and opened fire with his pistol but had not come close to hitting him. Will didn't bother firing but quickly looked at the man to see which weapons he had on his horse.

The man thundered away down the road to the north as Will ran the opposite direction and entered the livery to saddle Rusty. He had him ready to go in eight minutes. Otto, who had been sitting outside the church when he had bolted, was sitting nearby waiting orders.

"Let's go, Otto," he said as he mounted.

His marching orders received, Otto trotted after Rusty.

Will had the two weapons he needed for the chase, and as he trotted down the street, he saw a small crowd by Heffner's Dry Goods.

Charlie Lerner shouted, "Will! Heffner's been hit over the head. It looks like he's been robbed!"

Will continued past as he yelled back, "Take care of him! I'm going after the thief!"

He set Rusty into a fast trot, which Otto mimicked. Will didn't need exceptional tracking skills to see where the outlaw was going. The tracks of the galloping horse were like a beacon and Will knew the horse couldn't last long at that rate, so the rider must be an amateur. Robbing a mercantile would net him less than a hundred dollars, but the penalty for what he did would be just as severe as if he had robbed a bank. The rider was making mistakes in his getaway, too. Shooting at a lawman coming out of a church wouldn't go over well with a judge, but galloping the horse was the biggest mistake because he'd be easy to track and short on distance.

The galloping tracks finally left the road about three miles outside of town, so he pulled his Spencer as it might require the range. It had been so long since his last life-threatening situation, he had forgotten how much he relished the challenge. He just didn't expect this to be a challenge, as many mistakes as this guy had already made.

Will slowed Rusty to a walk across the mixed terrain. The tracks, while not so deep once the thief slowed his horse, were still very easy to track. He would alternate looking at the tracks and looking for possible ambush sites. Even an amateur could get lucky.

The tracks made a sudden turn to the east and Will had a suspicion about where the rider was headed. There was an abandoned silver mine about two miles that way and the old road to the mine was about a hundred yards east.

He picked up the pace to a medium trot, now sure that was where he was going, but the question was, why? If he went into the mine, he'd have no escape. The mine had only one entrance as far as he knew. If he was going to try to set up for defense inside the mine's entrance, it would be just as bad. Ricochets hurt just as much as regular gunshots.

He saw the man's horse ahead about four hundred yards and, as expected, it wasn't even hitched near the mouth of the old mine. He knew the man had a Winchester, but he could stand outside the range of his repeater and pepper the shaft with Spencer rounds.

He closed within two hundred yards and stepped down, just dropped Rusty's reins, cocked the Spencer's hammer, and walked normally toward the mine as if there wasn't a man with a gun that would try to kill him.

"Come on out, mister! You're a sitting duck in there!" he shouted.

The reply was a Winchester round that passed him on the left, but the flame from the rifle's muzzle identified his location.

Will stopped walking and yelled, "One last warning! If you don't give yourself up, you're going to die today. It's a lot worse than ten years in jail!"

The man finally shouted, "I ain't goin' to no jail!"

"You're going to go for murdering the English language if nothing else. Give it up. This is your final chance."

He fired again, and Will brought the Spencer level and just pointed it in the direction of the smoke and fired. He expected that the amateur bad man would see the impact of the heavier slug, realize the precarious position he was in and just give up, but he was wrong.

The man fired two more shots in rapid succession, and Will fired one. This went on for almost a full minute before Will realized he was out of ammunition in the Spencer. Rather than reload, he stepped back to Rusty, slid the empty Spencer into its scabbard, pulled his Winchester, then cocked the hammer as he walked back to his previous position, then continued toward the shooter. Once he was within a hundred and fifty yards, he ducked and began jogging, making small direction changes as he drew closer. The other shooter kept an erratic fusillade of fire as Will cut the gap, and he wondered how much ammunition the man had.

Once he was within a hundred yards, he rose to his full height but kept moving while he began firing. The bullets were literally buzzing past him like killer bees when Will stopped quickly and unloaded six shots in rapid succession at the last muzzle flare.

The incoming fire suddenly stopped, and Will stayed in place, waiting for the large cloud of gunsmoke to clear. Will wasn't sure if he was reloading or had taken a serious hit. He hadn't heard a scream, so he guessed that he was reloading or waiting for his barrel to cool from the excessive rate of fire. After Will slid his last spare .44s into his Winchester's loading gate, he estimated that he only had nine or ten shots left, so he needed to make them count.

He took a deep breath, then sprinted toward the mine, firing three more times to keep the shooter down before he finally stopped behind the man's horse and waited, but received no more return fire. The man couldn't take this long to reload, and the silence suggested that he was no longer living. If he'd been hit, which he had to have been with as many chunks of lead that Will had sent in his direction, there would have been some moaning.

Will sucked in a breath and walked the last thirty feet to the opening of the mine where he found the man lying in a pool of blood, his jacket, and pants covered with holes. He must have been hit seven or eight times.

Will pulled his Winchester out of his hands and was nervously surprised. It was a '76 model, which meant that he had been lucky, or the man was just a terrible shot. He thought it sounded different when he heard it fire but hadn't paid that much attention at the time. He'd keep the rifle for personal use, then looked at the dead man, not having a clue who he was. He rolled him onto his back, went through his pockets, and found a total of $23.11 cents on him. Then, he stood, walked to his horse, and checked his saddlebags. He found one box of the new .45 caliber cartridges for the Winchester and another of .44s for his pistol. He pulled the man's gunbelt off. It was a Smith & Wesson Model 3, which was different. He'd keep that, too. To the victor and all that.

Other than the ammunition, there was nothing of note. He boosted the body onto his saddle. It was an okay gelding, but nothing to write home about, so he'd let the horse and saddle go to auction to pay for his burial. He led the horse back to Rusty and moved the cartridges and gunbelt to his saddlebags, leaving the Winchester in his scabbard until he returned to town.

He mounted and returned to San Miguel forty minutes later, stopped at Heffner's, stepped down, and went inside. He found Ed Heffner still standing behind the counter with a bandage around his head.

"Get him, Will?" he asked.

"He's draped over his horse outside. I'm going to run him down to Simon. Here's all he had on him."

He handed Ed the money, who accepted it and asked, "Why'd he do this for such little money?"

"A man gets desperate, I guess. If he'd just given up, he'd be facing fifteen to twenty years for robbery, assault, and attempted murder of a law officer, just for a little more than twenty dollars."

Ed shook his head and said, "Thanks, Will."

"Not a problem, Ed."

After dropping off the horse and body, Will took the two new guns back to his office, cleaned and reloaded both weapons, then went back to his routine Sunday.

No one knew who the thief was and even telegrams to other law enforcement agencies didn't turn up anything. He was buried, and the sale of horse and saddle covered the cost. It was a complete fiasco on the thief's part, whoever he was.

It was the only real serious incident in San Miguel since Will had been sworn in and Will hoped it was the last. The whole almost unnecessary robbery and gunfight had left a bad taste in his mouth.

―――

Back in Gila City, there was no change in Mary's condition, but she was eating. She was eating more than she had when she had been aware that she was eating. Something had triggered in her a desire to eat, and neither the doctor nor anyone else could understand what it was. She'd had her monthly, so she wasn't pregnant. Despite her increased appetite, there was no overall improvement in her condition. They would walk Mary around the house several times a day to keep her muscles working and, surprisingly, she was gaining weight.

Jesus Fuentes had specialists brought down from Phoenix to see Mary to no avail, although each of them was astonished to see her physical well-being despite her mental absence. None of them had ever even heard of a case like hers.

―――

The late autumn months arrived, and even though it was still comfortable most days, the nights could be pretty chilly, so Will wore a heavy coat when he went on his evening rounds. By then, everyone knew his reputation and tended to mind their own business.

Christmas found Will in St. Mary's church, praying for his own Mary, but not receiving the one gift he prayed for. He did have a joyful holiday with Emma and Pearl and surprised them when he took them to see Sarah, who was very large with her child. He was pleased to note that Ralph had moved his mother into her own house, and she seemed almost pleasant when he met her again, meaning she didn't snap his head off.

———

The new year arrived, and a blanket of light snow covered the town. Will continued his routines and Mary was always on his mind. He'd keep his promise and wait for her, which frustrated a few of the young ladies in town who had set their caps for Will. He was friendly to everyone, so it wasn't as if he was morose; he just didn't socialize. He was banking almost his entire salary because he had nothing to spend it on and just lived his life in dreary monotony.

———

In February, Emma became a grandmother for the second time as Will reminded her. Sarah gave birth to a little girl, and she and Ralph named her Rachel.

Emma took the train to Santa Fe and stayed for two weeks with her new granddaughter, even as spring began to arrive.

———

Then, one day in May, things changed dramatically for everyone in San Miguel that would have far-reaching effects.

It was Mary's seventeenth birthday, but it really didn't mean much to the events that would shake Will's world.

Will was making his morning rounds, wearing his shotgun scabbard and his Colt when he saw three men ride into town. He stopped in the street and watched them for a minute to get a read on them. Generally, when strangers entered town, he could tell their purpose by watching their faces.

HUNTING PEARL

These three were scanning the town, and he didn't care for the look of them, so he walked purposefully to his office, cracked open his shotgun, pulled the bird shot out of the shotgun, and replaced it with #4 buckshot. He snapped the shotgun and replaced it in its scabbard, so it wasn't very visible.

He stepped back outside and glanced at the three men as they walked their horses down the street, trying not to be obvious, but being more noticeable because they were trying hard not to be noticed. Will knew that his badge made him a target, and it was a rare time that it became an issue. This was one of those rare times.

He knew they were watching him, noticed that all of them had their hammer loops off, and suspected they were heading for the bank, so he reached behind his back and pulled the shotgun which set everything in motion.

The three men all pulled their pistols at the same time that Will pulled his shotgun. He cocked both barrels as they cocked their hammers, but they fired first. One of the .44s caught him in the upper chest, but not before he pulled the trigger on the shotgun.

All three of the riders were killed by the blast and toppled to the dirt street, and their horses didn't fare much better as they reared and screamed in pain. But Will wasn't there to hear the horses or anything else as he collapsed to the dirt onto his back, and his breathing grew more difficult as he felt his blood soak his shirt and the ground.

All he could see was the bright sky overhead and as his eyes closed, he whispered, "Mary."

———

Three hundred and eighty-seven miles away, Mary shot into a sitting position and shouted, "Will!"

———

Will was wheezing and tried to reach over and stop the blood with his hands. He knew he wasn't making any difference as he felt the warm wetness cover his palms.

Otto stood over him, whining. Will opened his eyes, looked at the big brown eyes, and wished he could see a different pair of brown eyes just once more but knew he never would. He rubbed Otto one more time, then closed his eyes and said softly, "I love you, Mary. I'm so sorry."

That was all he remembered as his personal night overtook him.

———

Mary was struggling against the nurse, the housemaid, and the cook as she shouted, "I've got to go! Will needs me!"

Jesus and Maria rushed into the room and were astonished to see Mary not only awake but fighting to leave the bed. They thought she had lost her mind.

"Mary! Control yourself!" Maria shouted.

"I've got to leave! Now! Will needs me! He's hurt!" she screamed back as she continued to struggle.

"Mary, you're making no sense at all!" Maria yelled.

"I am, too! Let me get dressed and go to him! He's in San Miguel and he needs me!"

Jesus took control as he stepped to her bed, sat down, and said, "Mary, calm down, please. You can get dressed, and then I'll send a telegram to San Miguel. If Will is okay, you can relax. If he has been hurt, then you can go. Is that alright?"

Mary stopped fighting and thought about it. She was absolutely convinced Will was hurt badly, but she also knew that she couldn't go on her own.

"Alright. Please hurry!"

Jesus left the room and left the house to take the buggy. It had already been harnessed as he and Maria were planning on going to the ranch.

After he was gone, Maria thought she'd straighten Mary out, recovery or not.

"Mary, you're being hysterical and childish. There is nothing wrong with that boy. You're using this as an excuse to run away from your responsibilities. I won't have it, do you hear?"

Mary glared at her mother and said, "What have you ever done to earn my obedience? My father was trying to sell me to a whore house, and you did the same thing. You tried to sell me to Fernando. Well, mother, you succeeded in making me a whore. He took me because of you. The only person who has treated me with respect and love is now lying in a bed in San Miguel. If he dies, mother, I'll leave anyway. I'll go to San Miguel and be his widow for the rest of my life. He's the only one who is important to me, mother. Not you."

Maria was flabbergasted. *How dare she talk to her that way? After all she had done for her!* She stopped short of slapping her defiant daughter, then stood and stormed from the room.

———

Will had been moved to Emma's room in the boarding house where the doctor had sewn his two bullet holes, one in the front right side of his chest just below the clavicle and the second on the back side. The bullet had passed through his lung and the doctor gave him just a small chance of recovery. He didn't know how much damage had been done to the lung by the bullet or how much he was bleeding inside.

Emma and Pearl were devastated by the shooting. The three men were all wanted criminals with large rewards for multiple bank and train robberies and three murders, but that didn't matter now. Will was pale and breathing erratically and they were going to lose him.

There was a knock on the door that didn't surprise either of them. Visitors had been stopping by since Will had been taken into the house and Pearl was getting annoyed, but left Will's room, walked to the front door, and after swinging it open, found a messenger boy with a telegram. Pearl pulled a nickel off the dish on the sideboard and handed it to him as she accepted the yellow sheet.

She opened the telegram and read:

WILL HOUSTON OR RELATIVE SAN MIGUEL NEW MEXICO

PLEASE ADVISE IF WILL IS INJURED
MARY ALERT AND CONVINCED HE WAS SHOT
REPLY IMMEDIATELY

JESUS FUENTES GILA CITY ARIZONA

Pearl read it again with disbelieving eyes, then slowly turned, walked back to Will's room, and as she stood at the door, she said, "Mama, come and read this."

Emma rose, accepted the message, and didn't believe it either, but said she'd head to the Western Union office and send the reply.

––––––

An hour later, Mary was dressed and insisted on packing, even before a reply was received. At the front door, the bell rang, and the housemaid answered the door.

It was a messenger with a telegram for Mister Fuentes. She handed him his nickel and took the telegram to Jesus. He didn't bother unfolding it but walked with Maria trailing so he could open it in front of Mary, and she would know that it was the telegram from San Miguel that said her worries were unjustified.

When they entered her room, he said, "Mary, sit down. I just received a reply from San Miguel."

Mary quickly took a seat and said, "Hurry, Mister Fuentes. The train leaves in just over an hour from now."

He calmly opened the telegram, and as he read it, his eyes kept getting wider. Even Maria didn't believe what she was reading.

"Read it to me, please!" Mary exclaimed.

He read in a still numbed monotone:

"It says, Will shot in robbery attempt this morning. Shot in chest. Prognosis not good. It's from Emma Houston."

Mary didn't wail or weep, but said firmly, "Get me to the train station. I'm already packed."

Jesus took control of the situation again and immediately had the buggy brought around. He had the cook prepare some sandwiches for her trip then opened his wallet and gave her two hundred dollars.

Mary accepted the money and the food but didn't want to delay her departure with any unnecessary chatting, so she wordlessly grabbed her travel bag and followed Mister Fuentes out of her room to the front of the house.

In the rush, no one noticed, not even Mary, that there had been significant changes in her appearance. It had been so gradual over the months and all she had worn were nightdresses, but when she put on her dress, it had fit perfectly. But it wasn't a time to be joyful for her womanly changes, even if she had noticed. She only thought about Will and the need for her to be with him.

The buggy was brought around and Jesus himself drove Mary to the train station. He carried her travel bag to the ticket agent and paid for her ticket to San Miguel. She would be getting in at 9:40 at night.

Jesus kissed her on the cheek and told her to tell Will that he would send them a wedding present in the sincere hope that their wedding was even possible.

She smiled and then waited for her train, and less than an hour later, Mary Fleming was anxiously riding north at forty miles per hour, praying that God would save Will for her.

———

Pearl and Emma were alternating providing care for Will. There was nothing either could do to improve his chances. He was still breathing, but there were a few times when one or the other had been terrified when they thought he had stopped.

But Will hung on. He was a strong young man and whether he knew it or not, help was on the way.

Pearl was more upset than Emma, and that was saying something. She finally had been reunited with her son and now this had happened. After all the danger he'd been through, he had to face death where he'd been born. Pearl was sitting in the room with Will, sipping her cup of tea. She would talk to Will and sometimes kiss him on his forehead. He wasn't feverish, so there was hope.

The parade of visitors had finally slowed down to a trickle and stopped after seven o'clock. It was after nine now and it was quiet.

Emma came in to relieve her daughter and asked, "Is there any change, Pearl?"

"No, Mama. But he's not running a fever and his pulse is still strong. Doctor Frost said that a strong pulse means that his blood loss wasn't so bad."

"It's too bad that those men were all killed in the shotgun blast. I want to hang them myself."

"Did you read the wanted posters on them? Those were horrible men."

"Our Will saved a lot more people grief by doing his job."

"It seems like all he's done is help people, and now we can't help him at all."

Emma felt just as helpless as she replied, "All we can do is wait."

They heard the door to the outside open and close, which was probably one of the guests, but a few seconds later, there was a knock on the door to their private rooms.

"Don't those people know he needs his rest?" Emma snapped.

"I'll get it, Emma," Pearl said getting up from the chair that she had occupied for three hours.

She walked stiffly to the door and opened it, ready to send the person away, and didn't know who the young lady was. At first, Pearl thought it might have been Mary, with her big brown eyes and long black hair, but this pretty young woman was far from skinny.

Mary asked, "Mrs. Houston? Or are you Will's mother, Pearl?"

"Mary?" she asked incredulously.

"Yes. Could I see Will, please?"

Pearl replied, "Oh, yes, please come in, Mary," then she turned and said, "Emma, Mary is here."

"Will's Mary?" she asked from Will's room.

"I hope so," Mary answered as she hustled past Pearl, dropping her travel bag on the floor.

Once she reached the room, she walked slowly to Will's bed and wanted to start crying when she saw him but knew it wouldn't do any good for anyone. Instead, she stepped quietly to the bed, sat next to Will, and took his hand in hers.

She leaned close to him and said, "Will, I've come. You called for me and I'm here now."

Will was somewhere between consciousness and a dream world. Sounds would filter in and be woven into his dreams. Now, he was hearing Mary's voice and he smiled. He had wanted to hear her voice more than anything, and now it was here and sounded so near and so real.

Emma and Pearl saw the smile and clutched each other.

Mary took his hand and held it against her breast as she said in a soft voice, "I'm ready, Will. I need you to come back to me, so we can get married."

In Will's dream, Mary felt so soft, and she wanted to marry him now. He was so happy that he knew it must be heaven. He had died, and Mary was talking to him.

She leaned forward and kissed him ever-so softly on the lips, barely brushing hers against his.

Will felt her lips and kissed her back.

Mary felt the response and kissed him more deeply.

In Will's dream, Mary was kissing him, and he was kissing her, but this didn't feel like a dream. At first, it was so soft it had to be a dream, but now, it was different and so real. Suddenly, his mind shouted at him. This wasn't a dream Mary, this was his Mary.

He tried to see her, but his damned eyes didn't want to work.

"Mary?" he barely whispered.

Mary felt her heart quicken as she replied just a bit louder, "I'm right here, Will. I'll always be with you now."

Will was fighting with his eyelids. *Open!* There was some movement as they began to pry themselves apart.

"I said open, damn it!" he thought loudly.

They fluttered twice and then stayed open to an incredibly beautiful sight when they revealed two big, beautiful brown eyes just inches from his own.

"You came, Mary," he whispered as he smiled.

"I came. You called for me, Will. I had to come."

"I love you, Mary."

"I love you, Will."

"Mary, will you marry me now? Or was that just a dream."

"Yes, Will. I came here to marry you."

"Then it was worth taking a bullet to bring you to me."

Mary finally gave in and felt the tears welling in her eyes as she kissed Will again.

Emma and Pearl had been crying since Will had first opened his eyes.

After their lips parted, Will said hoarsely, "Mary, I'll get better soon now. I have to get ready for our wedding."

"Is that a promise, Will?"

"Yes."

"Then I know you'll get better because you promised me."

"Mary, could you ask one of my mothers to bring me some water?"

"I think they heard you, Will," Mary said as she turned and smiled at his two mothers.

Emma brought a half-full glass of water that she handed to Mary, who then put it to Will's lips and let him drink slowly. He drained the glass and felt better.

He smiled at her and said, "Mary, you need to get some sleep now. You and my mothers. They're tired like you. I'll be all right now that you're here."

"We'll do that, Will. You sleep yourself now."

"Can I have one more kiss before you leave, Mary?"

She smiled and kissed him again, then she stood and walked to Pearl as Will's eyes closed again. She hugged each of his mothers then they all walked to the kitchen.

Emma had tea ready and they each sat down with their cups before them.

Pearl asked, "Mary, Will told us you were in a state of shock for a long time. When did you come out of it?"

"Just this morning. I was gone and then, I suddenly felt a lightning bolt hit me and knew that Will was hurt and needed me. What is the date, anyway? No one told me, and I slept on the train."

"The twentieth of May."

Mary was shaken as she asked, "I've been out that long? It's almost been a year."

"That's about right. Will has been the town marshal now for about ten months."

Then after adjusting to the new date, she smiled and said, "It's my seventeenth birthday."

Emma smiled and said, "And you've given us the greatest gift of all, Mary. You've brought our Will back."

"No, I've been given the most incredible gift that I could have ever hoped for. I'll get to spend the rest of my life with Will."

"Mary," Pearl asked, "Will told me that he thought the reason you wouldn't marry him was because you were so thin."

"It was. Looking back now, I realize that it was such a foolish thing. He's been everything to me since the minute he found me in the desert, and I did something stupid like that. I should have realized how special he was for loving me as I was. Instead, I thought that having a good figure was important to making him happy."

"But you have a very nice figure," Emma said.

"I didn't even realize it until the train was in New Mexico. I slept most of the way and then when it got dark, I saw my reflection in the train window and almost didn't recognize myself."

"You got dressed and didn't notice?"

Mary shook her head, and said, "All I could think about was Will. I knew he was hurt, but they wouldn't let me leave until they received your telegram."

Pearl asked, "But how did you know in southwestern Arizona when Will was shot in northeastern New Mexico? It was almost the same instant."

Mary shrugged and replied, "I just don't know. As I just said, it's what broke me out of my condition as if I had been hit by lightning."

Emma said, "When we received the telegram, we were amazed and still are."

"I can't explain any of it. I just knew he was hurt and needed me."

"Well, we can all talk in the morning. We have some empty rooms, or would you rather sleep in Will's bedroom upstairs?"

"I'd like that."

"I'll show you where it is," said Pearl.

"Thank you, Mrs. Charlton."

Pearl smiled and said, "Mary, given what's happening, I think you should call me mama, and I never want to hear that name again anyway."

Emma chimed in, saying, "And you may as well call me mama, too. He calls us both mama."

Mary laughed and said, "It must get confusing at times."

"It can. Let me show you to his room."

"Where's Otto? I didn't see him out front."

"He's over at the marshal's office right now. I think he believes he's the acting marshal in Will's absence."

"He probably would do a good job, too."

Pearl showed Mary to Will's room and bade her goodnight. Mary entered, lit a lamp, and closed the door. She felt Will's presence everywhere as she fingered his gunbelt hanging on the bedpost. Put there by one of his mothers, no doubt. His other guns were in the corner and his Stetson was on the dresser. She smiled, put up her long black hair, and tucked it under the Stetson before slipping it onto her head, letting it slide to her eyebrows just as Will had done when he first thought of disguising her as a boy. She was pleased that she wouldn't be able to manage that deception now.

She finally undressed and looked at herself in the mirror, the first time she had been able to see the shapely young woman that she had always hoped to see looking back from the looking glass. All she could think was how pleased Will would be when he finally could see her. She slipped on her nightdress, turned off the lamp, and slid into the bed, almost exulting in the faint Will scents. She had returned to her Will.

CHAPTER 7

Mary's return was the most powerful medicine any doctor could have prescribed. The man had taken a .44 caliber bullet in the chest the day before and was near death. This morning, the doctor arrived and found Will in his bed eating bacon and eggs. He was left shaking his head and mumbling something about an article for a medical journal.

The word raced around San Miguel that the marshal would make a full recovery soon.

The three women in his life worked tirelessly to help Will recover. In two weeks, he was walking around the house unassisted. The doctor found his lungs clear and pronounced him fit. He had removed the sutures, and Will was happy not to have to do the job himself.

———

Will left the house just three weeks after being shot and returned to his office where he cleaned up some paperwork and found three vouchers for five hundred dollars each for the rewards on the three victims of his shotgun.

Otto was never further than ten feet away from him unless he was eating at the café or in the house, apparently believing he had failed in protecting him.

And then there was Mary. Mary and Will were almost inseparable, except at bedtime. He had moved back into his room and Mary was given a room three doors down. For two young people who were so attached and so obviously in love, it was a major feat of personal control for them to remain in their own rooms at night, but they did and for just one reason. They were going to be married on the first day of summer, and it was only four days away.

Will was in his office with Mary sitting on his desk and Otto was out front ensuring their privacy when he said, "Mary, we're going to be married in four days, and I'd like to give you an early wedding present."

"Will, grooms don't give brides wedding gifts, except on the wedding night," Mary said with a smile.

"Well, it's more of a gift for the two of us."

"Then that will be acceptable."

He stood, took her hand, and hated to admit it, but he was still mesmerized by her new figure. She was well aware of the effect it had on him and was glad that it did.

They left the office and walked toward the north side of town away from the train station, passed the general store and Will turned down a side street, then finally stopped in front of a large, but not fancy house.

"What do you think, Mary?" he asked as he smiled at her.

"The house?" she replied expectantly.

"The house. Even before you came, I wanted to be ready for you when you did. I knew that the house had been for sale for a few months, and I had been looking at it every day when I made my rounds. It's not that old and seemed in good condition, so I bought it and had Ferguson's Construction come in and fix the things it did need and added some improvements. I asked my mothers to see to the furnishings and other necessities, so it's ready for us to move in after we're married. Do you want to go inside?"

Mary was so excited that she didn't answer but just nodded and pulled Will's arm closer as they walked up the stairs.

Will unlocked the door, swung it open, and let her quickly enter as he followed her inside to appreciate Mary's impressive view.

Mary's head was on a swivel as she looked at everything and marveled knowing that this would be her home. She simply couldn't believe her eyes. It was like she had picked everything out herself. All of the furniture was so perfect!

She waited for Will and put her arm around his waist as they toured the house. There was a bathtub with an attached water pipe and valve, and when they reached the second floor, she found that there was a second complete bathroom upstairs. The bedrooms upstairs were just as well furnished, including their bedroom. It had the biggest bed she had ever seen, and when she mentioned it to Will, he just grinned at her.

Then she found the kitchen and was stunned into silence. It was enormous for one thing. Her old house in Gila City would have fit inside. There were pots and pans and two sets of dinnerware and flatware. It even had a full pantry and cold room. Everything that she needed to cook was there.

They walked out of the kitchen onto the back of the wraparound porch and just stared out into their large yard. Then she suddenly whipped around and hugged Will as she was on the verge of crying because she was so extraordinarily happy.

But Will had one big surprise left.

He looked into those smiling brown eyes, then smiled and said, "Mary, come with me. There's one room you haven't seen yet. It's right off the parlor."

Mary was skipping like she had when she was six as she held onto Will's arm while he strode down the long hallway and turned into the parlor.

He led her through the parlor and opened a door. She stepped inside, expecting to be thrilled, but saw shelves full of books, and her ebullient mood evaporated.

She looked at the books, then said, "But, Will..."

Will cut her off by kissing her and pulling her close. Mary forgot about her handicap and just melted as Will held her.

As he put his arm around her shoulders, he said, "Come inside. I'll show you something."

She walked with him into the library, then he turned to one of the shelves and pulled out a small volume.

He walked over to a couch and sat down before pulling her onto his lap. He laid the book on her lap, before putting his arms around her and flipping open the cover.

"Mary, this is McGuffey's Primer. It's the first book we all used to learn to read. I made you a promise when we were first together that I would help you to learn how to read. Now, because of circumstances, I wasn't able to get it done before your seventeenth birthday. But when we move into our home, I will start fulfilling that promise, and within a few months, my love, all those books will be open to you. You'll go to exotic places and have extraordinary adventures. We'll do it together, Mary. Like we'll do everything for the rest of our lives."

Mary felt the tears flowing as she leaned back and pulled his arms around her tighter. She knew he would keep his promise, because he always did.

Even before they left their new house, Will showed her how to write her name. She didn't need to understand the letters. It was just a simple mimic, but he wasn't showing her how to write Mary Fleming. He told her that she was writing Mary Houston. She knew that Will wanted her to be able to proudly write her name on the marriage certificate and worked hard to get it right. Her handwriting was quite natural and looked perfect after just a few hours.

———

The next three days crawled by for them both. Their stolen moments away from prying eyes left Will in a sorry state. Will found the softness that Mary wanted him to find, and Mary wasn't sure whether to laugh or commiserate with Will's discomfort. She was getting a bit excited herself, something she never could have imagined a year ago. When she thought of it, none of what was happening now was even a dream a year ago.

The highlight was when Emma, Pearl, and Mary took the short train ride to Santa Fe where they were met by Sarah, and all of Mary's new family helped her to pick out a wedding dress. After it had been chosen and impressively, required little alteration, Pearl and Emma took Mary to the jewelry store and had her choose their bridal ring set.

When not with Will, Mary spent time with Emma and Pearl, who had already accepted her as a daughter.

———

Sarah and Ralph had arrived with Rachel to celebrate the wedding and Mary was enchanted with the little girl and naturally, wanted one for her and Will. She and Sarah had bonded like sisters almost from the start, as they shared a common love for Will. Sarah told her stories about the young Will that even Emma hadn't heard.

———

Then the first day of summer arrived. The wedding was set for two o'clock that afternoon and Will had dressed in a suit that he had ordered, and Emma had spent a few days getting it to fit properly. In the absence of fathers, Mary asked Pearl to escort her down the aisle and Emma understood her request. After all, it was her grandson's search for Pearl that had led Will to her.

St. Mary's church was full of well-wishers. This was the fairytale wedding that everyone wanted to see. The incredible story of Mary's recovery at the moment of Will's fall was widely known. Whether it was believed or not wasn't important. His sudden recovery when she arrived had to be believed because they had all witnessed it.

Will was standing at the front of the church near the altar waiting for his bride. Emma was with him, and probably for the first time and only time, the best man standing next to the groom was standing on four feet, not two, as a freshly groomed Otto seemed to accept his important role. He wouldn't be able to sign as a witness, but Emma and Pearl could handle that.

Will was still finding himself so connected to Mary that he almost felt her entrance into the church before she arrived. He held his breath as the organist began to play, and his vision was locked to the back of the church. Mary and Pearl walked into view, and Will still couldn't breathe as his eyes beheld his Mary.

HUNTING PEARL

She was wearing a veiled ivory satin dress that accented every curve and movement as she slowly walked down the aisle toward him. He had fallen in love with the skinny girl but was marrying the beautiful, full-figured woman, yet it wouldn't have mattered to him for a second if she hadn't put on an ounce of weight since he'd first seen her. He would have been just as happy to see the thin young woman walking toward him with those big brown eyes smiling at him from behind the veil. They were both Mary...his Mary.

She walked slowly and elegantly toward him and he finally remembered to breathe just before he passed out. He took her hand from Pearl's and she stepped forward. The priest began the marriage ceremony, but it was all a blur to both Will and Mary as they had their eyes locked and were busy passing unspoken vows and promises meant only for each other. They exchanged their conventional vows and rings, and at some point, the priest must have pronounced them man and wife, because they were kissing each other, which sealed those vows and promises that they had just made to each other.

They walked back down the aisle of the church with arms locked and soon left the dark interior and stepped outside into the brilliant sunlight. They had anticipated walking back to their new home, but instead, a groom dressed in a black frock coat ushered them into a beautiful carriage being pulled by four matching black horses. They were a bit confused but climbed inside before the carriage turned and drove to their home, where they would await the family.

When they stepped out of the carriage to enter their home, the smiling but silent driver handed them an envelope and turned the carriage into their yard.

Will opened the envelope, found a letter, and when he unfolded the letter, found a bank draft inside.

Dear Will and Mary,

Congratulations on your wedding day. I am very happy for you both. If any two people were meant to be together in this world, it is you.

The carriage and horses are yours. The money is to build a carriage house.

When you have a child, please let me know so we can come and visit.

Jesus Fuentes

P.S. The extra $100 is because we found the money in Mary's pants pocket.

The draft was for eleven hundred dollars.

Will smiled as he turned to his new bride and said, "It's from Jesus Fuentes. The carriage and horses are ours and he sent a draft to cover the cost of a carriage house, but it's probably enough for two. He also sent an extra hundred dollars because they found that much money in your pants pocket."

Mary laughed and said, "I can't believe I forgot about the hundred dollars you gave me!"

Will took her hand as they walked onto the porch, then he opened the door and glanced down the street. He knew they had a couple of minutes before the family could walk from the church, so just as they prepared to pass over the threshold, he scooped her into his arms as she squealed in surprise.

"What's this for?" she asked as she giggled with her arms wrapped around his neck.

"I read about this tradition in some places and thought I'd try it. It's the way a new bride should make her first entry into her home," he replied as he turned sideways to walk through the doorway without smacking her head.

"But I've been in here before," she said as he kicked the door closed with his heel and then slowly set her back to her feet.

"Yes, ma'am, but not as my wife and now I'll be able to explore every bit of your wonderful curves and bulges that I somehow, heroically, yet tragically, have been unable to discover."

She laughed as he began his husbandly exploration in the brief minutes before the others arrived. As he did, Mary found that all her own pent-up frustrations had evaporated, and she did a bit of hand-wandering on her own.

But it didn't last long, and they barely had time to rearrange their marital attire before they heard the sounds of the approaching family and guests.

When they all entered, Will explained about the carriage, and the newest female member of the Houston family was the only one not allowed in the expansive kitchen to prepare food for everyone. While the food baked and cooked, everyone enjoyed coffee and tea with the cake that Emma, Pearl, and Sarah had made the night before.

As everyone chatted and passed the standard jibes and ribbing to the newlyweds about their wedding night, Will and Mary kept passing anxious looks at each other whenever they could. As much as they loved their family, they wanted desperately for them all to leave.

The sun was finally displaying a spectacular New Mexican sunset when Emma, Pearl, Ralph, Sarah, and Rachel finally made their farewells and walked back to the boarding house.

The newlyweds wasted no time, as they both raced pell-mell into their new bedroom with the large bed. Silk and wool flew through the air within minutes and were soon followed by cotton undergarments as the long-frustrated couple were finally able to fulfill the fantasies that had been threatening to erupt soon whether they had been married or not.

An hour later, Mary was contentedly laying on Will's left side as he slid his fingers across her damp skin.

He kissed the top of her head and asked, "Mary, do you remember the night we stayed in the same room in that cantina in Arizona City?"

"I'll never forget a moment of that first time we were together, just like I'll never forget this one."

"Remember you said you wouldn't be uncomfortable having me sleep in the bed with you and I said it was better if I slept on the floor?"

"Of course, I remember. It hurt me, Will. I thought you didn't see me as a female worthy of your attention."

"The problem, Mary was that I was too aware that you were a female. I wanted to climb into the bed and kiss you and hold you, but I didn't because of what had happened to you and was just so worried that it might bring back those memories. But as it was, I stayed awake a long time thinking of anything that could take my mind off you."

She turned her head up to look into his blue eyes and asked, "You did? Even then, when I was so thin?"

He pulled her closer, kissed her softly, then said, "I loved you even then, Mary. When I started that long, mostly frustrating search to find my mother, I could never have guessed that the most precious pearl I would find was you."

EPILOGUE

April 7, 1881

Will walked into the library carrying his cup of coffee and a cup of tea with cream and sugar for Mary, just the way she liked it.

As he left the parlor and entered the library, he saw her curled up on the tufted couch with her feet under her, reading, and smiled at the sight.

She looked up from her book, smiled at her husband, and set the book down as he placed her cup of tea on the nearby end table, then sat down on the couch beside her.

Mary swung her feet down to the floor and picked up the tea, saying, "Thank you, Will. You're spoiling me."

Will smiled and replied, "I enjoy it, Mary, besides it's getting harder for you to get around with that load you're carrying."

Mary took a sip of her tea, then rubbed her swollen belly and said, "Soon, I won't be carrying it around and you'll be able to do some of the work."

Will laughed and said, "I won't mind."

Mary took another sip of her tea and said, "We never did decide on a boy's name."

"Well, we did eliminate Joseph right away for some reason," he said with a grin.

Mary nodded and said, "Two despicable fathers named Joseph who weren't even our fathers anyway. That was an odd coincidence."

"To put it mildly. I always liked Sam, but that name has to stay in Texas, I think. How about plain old John? That has a nice Western flair to it, don't you think?"

"I like it, Will. Okay, we'll go with John if it's a boy and Grace if it's a girl."

Will took a sip of his black coffee, then asked, "Are you still reading *Journey to the Center of the Earth?* You've been on a real Jules Verne streak lately."

"No, this one is completely different, and I was going to tell you about it."

Will smiled at Mary, amazed at how quickly she had taken to reading. Just before they were married, he had to show her how to write her name, now she was going through a book a week, if not more.

"So, what do you want to tell me about this one?"

She smiled and said, "Have you read *The Scarlet Letter* by Hawthorne?"

"No, I've heard about it, but never read it. What's it about?"

"It takes place in Massachusetts in the seventeenth century and is the story about a woman named Hester Prynne who conceives a child out of wedlock and is ostracized for her sin."

"Now that sounds like a familiar story. Did you know that was the plot before you started reading the book?"

"No, I didn't, but the familiarity of the circumstances wasn't the most striking coincidence in the story. It was the name of her child that was startling."

"She named her boy Will?" he asked with wide eyes.

"No. She named her daughter Pearl."

BOOK LIST

1	Rock Creek	12/26/2016
2	North of Denton	01/02/2017
3	Fort Selden	01/07/2017
4	Scotts Bluff	01/14/2017
5	South of Denver	01/22/2017
6	Miles City	01/28/2017
7	Hopewell	02/04/2017
8	Nueva Luz	02/12/2017
9	The Witch of Dakota	02/19/2017
10	Baker City	03/13/2017
11	The Gun Smith	03/21/2017
12	Gus	03/24/2017
13	Wilmore	04/06/2017
14	Mister Thor	04/20/2017
15	Nora	04/26/2017
16	Max	05/09/2017
17	Hunting Pearl	05/14/2017
18	Bessie	05/25/2017
19	The Last Four	05/29/2017
20	Zack	06/12/2017
21	Finding Bucky	06/21/2017
22	The Debt	06/30/2017
23	The Scalawags	07/11/2017
24	The Stampede	08/23/2019

25	The Wake of the Bertrand	07/31/2017
26	Cole	08/09/2017
27	Luke	09/05/2017
28	The Eclipse	09/21/2017
29	A.J. Smith	10/03/2017
30	Slow John	11/05/2017
31	The Second Star	11/15/2017
32	Tate	12/03/2017
33	Virgil's Herd	12/14/2017
34	Marsh's Valley	01/01/2018
35	Alex Paine	01/18/2018
36	Ben Gray	02/05/2018
37	War Adams	03/05/2018
38	Mac's Cabin	03/21/2018
39	Will Scott	04/13/2018
40	Sheriff Joe	04/22/2018
41	Chance	05/17/2018
42	Doc Holt	06/17/2018
43	Ted Shepard	07/16/2018
44	Haven	07/30/2018
45	Sam's County	08/19/2018
46	Matt Dunne	09/07/2018
47	Conn Jackson	10/06/2018
48	Gabe Owens	10/27/2018
49	Abandoned	11/18/2018
50	Retribution	12/21/2018
51	Inevitable	02/04/2019
52	Scandal in Topeka	03/18/2019
53	Return to Hardeman County	04/10/2019
54	Deception	06/02.2019
55	The Silver Widows	06/27/2019
56	Hitch	08/22/2018
57	Dylan's Journey	10/10/2019
58	Bryn's War	11/05/2019
59	Huw's Legacy	11/30/2019
60	Lynn's Search	12/24/2019
61	Bethan's Choice	02/12/2020
62	Rhody Jones	03/11/2020
63	Alwen's Dream	06/14/2020

Made in the USA
Las Vegas, NV
28 September 2022

56103966R00194